BROTHERS
IN CRIME

THE JESSE DAMON SERIES

BROTHERS IN CRIME

KM ROCKWOOD

A Jesse Damon Crime Novel

WILDSIDE PRESS

*In memory of my brother, The Edward,
who left us much too soon.*

Published by Wildside Press LLC
www.wildsidepress.com

CHAPTER 1

"Jesse, you made the front page of the paper again."

"Yeah?" I paused next to the time clock, card in hand, ready to punch out. This couldn't be a good thing.

John, the foreman on my midnight-to-eight shift, held a folded copy of the *Rothsburg Register*, the local newspaper, in his hand. Bucky, day-shift foreman, stood next to him, a nasty smirk on his face.

"The picture looks like a mug shot. A recent one," John said. "You look kind of rough. Need a shave." He unfolded the paper.

"You may as well punch out," Bucky said to me. "Nobody's gonna pay you any overtime."

I took a deep breath and slammed my timecard into the slot with more force than necessary. The mechanism in the clock gave a "clunk," snagging the card and holding on.

That's what I got for being too rough with it. How was I going to tell John that I'd messed up the time clock?

The clock made a rasping metal-on-metal noise. I tugged on the card, and it came free. They hadn't seemed to notice. I put the card in its slot in the rack and decided not to say anything.

Shoving the newspaper toward me, John said, "It was written by that woman reporter who wrote about you before. Carissa Whoever. The headline's kind of snarky, but the article itself isn't bad."

"Yeah." Carissa Daniles was trying to build a name for herself as an investigative reporter, and she wasn't one to let truth or ethics stand in the way of a good story. Rothsburg was a small, depressed city that a lot of heavy industry had left behind. Not a whole lot of things to investigate.

I took the paper. The headline read, "Paroled Murderer Makes a Killing."

Just like Carissa. She'd think that was clever and amusing.

It might be clever, but I sure didn't find it amusing.

The picture made me wince. Any doubt that it might be a mug shot was dispelled by the fact that I was holding a plaque with a commitment number on it. On the wall behind me were marks to show height. It had been taken a few weeks ago when I'd gotten locked up. Not a terrible picture for a mug shot, but my face was bruised up a bit and I looked moderately deranged. I did need a shave, and I'd lost my hair tie, so my wiry brown hair stuck out in a bush around my head.

"That's about you getting a reward for that fancy cat collar you found," John said.

"And the article said it was stolen," Bucky said. "From a jeweler's. Probably Jesse who stole it in the first place."

I didn't see any point in rising to the bait Bucky was dangling in front of me. He was going to believe what he wanted to believe, and anything I said was not going to change his mind. Just might make him mad. And he was a foreman. I was just a laborer. Thank goodness not on his shift.

"It says 'substantial reward.' How much did you get, Jesse?" John asked.

"Nothing, so far," I answered. "The reward's supposed to be five thousand dollars, but there's no saying I'm really gonna get it."

"You found the collar, didn't you? And you turned it in."

"Kind of. I mean, there was this cat who showed up at my door wearing it. The collar was pretty heavy, and the cat was scratching at it, so I took it off. I didn't realize it had real jewels or anything. I tossed it aside and forgot about it until I was cleaning out my apartment. After it got flooded out."

"Five thousand dollars is a lot of money to anybody," Bucky said.

And especially to somebody like me. "True, that," I agreed.

"So." The smirk spread wider over Bucky's face. "You gonna use it all up on drugs right away, or save some of it for the next time you need to bail out?"

John shook his head and glanced around. By now, everybody else on the overnight shift at Quality Steel Fabrications had left and the dayshift was well under way. Machinery thundered, sparks flew, and the smoky smell of hot steel and oil filled the air.

"Maybe I best be going," I said to no one in particular. I folded the newspaper again.

"That's mine. Gimme it back," Bucky said, snatching it out of my hand.

"That might be a good idea, Jesse," John said. Turning away from me, he raised his clipboard and made a few marks with the stub of a pencil. "Here's where we left off in shipping, Bucky."

I grabbed my jacket from a hook along wall and put it on as I hurried toward the shop door.

The sunlight outside was so bright, it blinded me. Stepping out onto the sidewalk and closing my eyes against the glare, I paused to zip my jacket.

"See," a familiar deep voice said. It came from behind a black Lincoln parked next to a fire hydrant. "I told you if we waited long enough, Jesse would show up."

My gut froze. That voice belonged to one Detective Montgomery of the local police force.

"You were right," Detective Belkins, who often partnered with him, said. He was sitting in the passenger seat, the car door open. He shook his pale bulbous head. "I guess I lost that bet, huh?"

Montgomery came around the car, his impeccable gray overcoat buttoned against the gusty wind. Scraps of fast food wrappers and advertising flyers swirled around his polished shoes. He held a pair of black leather gloves in his perfectly manicured dark hand.

Belkins pushed the car door open farther and clambered out, his washed-out blue eyes blinking rapidly in the sunlight. His trench coat was disheveled, and what hair he had left blew in the wind. He tore a soggy, unlit cigar out of his mouth to loudly clear his throat. "Where were you last night, Damon?"

I stood still, careful to keep my hands where they could see them. No reason to give them any excuse to say they thought I was going for a weapon. I'd be slammed face down on the sidewalk before I could think. "Home," I said. "Until I left for work."

"And what time was that?"

"About eleven o'clock or so." It didn't take a whole hour to walk the distance to work, but I liked to get there early.

"And you stayed the whole shift?"

"Yeah." Of course I stayed the whole shift. What were they getting at?

He stuck the cigar back in his mouth and talked around it. "And people saw you the whole time?"

"Yeah. I mean, I drive a forklift. I'm moving around the plant, but people see me. And I worked the whole shift. Except for lunch."

"What time was that?"

I scratched my chin. I needed a shave again. "I dunno. Maybe about four thirty or so."

"And how long do you get for lunch?"

"Three-tenths of an hour. Eighteen minutes."

He rocked back on his heels. "How long did you *take* for lunch?"

"Eighteen minutes."

Montgomery took over. "Who would have seen you around two?"

I shrugged. "I'm not sure. The foreman. Maybe Hank, the plating room lead. Anybody who was working."

Belkins narrowed his eyes. "I don't believe you."

"Check with John," I said. "The shift foreman ought to know who's there and who's not."

He snatched the cigar out of his mouth again and looked at it. "I intend to do just that."

Where was all this leading?

Montgomery drew himself up to his full height of well over six feet.

"Jesse," he said. "You might as well come clean. We have a video of you breaking into that ATM this morning."

CHAPTER 2

Impossible. I'd been at work the whole shift. I *knew* I hadn't broken into any ATMs. I was on parole, and for someone in my position, that would be a quick ticket back to prison. I had another twenty years backup time on the last sentence. If I picked up another felony conviction, I'd be sent back to finish that up in addition to a new bit. I could just about kiss my life goodbye.

Belkins was frowning at the end of his cigar, as if it tasted bad. Of course it tasted bad. It was a cheap cigar to begin with, and he'd been chewing on it for heaven only knows how long, so it was all soggy. He turned to me. "You know the routine, Damon."

I did indeed. We were standing next to the car. I glanced at it, which, since it was parked by a fire hydrant, had a fair amount of room in front of it. "The front of the car or the wall?" I asked.

Montgomery laughed. "Wouldn't want anything to happen to the car. The wall, I think, Jesse."

Turning to face the grimy brick of the factory wall and taking the few steps over to it, I spread my legs and leaned forward on my hands.

Montgomery stepped up behind me. He removed my wallet and keys from my pockets and swept his gloved hands under my jacket, between my legs, and down around my ankles. "Still no ankle monitor, eh?"

"No. Mr. Ramirez took me off of home detention a while ago." Mr. Ramirez was my parole officer.

Belkins snorted. "Mistake, that. But then, paroling murderers is a mistake anyhow. Lock 'em up and let 'em rot."

"Incarceration's expensive," Montgomery pointed out. "You know how much of our tax dollars go to prisons? Infinitely cheaper for the taxpayer if someone's out on parole and holding down a job."

Belkins laughed. "You getting a head start on your political career with me? You ain't telling me nothing I don't know."

"Hold the position," Montgomery ordered me, stepping back.

"Some people need to be locked up." I heard Belkins spit on the sidewalk. "When they're out on the street, they like to do things like kill other people. Or break into ATMs."

Montgomery pulled one of my hands behind me, turned the palm outward. I felt the cold steel bite of handcuffs on my wrist. He was following standard procedure, intended to make it hard for me to attack either one of them or take off running while they questioned me. As long as they didn't call for transport down to the stationhouse, I could hope they were just going to talk to me and then let me go.

He repeated the move with my other hand.

"We have to figure out what happened there," Montgomery said.

"Nothing to figure out," Belkins said. "We have a damn *video* of Damon breaking into the blasted thing. It's pretty clear."

"There's the time discrepancy." They let me overhear the conversation. It was a technique they used in the hopes that I would get upset and possibly blurt out something.

I wasn't going to blurt out anything.

"The hell with the time discrepancy," Belkins said. "He snuck away from work for a while. Or the time on the tape is wrong. Or the guys he works with are covering for him."

Montgomery tugged on my arm. "You can turn around, Jesse." To Belkins, he said, "Why would anybody he works with do that?"

"Well, there's that girlfriend of his who's worked there for a long time." Belkins had thrown the soggy cigar down by the curb and pulled a new one, wrapped in cellophane, from the breast pocket of his trench coat. "Maybe they'd lie if she asked them to."

I wished Kelly were my girlfriend. Sometimes she acted like she was. After twenty years in prison, she'd introduced me to sex. And I liked nothing better than spending an evening at her house, fixing supper, reading stories to her two kids, and helping them with their homework. Made me feel like a regular guy, not just a paroled convict. Sometimes we caught a few hours in her soft bed before the babysitter came and we had to leave for work. But she refused to make any kind of commitment.

Belkins unwrapped the cigar and threw the cellophane next to the old cigar. "We haven't got a cage in that car. I'll call for transport."

My throat closed. They hadn't said they were arresting me or read me my Miranda rights, but they didn't have to. I'd signed away most of my rights when I'd signed the parole papers.

The patrol car responded so quickly, I wondered if it had been on backup around the corner or something. As it pulled up, lights flashing, the door to Quality Steel Fabrication's front office opened. Out stepped one of the executives, a tall man who often stalked the shop floor just before our shift ended. Accompanying him were another man and a woman I recognized as working in personnel.

They paused and watched Montgomery open the back door of the patrol car, still grasping me firmly by arm.

"Surely not one of *our* employees?" the executive asked.

"I'm afraid so," the personnel lady said. "One of the ones we got on the state's plan to hire paroled felons from the prison."

"Surely we don't hire drug addicts. Or anyone with a violent history."

"Well..." She frowned.

"We've already had a few drug problems here. And we definitely don't need anyone who might get mad and come back with a gun," he said.

"Not hiring anyone with a drug or violent history would pretty much cut out everyone we could hire under the program," she pointed out. "At least for shop workers."

"Hmm. Maybe we'll have to look into our participation in that plan."

"It does give us a really good tax break," she said. "And some pretty good workers."

"Then maybe we'll have to look at that particular employee. Do you know his name?"

She nodded. "Jesse Damon. Forklift driver on midnight to eight."

I was past my probationary period, so I was in the union. That gave me a little protection against them just letting me go, since we'd file a grievance. But if management decided they were going to fire me, they'd be able to find something. Nobody lives so they can't be targeted, and I had a big bull's eye on my back.

* * * *

My hands firmly cuffed behind my back, I sat in a battered chair in a dim interview room in the stationhouse. I'd been relieved of my belt and my steel-toed boots. They'd even taken my hair tie, so my hair fell in my face. I hadn't had a haircut—they cost money I could ill afford—since I'd been released from prison. Usually, I wore it in a neat ponytail that hung down past my shoulders. Now it sprang out in all directions. What did they think I was going to do with the hair tie?

The cuffs were too tight and cut into my wrists. My arms were stiff from being held in that uncomfortable position for too long. Fortunately, I'd worn handcuffs enough to know to sit a little sideways in the chair so my hands wouldn't be completely numb when I got up.

Another chair and an equally battered table were in front of me. The table had dark irregular stains in the wood. *Blood?* I shivered.

A long dark window overlooked the room. A one-way mirror. I had no doubt that someone was keeping a very close eye on me.

I knew the routine. I'd be kept waiting until they were good and ready to come in and start asking questions, trying to trick me into contradicting myself. Since I was on parole, I didn't dare refuse to answer. Or complain about the wait. They'd report me to Mr. Ramirez as being uncooperative. And he'd start to wonder if he should lock me up and schedule a parole violation hearing. All it would take was his signature on a piece of paper.

Time passed, but I had no way of knowing how much. My stomach growled. If they had put me in a holding cell, I'd get fed. But that wasn't likely to happen here.

What did they think they had on me? I certainly hadn't done anything like breaking into an ATM, so any video of that had to be bogus. And if Montgomery was right about the timing, I'd been at work. Any number of people, including John, the foreman, would vouch for me. No way could I have left long enough to get to an ATM, much less break into one.

Or was this an attempt to get me to roll over on somebody else? If it was, we would all be out of luck. While I knew of a few things going on at work that weren't strictly legal, like the bennies the truckers traded and the joints that came out in the back of the plant, I doubted I had any information the police didn't already have.

Dropping my chin on my chest, I tried to catch a few winks. The more tired and hungry I was, the easier it would be for them to trip me up in my answers.

Almost immediately, the door opened. Of course they'd been watching me, trying to gauge how stressed I was. If I could doze off, I couldn't be anywhere near as stressed as they wanted me to be. I didn't turn my head to look toward the door.

The odor of stale cigar and whiskey reached me. Detective Belkins stepped into my field of vision. He didn't look happy.

Great. The team of Belkins and Montgomery was something I could handle. They played a version of good cop/bad cop that I understood and could deal with. Montgomery was bucking for a promotion, and he wanted to be seen as squeaky clean. He was well aware that, as a paroled murderer, I was a high profile suspect, with my picture likely to end up splashed all over the front page of the newspaper if I caught any new charges. The whole trial would be covered closely, and he'd want to be very careful that any information they extracted from me would stand up in court.

But Belkins by himself was bad news. He wouldn't even consider the possibility that I wasn't guilty, and he'd be working to make the evidence support that. He'd be looking for a statement he could twist around and claim was a confession. He wouldn't be fussy about how he went about getting evidence, either. An old-school cop, he would try to bully me into saying something unwise.

He wouldn't completely succeed with that tactic, since I would never say I was guilty of something I knew I wasn't, but he might make things up or twist my words around and make it seem like I was lying. And he wasn't above the occasional smack to the back of the head, where no bruises would show up.

I didn't want to provoke Belkins into using any physical force, so I sat very still.

"Well," he said, walking around behind me. The hairs on the back of my neck bristled, but I didn't turn to look at him.

Silence filled the room. He was waiting for me to say something. Most people can't stand an extended silence and start talking to fill it just because they're uncomfortable.

I'm not most people. Over the years, I'd been interrogated by the best. And Belkins was far from the best. I was pretty uncomfortable, but I knew better than to start babbling just to break the silence. Belkins would have to ask me a direct question if he wanted me to say anything. The silence stretched on.

His patience wore out first.

Slamming his fist on the table in front of me, he said, "Damn it, what have you got to say about the ATM break in this morning?"

I didn't look at him. "Nothing."

"What the hell do you mean, nothing?"

"I didn't know anything about it until you and Montgomery picked me up this morning. Detective Montgomery," I corrected myself. No point in giving him a chance to think I was being disrespectful.

He slipped into the chair across the table from me and looked straight into my face. I didn't move, but I averted my eyes. "We've got you on video tape, dead to rights. You dumb enough to think they don't have surveillance videos of ATMs going twenty-four-seven?"

"I never thought about it. I don't have a bank account, and I sure don't use ATMs. But it would make sense to have surveillance videos of them going all the time."

"Damn straight they do." He got up from the table and walked around in back of me again.

My neck muscles tightened, but I didn't turn my head. Silence stretched out once more.

Again, he grew impatient first. "How can you explain a video of you smashing an ATM and grabbing the money? With a crowbar? And taking off?"

"I can't explain it. It wasn't me. I'm surprised it didn't set off some kind of alarm."

"It did set off an alarm, stupid. How do you think we got the tape and all?"

All I said was, "Oh."

Belkins paced the floor behind me. He tried a new tactic. "Refresh my memory. You're on parole, right?"

He knew I was. "Yes, sir."

"And how long ago were you released from prison?"

"It's been about five months now."

"And you're reporting regularly to your parole officer?"

What did he expect me to say? "Yes, sir."

"Haven't violated your parole?"

Maybe I had, a few times. Small stuff. But I hadn't been caught, that I knew of. So I said, "No, sir."

He snorted. "And what was the original conviction?"

I wasn't telling him anything he didn't already know. "Murder. Possession of a handgun during commission of a felony. Conspiracy."

"You pled guilty?"

"Alford plea." That plea—not admitting I was guilty, but agreeing that the state had enough evidence to convict me—had been a problem from the beginning. Counselors and parole boards want to hear remorse. That's hard to come up with when the plea itself denies I'd done it.

"Refused to accept responsibility, eh?"

I didn't have an answer for that.

"What happened to the other charges?"

"Dropped in the plea bargain."

He walked back into my field of vision and slipped into the chair again. "Weren't there possession of a controlled dangerous substance with intent to deliver charges, too?"

"Yeah. But they were dropped."

"And—" he tapped the table, as if he were making a startling revelation "—armed robbery?"

"Dropped." I didn't see how it made much difference.

He leaned close so I could smell his sour breath. "You tried to steal money once. It's not so far from that to breaking into an ATM. The same type of crime."

I was tempted to point out that in reality, armed robbery was a violent offense and carried much heavier penalties than a smash-and-grab that didn't involve any actual human beings. But it probably wasn't a good idea to say that. All things considered, Belkins was being very reasonable. I didn't want to do anything to change that.

The door opened and bright lights switched on, bathing the dismal room in a harsh glare.

"I thought you were going to wait for me," Montgomery said, a touch of irritation in his smooth voice.

Belkins jumped to his feet. "You was taking too long."

"I wanted to talk to a few of the people on the midnight shift," he said. "Find out what they had to say. I caught the foreman before he left and talked to the plating room line boss at his house."

"And?"

"And," Montgomery said, "they both agree it would be impossible for Jesse to have been gone for longer than fifteen minutes without them noticing."

Belkins paced across the room. "They're just two people. They could be wrong."

"I'm going in tonight to talk to others." Montgomery perched on the edge of the battered table. Against his slender dark hand, the green stone in his ring winked in the bright light. I caught a whiff of cologne and mint mouthwash.

Belkins moved restlessly. "How about the time on the video? That could be off."

"Maybe. But not by much. A patrol car responded to the alarm within minutes of it going off."

"But the perp was already gone," Belkins said.

Montgomery nodded. "The perp was already gone."

Belkins swung to look at me. "Made it back to work, huh? You were lucky."

I hadn't been part of the conversation up until now, and I had no intention of joining it now unless I had to.

"You find out anything from Jesse?" Montgomery asked.

Belkins lifted his pudgy hand up and rubbed the misshapen red nose on his fish-belly white face. "Not much. But if we keep at it, we'll get something."

Montgomery hoisted himself up higher on the table and began to swing his long, thin leg. "I'm not so sure about that. Jesse's not going to tell us anything he doesn't want to."

Belkins coughed. "We got a few things we ought to go over. Not in front of him. You wanna come out in the hallway for a minute?"

"I don't think that's necessary," Montgomery said. "Jesse's pretty familiar with how these interviews work. Aren't you, Jesse?"

He peered at me.

I shrugged.

"You want a cup of coffee?" he asked me.

That sounded really good and I was tempted to say yes, but to drink it, I'd have to ask to have my hands uncuffed. Or at least moved to the front. That would give Montgomery a slight psychological advantage. "No, thanks."

"Suit yourself." He got up walked around behind me. "Have you got anything to say about where you were at two this morning?"

"At work," I answered.

"You know, a surveillance video is damning evidence. And even though it's nighttime, this one is pretty clear. Got lots of good footage of you coming and going. And some pretty good shots of your face."

I had no idea what to say, so I just kept quiet.

Montgomery perched on the edge of the table again and picked an imaginary piece of lint off his gray striped trousers. "I can see where you'd get into a situation where you needed money fast," he said. "You're supposed to get that reward for the cat collar, but it hasn't come through yet, has it? Maybe you spend a little too much, expecting that?"

I looked down at the table. "I'll be surprised if I ever do get that reward. I sure as hell haven't been spending anything extra, expecting to get it anytime soon."

"And what would you do with it if you did get it?" he asked.

"I dunno. I got to find a new place to live, so I could use a down payment."

Montgomery looked at his watch. "That's right. Your old place got flooded out, didn't it? Where have you been staying?"

"A few nights here, a few nights there." If I didn't have to, I wasn't going to tell him I'd been house sitting for Mandy. She was a respectable woman who worked at the public library. I'd met her when I first applied for a library card. She hadn't blinked an eyelash when I'd handed her my prison ID and the lease on a crummy one-room apartment to qualify for a library card. I'd always be grateful for that.

When I first knew her, she was in a disastrous marriage to a man who was an executive at Quality Steel Fabrications, where I worked. He got caught in some kind of counterfeited identity scheme and ended up killing one of his accomplices. She'd since settled down with Nicole, another woman, and because she had the money to push it, her divorce had come through pretty fast. Or maybe it was an annulment. Whatever it was, her lawyer handled it. With gay marriage now legal, she and Nicole had gotten married. Now they were on their honeymoon, and I was staying in the carriage house behind the lovely old Victorian house that Mandy had inherited from her parents. As long as she wanted me to stay there and keep an eye on it, she was letting me stay for free. It was a big help, and it meant the place wasn't empty while they were away.

"Not staying at the girlfriend's house?"

"Sometimes." I wish. But we weren't ready for that type of commitment. At least, she wasn't.

"I understand," Montgomery said, "that she's got money problems, too."

"Well, yeah. We was out of work for a while. When the flood knocked out electric power, Quality Steel shut down. She got unemployment compensation, but that's not at all like a real paycheck. And her car's been giving her grief. Needs a new clutch. That ain't cheap."

"How about you? Did you get unemployment compensation?"

"Nah." I shook my head. "You have to have so many quarters of employment credit before you're eligible, and I don't have enough."

Belkins laughed. "They don't give credit for working in the prison kitchen?"

"Actually, I worked in the laundry," I said.

He snorted. "Same difference. What'd you get, a dollar a day?"

That was the standard inmate pay rate. "Yeah."

"So." Montgomery took over again. "Your girlfriend's short of money. And what with the divorce and custody battle for her kids, she's got lawyer fees and court costs. And the car. You think maybe you should help her out?"

"She's pretty independent," I said. "I think she'd feel funny about taking much from me. Even if I had it. She'd think it was creating some kind of obligation or something."

He leaned back. "A security deposit on the kind of rat hole you'd live in wouldn't take the whole five thou, if you get the reward. What else would you do with it?"

Extra money. A dizzying thought. I blurted out, "I'd look into getting my driver's license." Even to me, I sounded too eager.

"Your driver's license." Montgomery stroked his chiseled chin thoughtfully. "Why don't you just go get a learner's permit? Don't you already know how to drive?"

"I kind of do. And I could get somebody to let me practice." Who, I didn't know. Maybe Kelly?

"So what's the problem? It doesn't cost *that* much."

"I never had a license. So I'd might need to pay for one of those stupid driver's education courses. And I have moving violations."

He laughed. "Moving violations, huh? And you never had a license. That's a good trick. I take it that's from before you got locked up?"

"Yeah."

"So they're, like, twenty some years old?"

"Yeah. But they don't go away." I'd checked. "I still got to pay the fines."

"I hope they don't charge interest on what you owe."

"No. But I do have to pay them before they'll even think about giving me a learner's permit."

Belkins plunked himself down in the chair again. "This isn't a damn counseling session. You're not finding out anything. I say we lock him up for a while. Let him stew about this. Maybe he'll decide to cooperate."

"And what kind of conclusion would he come to?" Montgomery asked.

Belkins smiled his mean little smile. "We could maybe cut him a deal, especially if he returned the money. Guilty plea, a short sentence, maybe even probation. Save everybody a lot of trouble."

Did he think I was stupid? A new felony conviction would send me straight back to prison for years.

Montgomery got to his feet. "You're right we're not getting anywhere. But I'm not so sure we'll get any further locking him up. That costs the taxpayers money. And he might lose his job. If he can't pay his own way, it'll cost even more."

Belkins spat on the floor. "There you go, running for office again. The jail's already there. Don't cost much more to add one more person. He's not gonna hold down the job long-term, anyhow. Look at the recidivism rates for violent offenders who have spent that long in prison."

I was aware of them, too. If there was any way for me to beat those odds, I was determined to do so.

"And he might take off anytime," Belkins added. "Or commit who knows what new offense. Kill somebody else."

"This is a property crime. I'm sure they'd set bail," Montgomery said, "so he could still take off if he wanted to anyhow."

Belkins pounded his fist on the table. "He could never make any bail himself. If somebody did bail him out, we'd get a good look at whoever's in this with him. Like the girlfriend."

He was right. Any bail they set would be too high for me to even think about making, even if I could find a bail bondsman who was willing to handle it. Which was doubtful. And Kelly could never come up with the required ten percent, even if she wanted to.

Once again, they were trying to see if I wouldn't jump in and say something stupid. They'd have a long time to wait. But they were also trying to ramp up my stress level.

And that was working pretty well. I felt sweat gathering at the base of my neck. But even if they managed to pressure me into saying something, I didn't know anything at all about the ATM break-in, so it wouldn't be much help.

"I don't know." Montgomery got up and took a step toward the door. "I want to take one more look at that video before I fill out my report and take it over to the district attorney. And talk to Damon's parole officer."

They both went out the door, turning off the bright overhead light as they left.

Once again, I sat in the dim interview room by myself, waiting for who knows what. Actually, I knew damn well what. Release or jail.

I shifted restlessly in the chair. They could have at least given me a chance to use the john before they left.

CHAPTER 3

After what seemed like hours, but couldn't have been anywhere near that long, the door to the interview room opened and a uniformed corrections officer came in.

Not a police officer or sheriff's deputy. Corrections officer. Not a good sign.

"Come on," the CO said. "You're wanted downstairs."

I lurched to my feet, my arms and legs stiff from sitting so long in an awkward position. He grabbed my arm and steadied me.

Best bet would be to keep quiet, but I couldn't help asking, "What'd they want me for?"

"I dunno." He shrugged. "I was just told to bring you downstairs. Maybe they need the room for somebody else."

Doubtful.

I was grateful for the firm grip he kept on my arm as we descended the noisy metal staircase. At least I wasn't wearing leg irons. Although I could manage the transported-inmate shuffle all right on flat ground, I'd never quite mastered doing stairs with my ankles shackled.

When we reached the bottom of the stairs, he steered me left toward Central Booking, where incoming prisoners were processed. My stomach twisted. I tried to take a big breath to calm myself, but I could hardly force air into my lungs.

Montgomery stood at the desk, leaning on an elegant elbow. I kept my head down. I couldn't bring myself to look at his face. I was afraid of what I might read from his expression.

"Well, Jesse," he said. "Got anything more you'd like to tell me?"

I didn't trust myself to speak. I shook my head.

"Still say it wasn't you on that surveillance video?"

My mouth was dry. "Yeah," I managed to say.

"You know," he said, "I've been trying to figure out how you could have managed that. The video maybe has a lot of shadows, but there's a couple of reasonable face shots. Full on. I could swear it's *you* on it."

I didn't say anything.

"But your alibi checks out. At least for now."

So if my alibi checked out, what was I doing standing here at the intake desk? In handcuffs. Nobody was going to care what I thought, though, so there was no point in protesting. I maintained my silence.

"You know what?" Montgomery said. "I talked to the state's attorney. He doesn't like that a whole bunch of solid citizen types say you were at work with them when the break-in went down."

Glancing up at him, I said, "And…?"

"And he's not charging you. At least right now."

So they weren't charging me. That was one major step in the right direction. But was I going to be held for a parole violation hearing? I licked my lips. "What does that mean for me?" My voice came out dry and raspy.

"It means," he said, "that you can go now. Turn around so the CO can take the cuffs off."

As I turned, my socked foot slid on the tile floor. Once again, the alert CO caught my arm and steadied me. The guy had kept me from falling a few times. At this rate, I was gonna owe him big time.

He undid the handcuffs and snapped them back onto his belt. "That all?" he said to Montgomery.

"I think so. Thank you," Montgomery answered.

My wrists tingled. I resisted the urge to rub them to restore the blood circulation in my hands.

"I'll take you to get your stuff," Montgomery said.

With a detective at the property room window with me, I didn't have to wait at all. And all my things—wallet, keychain, belt, boots, jacket, even my hair tie—were produced without a problem.

"Sign this," the clerk growled, pushing a receipt toward me.

I signed. I didn't bother to check it closely since I hadn't had much to begin with. I glanced in my wallet. Both my IDs—the employee one from Quality Steel and my old prison ID—were there. So was my library card. And the pathetic few dollars I had until my next paycheck.

Montgomery stood next to me as I threaded the belt through the loops on my jeans and then sat down to put on the boots. Then he walked me to the front door.

"You know," he said, "I'm going to get to the bottom of this. Figure out who was in that video, if it wasn't you. Or if it was you, how you managed to pull it off."

"It wasn't me."

He laughed. "If you find out anything that might help, or think of anything, give me a call. Tell them you need to talk to me, but don't leave a message. Might save your bacon."

I had no idea what I could find out, or how, but I nodded. "Will do."

He turned to go back inside.

"And Detective…" I said.

Pausing, he said, "Yes?"

"Thanks."

"Thanks? For what?"

I drew a deep breath. "I figure it must have been you talked to the state's attorney to let him know he might not have a case. And included the stuff about an alibi, all the people saying I'd been at work. If it was Belkins, he would have left out that part. And I'd be locked up. So thanks."

Montgomery laughed. "And Belkins doesn't think you're very, shall we say, astute."

I hurried down the outside stairs and away from the county buildings. A few drops of rain fell as I headed back to the carriage house behind Mandy's big Victorian mansion where I was staying while she was away. I had to report to work at midnight tonight. After what had gone on so far today, I needed to remember to appreciate that opportunity. It was a good job for anyone, much less a paroled convict, and I'd never find one half as good if I lost it.

I should try to get some sleep. Driving a forklift and working around heavy steel fabrication equipment and welders wasn't a good idea if I was exhausted. I was all stressed out and knew sleep wouldn't come easy, but I'd learned over the years to force myself to catch a few winks whenever I had the opportunity, even if my mind was racing.

Luck had been with me to come by this house-sitting gig. The carriage house was the most comfortable place I'd ever lived in and the nicest neighborhood. The opportunity had come just when I really needed a place to stay, after a major flood had ruined my apartment. The building was old and mostly vacant. I could see why the landlord was taking his own sweet time about making repairs. If he made them at all.

I had no control over this, like an unfortunate number of things in my life. But it was getting better. When I was first released from prison, I was on home detention, only allowed to leave my basement apartment for work, parole meetings, and a few hurried hours for running errands like laundry and shopping. Those few hours were the first time in my life I ever felt free to do whatever I wanted. I tried to fit in visits to the library.

For all those years I was locked up, I'd read everything I could get my hands on. For someone like me who could never afford a TV, it passed the time and served as a distraction from the monotonous routine of prison life. I came to appreciate the value of the prison library and made a beeline for the local public library as soon as I could.

Mandy had made me feel welcome, not like a dangerous felon she maybe had to let in the library because it was a public place, but who everybody knew didn't really belong there. She'd actually smiled at me when she handed me my new library card.

I'd certainly been on the receiving end of smirks, but no one, especially not a woman, had smiled kindly at me in years. I'd looked Mandy up every time I was in the library, and if she had a minute, talked to her a bit.

At the time, she was in the ill-considered marriage with Sterling Radman, who'd recently come to town to work for Quality Steel. He was a man who was not particularly interested in her, but just her substantial inheritance. Then she discovered her new husband was involved in a number of illegal schemes and was making plans to mortgage her house, clean out her bank accounts, and abscond. When she realized he might also be intending to arrange her demise to inherit, she asked me if I would kill him for her first.

Not likely. For one thing, we weren't going to get away with it. I'd had more than enough of the criminal justice system. And she'd hate prison just as much as I had. Probably more, since she'd always lived a comfortable upper-middle-class existence. I convinced her that's what divorce courts were for and dragged her to her family's lawyer. He arranged for her to stay in a safe house until Sterling was arrested.

I wasn't sure at what point she'd come to the conclusion that, for her, it wasn't just the marriage to Sterling that was ill-considered. It was marriage to a *man*. But that wasn't any of my business. And now she'd found Nicole. I was happy for her.

The windows of the carriage house overlooked the alley that ran behind the house, but the door opened into the fenced yard. While the exterior doors for the horses and the carriage itself were still visible on the exterior, they weren't functional. Inside, they had been walled over and a roomy living room/kitchen combination fitted where the stalls used to be. Upstairs, under the eaves, was a cozy bedroom and bath. It was altogether a comfortable place to live. Too bad it was temporary.

I opened the tall gate and stepped onto a path among the well-kept flower beds. And stopped.

A young woman was sitting on the steps to the carriage house, a suitcase by her side and her head bent over a bundle in her lap. She was shivering.

Was that a *baby* in her arms?

She lifted a tear-streaked face and stared at me. "Who are you?"

"I was going to ask you the same thing," I said.

"I'm Eileen McCormick. My aunt, Nicole Smithson, lives here."

"My name's Jesse Damon. Your aunt is away for a while. She and Mandy went on a trip." I didn't want to say honeymoon, since if Nicole hadn't made her family aware of her sexual orientation, it sure wasn't my place to blab it to her niece. "Mandy owns the house. I'm staying in the carriage house and keeping an eye on the place while they're gone."

Tears welled up in her eyes. "When will they be back?"

"Another week or so. Maybe longer."

The tears trickled down her cheeks. "What am I going to do?" she wailed.

"What do you mean?" I asked.

She reached into her pocket, pulled out a piece of paper covered with handwriting, and offered it to me. "Aunt Nicole told me I could bring the baby and come stay with her if things got any worse at home with my husband." She took out a soggy tissue and wiped her nose. "They got worse. So I walked out. And if Aunt Nicole isn't here now, I've got no place to go."

I took the proffered paper and read it over quickly. Sure enough, it was a letter. And it said exactly what she said it did.

"Well, let's at least go inside. Get you and the baby out of the weather." I unlocked the door and grabbed the suitcase.

Once inside, I laid the suitcase on a chair and reached for Eileen's coat as she slipped out of it, juggling the baby from one arm to the other. The coat was just a shell with no lining. It wasn't freezing outside, but the coat couldn't have kept her warm. Underneath, she wore a thin cotton dress. No wonder she'd been shivering.

She was pale, with lank brown hair and dark circles under her eyes. Her shoulders drooped. Bruises surrounded her thin upper arms and her neck. Finger marks.

I gestured at the sofa. "Sit down."

Clutching the baby tightly, she sat. I grabbed an afghan from a chair by the window and wrapped it around her shoulders.

"Want a cup of coffee?" I asked. "All I got is instant."

"I'd love a cup of coffee. Instant is fine."

Taking two mugs out of the cupboard, I filled them with water and put them in the microwave.

Opening the refrigerator door, I said, "I haven't eaten all day. I was gonna fix something. You hungry?"

She nodded without looking up at me.

My grocery supply was pretty limited. I'd planned on frying slices of hot dog and adding them to a package of ramen noodles for my lunch, but I wanted to feed her better than that. "Omelet okay?" I asked.

"Omelet sound wonderful," she said.

The microwave buzzer sounded. I took out the mugs and spooned dark coffee crystals into the hot water. I drank my coffee black.

"You want a little milk in that?" I had splurged on a gallon of milk. I hadn't bought any sugar, but there was a sugar bowl in the cupboard. I took the lid off and peered in. It was about half full. "Or sugar?"

"Yes, please," she said.

I guess that meant both. I stirred milk and sugar into her mug, carried it over, and put it on the end table next to her.

She pulled a hand out from under the bundled baby and picked up the mug. "Thanks." She took a sip.

Taking a quick gulp of my own coffee, I put the frying pan on the stovetop to heat up. I chopped up some onion and green peppers and then whisked a half dozen eggs with a little water in a bowl. I put the eggs in the frying pan, added the veggies, and drained a small can of tomato bits and added that, too. I hesitated over the slices of cheese. It was an extravagance, but I put a few of those in. They melted nicely.

Toast would be a good addition. All I had was a loaf of cheap white bread and a tub of margarine. I put a couple of slices in the toaster while the omelet cooked.

Finally, everything was done. I slipped the omelet onto a plate and cut it in half, transferring half to another plate and adding the toast.

Putting the plates on the table, I said, "You wanna come over here and eat?"

Eileen frowned down at the baby in her arms.

"Is he okay?" I asked. "I mean, he hasn't made a sound."

"*She*. Abigail. I think she's just tired. Her daddy and me were up all last night fighting, and she cried all night."

I scratched my head. Unless Abigail could drink plain milk, and I knew babies were supposed to get some kind of fancy formula that cost a fortune, I didn't have anything to feed a baby. "Did you bring anything for her to eat?"

With a shy smile, Eileen nodded. "I *always* have something for her to eat. She's breastfed."

"Oh." That took care of that problem. I hoped she wouldn't whip out her breast and start feeding the kid right now, though.

She didn't. "If you could spread out a blanket or something, I could lay her on the floor while I eat," she said. "There's one in my suitcase."

Rummaging around in her suitcase seemed like the wrong thing for me to do. "You want me to get it out?"

"If you could."

I went over to the suitcase and unzipped it. A soft pink baby blanket with a satin edging was on top. Gingerly, I lifted it out and unfolded it.

"Just spread it on the floor," Eileen said.

I did so. She stood up and carried the baby over. Kneeling, she laid her gently on the blanket. Abigail made a few mewing sounds and stuck her fist in her mouth, but she didn't wake up.

Eileen and I sat down to eat. I was hungry, but she practically inhaled her food. I got up to make us a couple more cups of coffee. "You want some more toast?" I asked. "I got some peanut butter you could put on it if you wanted."

"No. Thank you. If I eat any more, I might get sick. But that was good."

I put the refilled mugs on the table. "You got some way of getting hold of your aunt?" I asked. "A cell phone or something?" I didn't have a cell phone, but it seemed like everyone else on the face of the earth did.

She looked down. "Gary—that's my husband—he keeps the cell phone. He says if I ever needed to use it, he'd put the call through for me."

I knew the type. "And I bet he said you didn't need a landline in the house, either."

She nodded.

"Or a car. Or money. Or friends."

"You've been reading my mail." She gave me a wan smile.

I smiled back. "If he let you get any mail."

She laughed, but tears gathered in her eyes. "You've got that right. I had to have Aunt Nicole send her letters to General Delivery. Gary goes to get his hair cut every two weeks, and I go to the grocery store, which is right next to the post office. I had trouble getting the letters at first because I don't have any picture ID, but in the end, they gave them to me."

"Does he know where you're at?" In my experience, people like Gary didn't give up easily. And they could be a problem.

"I don't think so. I haven't been in touch with any of my friends since we got married. He knows I have a few relatives, and he knows Aunt Nicole lives here in Rothsburg, but not exactly where."

"How did you get here?" I took a sip of my coffee.

She hugged herself. "I drove. Gary has a job out of town for a few days. A friend picked him up this morning, so he left the car."

"I'm surprised he left you the keys."

"He didn't." She rubbed her eyes. "And he thought that since I don't have a valid driver's license anymore, I couldn't drive it. But I know where he hides his spare key. And I used to drive. Before we started going out."

I drained my mug. "When's he gonna be back?"

"Maybe tomorrow night. Maybe not for a few days."

"And what's he gonna do when he finds you're gone?"

Her voice dropped to a whisper. "Probably start looking for us. He'll be mad."

"Where's the car now?" I asked.

"I left it in the driveway out front. You can't see it that well from the street."

I stood up. "But I bet you can if you really look. Let me put it in the garage."

She looked at me doubtfully, but she reached in her pocket and got out a key.

"I'll be right back."

The car was a dented station wagon with Ohio plates. It was too old to have an onboard GPS system. I could only hope Gary hadn't installed some kind of LoJack or other locator on it. When I got in and started it, the gas gauge was on empty. She'd barely made it here. I pulled it into the garage space in the garage that Mandy's BMW usually occupied. That was parked at the airport now. I closed the door and peered through the windows. It was evident that there was a car there, but it would be almost impossible to tell what kind. And the license plates were totally unreadable.

When I got back to the carriage house, Eileen had picked up the baby. The baby blanket was over her shoulder, and Abigail's head was tucked underneath it. The baby was making wet "mmming" sounds. She was getting her supper.

I was grateful Eileen had managed to handle that discreetly. I had no idea how I was supposed to react to a woman breastfeeding a baby. Only that the whole idea made me uncomfortable. Which it shouldn't. I mean, of course that's how babies got fed.

Sitting down at the table again, I looked away from her and the baby. "So you don't have a cell phone. I don't have a cell phone. I don't think Mandy has a landline in the house. And even if we dredge up a phone, I don't have a good number for either her or Nicole. Do you?"

"I did, for Aunt Nicole, but I didn't remember to bring it with me. I had it hidden, taped under a jar of pickles at the back of a cabinet in the kitchen. It's in a code, so Gary won't be able to figure out what it is even if he finds it."

Eileen seemed like a nice enough lady. How could she have ended up in this nightmare marriage? And stayed in it long enough to have a baby? "Mandy left me an e-mail address," I said, "but she said they might not be checking it much. You need a computer to send a message. And you need to know how to use it."

"I know how to use it at least well enough to send an e-mail," Eileen said. "Is there a computer in the house?"

"If there is, I don't know where it would be. Mandy has one of them laptop things. Maybe she took it with her. The library has one you can use. But I think they're closed right now. What with the budget cuts, they're not open every day anymore. You'd have to wait until tomorrow to send an e-mail from there."

Eileen eased Abigail out from under the blanket and held her up on her shoulder, patting her back. "And then there's no guarantee they'll get it anytime soon," she said.

"True, that." I stood up and gathered the dirty dishes.

Abigail belched loudly. I'd had a little experience with babies and their often-messy burps, so I grabbed for a paper towel and handed it to Eileen, but she didn't need it.

Eileen smiled fondly. "She's not a spitter," she said. "She's really an easy baby. Thank goodness."

I carried the dishes to the sink. "Mandy told me to make sure I didn't let anybody stay in the house while they were gone. She probably didn't have you in mind, but still…"

"If she said not to let anybody stay in the house, you have to do what she wants," Eileen said firmly. "I guess I can sleep in the car. I've certainly done it before. Do you think it's okay to leave it in the garage? I'd feel safer there."

"You sure as hell ain't gonna be sleeping in any car," I said. "Not cold as it is. And not with that baby."

She wiped her eye with the paper towel. "I haven't got money for a hotel."

I sighed. "If anybody sleeps in the car, it'll be me."

"This is your place for now. I can't put you out," she said.

"Yeah, well, that baby can't stay overnight in no car. It's too cold."

"Maybe I could sleep on the couch?" she said doubtfully.

Turning on the water in the sink, I turned to face her. "If we have to go there, you can take the bedroom. But in them letters, did your aunt ever say anything about me?"

"I don't think so." She felt the baby's diaper. "Wait. Did you say your name was Jesse?"

"Yeah."

Her eyes opened wider. "Mandy's friend Jesse."

"Yeah."

"The murderer."

CHAPTER 4

"Yeah." If she was going to be staying overnight in the same place as me, she had a right to know what she was getting herself into. At least Nicole had told her enough that it saved me from figuring out how to bring it up and explain it. I never quite knew how to have this awkward conversation with regular people.

Eileen sat quietly, gripping Abigail so closely that the baby started to squirm and let out a whimper.

She relaxed her hold and looked at me. She took a deep breath. "Mandy must trust you. She's left you keeping an eye on her house."

"I guess." I rinsed off the dishes.

"Aunt Nicole says Mandy has lots of valuable antiques and things. She wouldn't have left you to take care of everything if she thought you'd start selling it off or anything."

I looked over my shoulder at her and grinned. "Yeah. I may be a convicted murderer, but I ain't no thief."

In spite of the tension, she laughed. "Are you guilty? Of the murder, I mean."

Shrugging, I said, "Technically, yeah. I mean, in this state, anyone who was involved in a felony where somebody ends up dead is guilty of murder, whether they were the actual killer or not."

"So you didn't actually kill anybody?"

"Nah. I was a dumb sixteen-year-old kid. My older brothers had me stand lookout outside while they went in to a crack house to rob a drug dealer. Dumb as I was, I thought they went in to make a buy. But the drug dealer ended up shot to death. And my brothers took off. The cops thought I did it."

"Sixteen? Wouldn't that put you in juvenile court?" she asked.

"I thought that, too, but I found out different quick enough. Murder charges go straight to adult court."

Abigail whimpered again, and Eileen shifted her position. "But you didn't pull the trigger. You weren't even in the apartment. And you didn't even know they were planning to rob him. How could they charge you?"

"The drug buy itself was a felony. I knew about that, and I was participating. So no matter how you look at it, it's a legitimate conviction.

I didn't know anybody was dead when I was arrested, and we'd agreed that if anything went wrong with the buy, I'd accept responsibility for pretty much everything. We figured that since I was a juvenile, the most I'd prob'ly get was a few months in juvie hall. Or rehab. So I didn't deny it when they started questioning me."

"Weren't there any witnesses?"

I scratched my cheek. I still needed a shave. "Yeah. Even an undercover cop saw it. But the light wasn't good, and I look a lot like my brothers. By the time I figured out what was happening, it was too late to try to explain anything. Nobody wanted to listen. And I had a public defender; he was looking for the best possible deal, not an acquittal."

"So what kind of sentence did they give you?" she asked.

"I copped an Alford plea—that's when you don't admit guilt, but agree that the state has enough evidence to convict you—and picked up a little over forty years. The lawyer said he thought that was about the best he could do. I was a scared young kid, looking at the death penalty. Or life without parole. Forty years wasn't great, but it sure sounded better than then being executed. Or spending the rest of my life in prison."

"Forty years! They wouldn't have executed a sixteen-year-old, would they?"

I shook my head. "Twenty some years ago? Yeah, they might have. It's only been lately that the courts have decided minors shouldn't be given the death penalty. Or automatic life without parole."

"How long were you in prison?"

"Almost twenty years. And I was lucky to get parole then. I was young when I got locked up and hadn't had any disciplinary infractions for over fifteen years. So I wasn't a bad candidate when they really started looking for people to release. The money crunch helped; if they parole enough people, they can stop thinking about building so many new prisons."

"So you're going to be on parole for a while?"

"Yeah. I got another twenty years of that to go." Twenty years of parole restrictions. That wasn't going to be much fun. But it sure beat twenty more years locked up.

"And you haven't been in any trouble since your release?"

That wasn't exactly the case. "Well, they do have a tendency to think paroled convicts are likely to reoffend. So sometimes when something happens, I get picked up and questioned about it." I saw no point in saying that had just happened today.

Eileen got up and went to the suitcase. "I have to change Abbie's diaper," she said, pulling a folded disposable diaper out. "Do you have a plastic shopping bag I can wrap the old one in?"

I got a used plastic shopping bag from the stash under the sink. While she handled that task, I finished rinsing the dishes and put them in the dishwasher.

"So," she said when she was done and Abigail was dressed again. "Is that offer to stay here still good?"

"Of course."

"I can't put you out of your bed, though."

"Look." I glanced at the clock. "I work a midnight to eight in the morning shift. I got to get some sleep before that. But it does mean that you got the place to yourself from about eleven fifteen until sometime in the morning. How about I catch some sleep upstairs for a few hours now, and then you can have the bedroom? Then nobody has to sleep on the couch. Or in the car."

She reached over and gave me a hug, the baby between us. "That sounds like a great plan. I can't thank you enough."

* * * *

The alarm clock woke me from a deep sleep. Groaning, I rolled over and hit the snooze button. The security light in the alley shone dimly through the sheer curtains.

I was still tired, but it was time to get ready for work.

When I got downstairs, Eileen was sitting on the sofa watching TV. The baby slept peacefully on the pink blanket at her feet.

I pulled my hair back and secured it with a hair tie. "How're you doing?" I asked Eileen.

"Fine. Thanks to you." She pressed a button on the remote control and muted the TV.

Grinning, I said, "You're gonna have to show me how to work that TV. It looks complicated, and I didn't want to mess it up, so I haven't been using it."

"Really?" she said. "Didn't you miss not having TV?"

"Nah. I never had one when I was locked up—you could buy them, if you had enough money, but they were pretty expensive, so I never got one of my own—and all anybody ever wanted to watch on the dayroom TV was cartoons or sports stuff. So I just didn't bother."

"It's really not that hard. Do you want me to show you?"

"Not now. I got to fix something to eat and make a lunch."

"What time do you get lunch?" she asked.

"Around four a.m." I took a square of ramen noodle soup mix out of the cupboard. "Do you want something to eat?"

"No, thanks."

I was just as glad she said that. My food supply was pretty limited. "You can always fix yourself something later. If you can find anything you want."

"I'm not fussy," she said. "Besides, beggars can't be choosers."

"Huh?"

"I'm staying here under your good graces. And I'm eating your food. It would be pretty outrageous of me to object to what you can provide."

I hadn't thought of it that way, but she had a point. I crunched the ramen noodles into a bowl, added water, and stuck it in the microwave. Since I didn't have a lot of time, I would forego frying up some sliced hot dogs to add to it. I pulled out my loaf of bread and made a couple of peanut butter sandwiches. Not exactly a gourmet meal, but come lunchtime, I'd be glad I had it. I made instant coffee and poured it into my thermos. I put that and the sandwiches in my battered lunch box. When I was first released a few months ago, I'd paid five dollars for it at Goodwill. Thermos included. It worked.

When the microwave buzzed, I took the bowl out and stirred the seasoning packet into the noodles. It wasn't much, but it would do.

"Where do you work?" Eileen asked.

"Quality Steel Fabrications. Mostly, I drive a forklift. It's a good job, especially for a convict on parole. Now that I got in the union, it's got benefits and everything. I really lucked out."

She nodded. "What time do you get home?"

"I get off at eight. Sometimes it takes me a little while to get the forklift hooked up so the battery can recharge and run over the end of shift checklist. I don't get paid no overtime for it, but I want to make sure it's all right. So I usually get home maybe at nine or so."

"How do you get there?"

"I walk. It's not that far."

"I suppose you could take my car. If it's got enough gas."

"Thanks, but I don't got a driver's license. And I sure don't want to get caught driving without one. That'd be a quick way to violate my parole." I slipped on my jacket and picked up my lunchbox. "Besides, you don't want that car out on the street anywhere if your husband comes around looking for it."

"I suppose you're right on that." She lifted the back of her hand to wipe her eye.

She looked so vulnerable, I hated to leave her. "You ought to be all right," I said, as much to reassure myself as her. "Nobody should be coming around this time of night. If I was you, I wouldn't answer the door if someone did come by."

"You're probably right." She smiled. "I'll see you in the morning."

"Okay. Get yourself some good sleep."

The wind was picking up as I walked down the alley toward the factory. I looked around and marveled that no trash was swirling in the corners, like it would have been in my old neighborhood. Or around the steel plant. Classy part of town, this was.

It was a good hike, almost two miles, to work. That was the industrial part of town, nearer to the river. All downhill.

My old place had been closer, in an apartment in the basement of a defunct pizza parlor that had a brief resurrection as a store-front church that was now also defunct. When the spring snow melt in the mountains had coincided with heavy spring rains a few weeks ago, the river had overflowed its banks and flooded half the city. Including my apartment. So far, the landlord showed no inclination to spend the money to fix up an already decrepit building. Depressing. I would need to find a new place to live. I couldn't afford much. I thought wistfully of Kelly's big house, with its cozy—if somewhat dysfunctional—family and her big soft bed. I'd love to move in there, but she wasn't likely to ask me.

When Mandy and Nicole asked me to house sit, we hadn't really discussed how long I'd stay in the carriage house, just that I'd stay for sure until they got back. I felt a bit bad about not pointing out to them that I could end up locked up again pretty much any time, but Mandy knew that. I'd hoped they'd let me stay until I found somewhere, but Eileen's arrival may have changed things. Of course Nicole would want Eileen and the baby to stay there.

Shivering, I pulled my jacket closer. During the daytime, the air held a promise of warmer weather, but the night wind was chilly. I pulled my watch cap down tighter and flipped up the hood on the jacket. It would definitely not have been a good night for Eileen and the baby to spend in the car.

Walking in this neighborhood after eleven at night made me nervous, and I usually stuck to the alleys where I was less likely to be observed. That was a calculated risk, because of course if someone did see me in the alley instead of out front on the sidewalk, I'd look all the more suspicious.

Production was winding down on the evening four to midnight shift as I made my way to the time clock to punch in. The smell of hot steel and oil filled the air, and sparks flew. The shop floor vibrated like something alive, and the continual dull thunder of machinery pounded in my ears. At midnight sharp, the factory whistle would blow and most of the work would cease.

Midnight to eight, my shift, ran a reduced workload and staff. The twenty-four-hour continual operations, like the plating and packing lines, would continue, as would a few of the production stations. Shipping would be busy, since a lot of truckers took advantage of the lighter nighttime traffic to drop off or pick up their loads. They were anxious to be away from town and out on the highway before the morning commuters hit the roads.

John, the foreman, was standing near the time clock, a battered clipboard and the chewed stub of a pencil in his hands. "Jesse," he called to me as I punched in.

I grabbed my hard hat and gloves. "Yeah?"

"We got a shipment of chemicals for the plating room." He looked down at the clipboard. "It came hours ago. I don't know why second shift didn't get it moved. But they didn't. When you get everything settled and get a chance, put them in the locked storage area behind the platers."

"Okay."

"It's fifty-five gallon drums on pallets. The plating room lead has the key in his office. And he can show you where they need to be put."

"That'd be Hank, wouldn't it?" I asked.

"Yep. He knows where everything goes."

I headed out to the charging bay where the forklifts were plugged in, recharging their batteries. Taking down the clipboard next to the one I usually drove, I started going over the pre-shift checklist.

The roar of the machinery was not as loud here. A soft voice behind me said, "Hi, Jesse."

Turning, I grinned at Kelly, the sometimes girlfriend. Her long dark hair was gathered in a ponytail that hung down her back and brushed her ample rear. It was all I could do not to reach over and run my fingers through it. She was the other forklift driver on the shift. Her usual assignment was the shipping room, loading and unloading trucks, and the lift she drove was bigger than mine. Since I had to supply parts and remove pallets of finished products from the production stations all over the shop, mine had to fit in smaller spaces.

With an effort, I kept my hands to myself, clutching the clipboard hard. We both knew if I had my druthers, Kelly'd be a lot more than a sometimes girlfriend. But I settled for what I could get. Maybe someday, she'd see things differently. Or maybe someday, I'd be in a better position and be able to offer her and the kids some stability.

Maybe someday, the sun wouldn't rise.

"Look," she said, taking down the clipboard next to her forklift. "Did you mean it when you said you'd come over and keep an eye on the kids so I could go to an AA meeting?"

"Yeah. Sure." I'd been encouraging her to join AA. She'd been using alcohol as a mental escape sometimes, and she'd had a lot to escape lately. Finances were always tight, and the recent plant closing due to the flooding had hit both of us hard. She was trying hard to hang on to the house she'd been awarded in her divorce, since it was in a good school district and the kids didn't need any more changes in their lives, but the mortgage payments took a good hunk of her income. And now with her car giving her grief, things had to be even tighter. It might not be worth it to fix the slipping clutch on her battered old station wagon. That was a couple thousand dollars, and something else was sure to go wrong as soon as that was fixed. She really needed a new car.

Her ex was challenging her for custody of the kids, and while it didn't look like he had much of a chance—he had an alcohol problem, too, and a number of DUIs, at least one with the kids in the car—it was stressful and the attorney fees added up. Added to all that, she'd let her dad use her address for a home plan when he'd been up for parole from the same prison where I'd spent so many years.

That had turned into a major mistake. He was an old biker, and she thought he'd spend most of his time with the Predators, his bike club buddies, up at their clubhouse in the hills. He'd spent a lot of time with the bikers, all right—but mostly at Kelly's place in town. One night when he wasn't there, she'd been attacked and raped by one of the Predators.

Her father was locked up again now, and the rapist was dead, but things like that have a way of messing with a person's head.

As far as I could see, the wonder wasn't that she was drinking too much; it was that she was functioning at all. But she knew she needed to get her act together, especially for the kids. If she let it, AA could provide a solid base for her while she struggled with her demons.

She chewed on the end of her pencil and started inspecting her lift and checking items off her list. I stood still and stared at her with hungry eyes.

"I went to a meeting last weekend when Fred had the kids," she said. "And I've only had a drink once since. I think I've got a fighting chance to get this thing under control. But I bet I'd do better if I went to a midweek meeting, too."

"Of course you would. If you can get to a meeting when everything is closing in, it's a whole hell of a lot better than taking a drink. And you'll probably find a mentor you can call if you need to." I couldn't think of any way I'd rather spend time than go over Kelly's place, fix supper, and help the kids with their homework. I could put the years locked in a six by nine foot cell behind me. Of course, I would like it better if Kelly were there with us, too, but she wouldn't be gone all that long.

"Want me to come pick you up?" she asked.

"Nah. I can walk over. What time?" She shouldn't be driving that car any more than she absolutely had to, and I'd stop at the store and get something to fix for supper. Money was in short supply all around, but I could afford to buy something to fix them.

"How about five or so?" she said. "You can eat with the kids. The meeting shouldn't be too long, and I can drive us to work. After we catch a few hours' sleep."

I finally gave in and reached over to run my hand down that ponytail and over her rump. "Is that all we're gonna do in that big old bed? Sleep?"

She laughed. "Not if you can think of something else to do."

"Oh, I promise you I can think of something." I grinned.

"Well, I just might hold you to that promise." She hung her clipboard back up on its hook, flipped her hair back, and swung into the forklift's seat.

I watched her until she rounded the corner. Then I went back to finish my own checklist.

CHAPTER 5

The whistle signaled the shift change as I eased the lift out of the charging bay. Most of the machinery fell silent. The ruckus, somewhat diminished, would start up again in two minutes.

Diffy, one of the lift drivers on the four to midnight shift, came roaring down the hallway, skidding alarmingly close to the back of my lift as I pulled it into the aisle.

"Watch where you're going with that thing," he growled.

Diffy didn't like me much. He didn't have to like me much, but sometimes, he tried to get me in trouble. Sometimes he succeeded. Like a few weeks ago, when somebody'd crashed my assigned forklift over a loading dock when I was in the john. I didn't have any proof it was him, but I knew my foreman thought he'd done it, and the union backed me, so I hadn't suffered any serious negative consequences for the wrecked lift.

I straightened out my lift and braced myself for a possible minor collision. Which he would blame on me.

But he just pulled his into its place and climbed off, muttering to himself, and reached for the clipboard.

Just as happy to avoid a conflict and let the situation ride if I could, I headed out on the floor to make my rounds. To my pleasant surprise, all the work stations were well-stocked with parts and all the full pallets of completed products had been removed to the warehouse. Diffy always did an adequate enough job so that he wouldn't get in trouble, but usually, he left anything he could for me to take care of.

I headed to the plating room. Operators stood on wooden platforms in front of the four massive platers which stretched back into the cavernous gloom. Each squat behemoth had an overhead conveyor with a set of hooks. As the conveyor came down from the plating tanks in front of the operators, they took the shiny plated parts off the hooks with a practiced motion and replaced them with dull unfinished ones. The new ones were whisked away up to the first tank. The motion of both men and machinery was monotonous and unceasing. I'd worked the platers for a while before I was assigned to the forklift, and I knew the operators made it look much easier than it really was. Pungent chemical fumes and a thunderous roar filled the air. Everyone who worked here was offered masks and hearing protection, but it was uncomfortable to wear the bulky earmuffs with the required hard hat, so most people on this shift skipped them, although some wore earplugs. On the day shift, when all the supervisors and inspectors were present, people were much more inclined to wear the protective gear.

The platers were well-supplied with parts, and none of the pallets of finished products were anywhere near full. Diffy had done an unusually thorough job here, too. Maybe he'd tried to keep busy so he could avoid having to move the chemicals into the storage room.

Pulling up and parking by the plating room office, I swung off the forklift and opened the door to the office. Hank, the plating room lead, leaned his huge bulk back in the desk chair, his heavy boots up on the battered desk, peering at a stack of paperwork.

"I think I got this, Jesse," he said. "You wanna take a look at it for me?"

Since I'd started work here just a few months ago, the management had instituted a new, computerized system for issuing and tracking the work orders. One-page lists with part numbers and quantities scribbled on them had been replaced by multi-page computer printouts with dense blocks of information and paragraphs of text.

That might work well for the office staff that generated the paperwork, but it was a potential disaster for some of the shop workers, many of whom had worked at Quality Steel for years, way before it occurred to anyone doing the hiring that maybe new hires should be asked if they could read. A lot of them didn't. Hank was one of those people. So was Kelly. I could read pretty well, so I helped out where I could.

I took the paperwork from Hank. Using the order numbers in the corner of each page and the page numbers, he'd organized it and stapled each bunch together. Quantities and part numbers were highlighted in yellow. I flipped through the stack. "Way to go. What are you gonna run tonight?" I felt like one of my old high school teachers encouraging an unlikely but willing student. The ones who'd told me I could graduate and go on to college if I wanted to and worked at it.

Instead, I went to prison and got my GED.

Underneath his bushy mustache and full beard, Hank beamed. "Those u-shaped shelving units. In three different sizes. No way will we get through them all on this shift, so I don't got to worry about nothing else."

"That's right." I read over the paperwork. "They have a rush order on them—probably need them for a new store opening or something. They want 'em shipped on Friday morning."

Hank's smile faded. "I never could have figured out all that."

"Maybe not, but you had the essential information. You could've run all night fine without knowing any more than you had figured out. And you could have asked the foreman a few questions when he came around if you needed to."

He scratched under his beard. "Yeah, well, that works as long as it's John working. If'n it was another foreman on, I might not be able to ask nothing."

"But think of how much better you are at figuring it out than you were when they first switched to this system. And it was only a few weeks ago. Back then, you couldn't have gotten all this stuff put together right. So you're learning. In a little while, you'll have it down and won't need to be asking nobody nothing."

He grinned again. "Don't know that it'll ever come to that, but you sure been a help, showing me how to look for the numbers and all."

That was the closest Hank would ever come to a thank you. But it was really me that owed Hank. When I'd started working here and was still a probationary employee, I was assigned to operate a plater. At first glance, it didn't look like it would be that hard to learn, but when I watched the operators closely before I started, I realized it was a carefully orchestrated dance and not nearly as easy as it looked. Hank was patient with me, showing me how to handle the endless rhythm of the machinery and giving me the time I needed to master it.

"John told me there was some plating chemicals that came in today. He wants me to move them to the storage area when I can."

"Hope they got some potassium cyanide in." Hank removed his feet from the desk and stood up with surprising ease for a man of his size. He reached a hand the size of a small ham to get a key hanging on a hook above the desk. "We're running low on that. I'll put the key in my pocket, so when you get the stuff, just come and find me and I'll unlock the gate."

I'd never been in the plating storage area. "Okay. Will you show me where you want me to put it?"

He nodded. "Should be pretty obvious, though. Just match up the drums and put it with the same stuff."

"Rotate stock?"

"Yeah. Always. We use the old supplies up first."

Hank held up the key. "Only two keys for this lock," he said. "This one and the one the watchman has."

"Why is that?"

"Same reason they keep the damn stuff locked up. Some of these chemicals are pretty nasty. They don't want folks who don't know what they're doing fooling around with them. I know they don't want them out on the floor anywhere when the day shift people come in."

"I should be able to get started on it before first break," I said.

Hank nodded. "Truck must have been late, or they should have gotten those pallets moved in here on the last shift. Just you be careful."

Swinging back up onto the forklift, I went out to the loading dock to see what needed to be done out there.

Four trucks were backed into bays. Kelly had her work cut out for her. The load for each truck was assembled in a neat line on the shipping room floor near the loading bay, paperwork attached to the last pallet of each group.

Once again, I was surprised. Diffy usually left as much work for us as he could. And he usually dumped loads in a haphazard bunch. He must have really hustled to pull all that out of the warehouse and get the paperwork ready.

The drums of chemicals were tucked in a corner of the shipping room floor and had yellow "Restricted Area—Do Not Enter" tape draped around them. Some of the drums had diamond-shaped skull-and-crossbones stickers on them that said "Poison" with the number 6.1 in the bottom corner of the diamond. I looked closer. "Potassium Cyanide" was stenciled on the sides. That was what Hank was looking for.

Nobody on this shift was likely to bother them unless they were told to.

I took a few minutes to check the paperwork for Kelly. She was pretty good at matching the product number on the paperwork to the tags on the pallets, and she knew where the quantity should be written, so she could count to make sure she had the right number. But the bills of lading could get complicated, and some of the truckers would want her to go over them.

A truck driver leaned against the wall next to where the overhead door was open to his trailer. His log book was tucked under his arm, and he checked his watch as I skimmed the paperwork for his load.

"Look," he said. "I'm running late. I'm gonna be even later if I have to wait for Kelly to get to me. You think you could load me? Ain't nothing really heavy there—pretty much all wire baskets. Shouldn't be a problem for your smaller lift."

I glanced down the row. Kelly was waiting while a driver checked over his paperwork and signed it. He nodded, folded his copy up, put it in his pocket, and headed out to climb into his cab. Kelly went to close the overhead door as soon as he pulled out.

She had two other trucks to load before she got to this one.

"I done checked over the packing list and stuff," the guy said. "It's okay. It won't take you but a little while to load it, and then I can be on my way."

He was right. John expected Kelly and me to work together to keep the work flowing. If Kelly got swamped, I loaded trucks. If I got swamped, Kelly moved parts in the shop and warehouse.

When Kelly turned her lift in my direction, I caught her eye and nodded to the load, pointed to myself and then the truck. She smiled and gave me a thumbs up.

"Okay." I tucked the paperwork under my butt and swung around to pick up the first pallet.

Kelly had more experience maneuvering in the confined space of the trailer, and she would have been quicker about it, but I knew how to distribute the load and what needed to be tied down where, so it would be done and the driver on his way long before Kelly could have even started.

I finished up. The driver signed the paperwork, shut his trailer door, and went to climb into his cab. I delivered the paperwork to Kelly.

"Thanks," she said, raising her voice against the echoing noise in the shipping room. "I don't know what's going on here tonight. It sure is busy."

Returning to the corner where the chemical drums sat behind their tape, I undid the tape and eased my forks under the first pallet. Gently, I lifted them a few inches and raised the front of the forks so the load nestled back securely. Although I'd had routine training on handling the hazardous materials in the factory, I'd never actually moved the dangerous stuff like potassium cyanide before. Now would not be a good time for me to drop a load. Or worse.

Easing around the corner, I pulled up in front of the locked gate, parked, and went to find Hank and the key.

He was up on the catwalk around plater number two, helping the operator fish a bent shelf out of one of the tall narrow tanks. Seeing me, he patted the pocket where he'd put the key and held up an index finger.

I waited.

Hank walked to the end of the catwalk and tossed the bent shelf down. He turned back to the tank. No reasonable conversation was possible over the din of the machinery.

Picking up the shelf, I moved it off the platform to a pallet of rejects. Hank pulled on the conveyor hook, which had caught on the side of the tank and was jammed tight. When it wouldn't budge, he climbed up on the edge of the tank to get better leverage.

I tensed. Not a smart idea. Everything up there was wet and slippery. He grabbed the hook and yanked. It came loose, and he teetered sideways. He looked like he was about to fall into the tank, but caught himself on a gear of the overhead conveyor. His hard hat tumbled off, into the tank. The operator, who had been standing back watching, grabbed at Hank's arm and pulled him back onto the catwalk. He then reached into the tank, pulled out the hat, and handed it to Hank.

Taking the wet hat in one hand and the mangled hook in the other, Hank signaled to the other guy and headed toward the ladder. They trooped down.

When they were on firm footing on the platform in front of the plater, Hank hollered to the operator, "You can start up again. You'll be short a hook, but ain't nobody on this shift who can fix that. So just run it."

The operator nodded and pushed the emergency button to restart the plater. He reached for the shelf on the next set of hooks.

Hank and I stopped at the office so he could hang up the wet hat and take another one from a shelf. He tossed his wet gloves on the desk and took a new pair from a box. "Good thing that was a rinse tank," he said. "Cool water. I wouldn't want to explain what happened to that hat if there'd been anything corrosive in that tank. It'd just have to disappear." He didn't seem to worry about what would have happened to him if *he'd* landed in a tank that contained something corrosive.

Hank pulled the key from his pocket as we headed toward where I'd left the lift with its load.

The gate was open a few inches. "It like that when you got here?" he asked.

"No. It was locked up tight."

He pushed the gate open a little more. "Steb?" he called. "Steb, you in here?"

"Is that the watchman?" I asked. I'd seen him almost every night, but I'd never known his name.

"Sure is." Clutching the gate, he peered into the room. "Stebril Jenkins," he called, "if you're in here, you'd best say something, or I'm gonna go call the foreman."

A voice sounded from the dimness within. "Don't call John! It's me!"

Hank switched on the light. "What you doing in there in the dark?"

"Punching the check clock," he said. He had a punch card, and as he visited each check-in site on his round, he'd punch in on a clock which recorded the time.

Hank stepped past the gate. "What the hell's taking you so long?"

"I…" Steb said, his voice faltering. "Just look. What's this white powder stuff that's spilled on the floor here?"

Hurrying around some stacked drums, Hank stopped short.

A fifty-five gallon drum lay on its side. It had the diamond label on it, the skull grinning up at us. The drum had a large slash in it. A while granulated powder had spilled out onto the floor.

"Holy shit," Hank said. "That's potassium cyanide. We got to get that cleaned up, quick." He backed out the gate into the hallway. "Jesse, I'm gonna go find John. You make sure nobody else gets in here."

Steb, an old scrawny man with a grey beard and hair, twisted his punch card in his hands. "What should we do?" His skin was a strange flushed red color.

"Nothin'." Hank looked at the trail of white powder that led to Steb's boots. "You walk through that shit?"

"Must have." Steb leaned against the wall and lifted his boot to look at the sole. It was covered with the white powder.

"You just stay still. Don't move," Hank said over his shoulder as he left. "John'll be here in a minute. He'll tell us what to do."

I stood well back from the spill. The drum had tumbled off a pallet just like the one on my forklift. An odd odor reached my nose. Bitter almonds.

"I got to clean this off of my boots," Steb said to me. "Get me a fire hose. There's a standpipe back in here. Got to be a fire hose somewhere, too."

"Dude," I said. "You don't want to be putting water on that stuff til you know how to handle it. John'll bring the hazmat sheet."

Steb put his hand to his head. "I got a headache. Prob'ly from breathing that dust. You gonna get me a fire hose or not?"

"Not. Just hang tight."

"Never mind. I'll go get one myself."

I wasn't sure if I should try to physically block him or not as he came toward me. I knew we didn't want the potassium cyanide spread any farther than it already was.

John came running up. I'd never seen John run before.

"Steb wants a fire hose to wash off his boots," I said.

John skidded to a halt. His face paled. "My God! No! Put water on that stuff, and you got hydrogen cyanide gas. That's not only toxic to breathe; it can explode if a spark reaches it."

A steel fabrication plant has no shortage of sparks.

Hank lumbered up, lugging a big black loose-leaf binder with the skull and crossbones diamond on the front and on the spine.

John gestured toward the book. "Hank, look up the potassium cyanide section in there. I got to be sure I remember right what we got to do."

Hank's eyes opened wide, and he hefted the book. "I...I...I..." he stammered.

I grabbed it from him. "Potassium cyanide?" I said, flipping through the pages.

Steb took a couple more steps forward. "I got to wash this crap off my boots."

John's voice was tense. "Hank, pick him up and set him on the fork-lift seat. Then take his boots off. Try not to knock around that powder any more than you have to. Be sure you're wearing gloves."

Hank leaned down, slipping his big hands under Steb's armpits and easily lifting him off his feet. He carried him over to the forklift and plunked him in the seat. Steb's foot hit the controls, and the lift shuddered.

"Shut the damn thing off," John directed me.

"Here's the pages on potassium cyanide." I laid the book on top of one of the drums on the lift's forks and reached over to turn it off and pull the key.

"Leave my boots alone!" Steb hollered as Hank unlaced them and started to yank them off his feet, none too gently. "They're almost new, and they cost me over a hundred dollars!"

I could believe that. I worried about something happening to my steel-toed work boots, too. Replacing them would be a major expense.

Victor, the union steward, hurried up, his breathing labored. "What's going on?"

John didn't look at him. "Potassium cyanide spill. Steb's walked through it. And to hear him breathe, he prob'ly inhaled some. Jesse, what are the effects of breathing it?"

I looked at the page. "It says, 'irritate nose, throat, lungs, causing coughing and sneezing.'"

Steb sneezed.

"Also, 'high exposure can cause headache, confusion, dizziness, anxiety, pounding of the heart, even unconsciousness and death.' It says to seek immediate medical treatment," I continued.

John let out a sigh. "Victor, can you take Steb to the emergency room? Hank, go call the hospital and tell them we got somebody coming in who's breathed potassium cyanide. Possible skin exposure."

Hank took off for the plating room office.

"I need my boots," Steb said.

"We'll take good care of them for you," John promised. "Clean them up good and everything. You go with Victor."

"How'm I gonna go with Victor?" Steb asked. "I got no boots. I sure as hell ain't gonna go walking around here in my stocking feet."

"Well…" John scratched his head.

"He's skinny," I said. "If he shoves over, we can both fit in the lift seat. I can take him to the loading dock."

John nodded. "Okay. But be real careful. We don't need him falling off in addition to the chemical exposure. Victor, can you get your car and meet them at the dock?"

Victor nodded and headed out toward the parking lot.

I climbed up and perched on the edge of the forklift seat, pushing Steb over as gently as I could. Holding my breath, I tried to start the engine. The electric lifts could be fussy sometimes about starting when they didn't have a full charge, which was the main reason we usually left them idling while we did other tasks. Technically, that was against the regulations, but we all did it.

Fortunately, it started on the second try. I eased it around to the side of the hallway, dropping the pallet that I still had on the forks out of the way against the wall, and swung around toward the loading dock.

Steb wiped his nose with his sleeve. The sleeve came away red. "I got a nose bleed," he said. "I got to find some tissues."

For the minute, I ignored him. The last thing any of us needed was potential exposure to blood-borne pathogens.

When we got out to the shipping room, Kelly drove up, frowning. "John sees you fooling around like that, he's gonna write you up. Get him off right now."

"Accident," I hollered back at her. "Victor's picking him up at the dock and taking him to the emergency room." I looked at the bright red blood on Steb's face and hands. "You got any shop towels?"

"I can get some." She frowned. "Is that blood all over his face?"

"Yep." I pulled up by the last truck bay, which was empty. A doorway next to it led to a flight of stairs down to the asphalt surface of the truck yard. Climbing off the lift, I pushed the button to open the overhead door and flicked on the bright light. I hoped Victor had enough sense to drive down this far.

Kelly pulled up and handed me a wad of shop towels. I gave them to Steb. "Press them on your nose," I told him, remembering the procedure from our safety lessons.

Steb took the towels and dabbed at his face. "Haven't had a nosebleed in a month of Sundays," he said. "Wonder if it was breathing that chemical."

I was sure it was.

A car roared up beside the bottom of the stairs. "Come on, Steb," I said. "We got to get you into Victor's car."

He just sat there. "I can't go without my boots," he said.

Kelly looked from him to me to Victor, who was climbing out of his car and opening the passenger door. "Come on, Steb," she said, taking him by the arm. "We'll get you your boots. But first you have to get in Victor's car."

He slid off the seat. The light blue shop towels he had pressed to his nose were turning red. "The floor's cold."

"Yes," Kelly said soothingly. "That's why you need to get in Victor's car fast. He'll turn the heat up, and your feet will get nice and warm."

Her grip firm on his arm, she propelled him to the stairs and down them. Victor took over. He wasn't as gentle as Kelly and manhandled Steb into the car, slamming the door after him. He ran around to the driver's seat and slammed that door. Backing recklessly, he swung around and headed out of the truck yard at an unsafe speed.

Kelly came back up the stairs. "What the hell was that all about?"

"I'm not really sure of all the details. But there was a chemical spill in the plating room storage area, and Steb traipsed through it. I think he must have gotten a real snoot full. The hazmat sheet says one of the side effects of breathing the damn stuff is mental confusion, and he sure acted mentally confused."

"And nosebleeds?"

"Yeah."

Kelly hit the switch that closed the overhead door and turned off the light in that bay. "Steb isn't the sharpest crayon in the box under the best of circumstances. They basically gave him that watchman job because he was hurt on the job. It's better than workman's comp for the rest of his life, both for him and for the company."

"You'd think they'd want somebody pretty sharp to be the watchman," I said. "After all, isn't he the one who has to respond to emergencies?"

"Nah. He's supposed to report problems to the foreman. His real title is *fire* watchman. All this oil and chemicals soaked into this old wooden flooring over the years. And all the sparks thrown by the equipment. We don't get them as much as we used to, but small fires happen. The trick is to keep them small. He's supposed to find them before they get out of hand. The foreman handles it from there."

"I'm just as glad I haven't seen none of them since I been working here."

"You work here long enough, you will."

I climbed back on my lift. "It can wait a long time, thank you."

"What was it that spilled?"

"Potassium cyanide."

Kelly frowned. "That's about the worst stuff we have. Did it get into the drains?"

"I don't think so. But Steb wanted to use a fire hose on it. John told him not to, though. Something about poisonous gas."

"Yeah. Hydrogen cyanide gas. They've used it in war. And it's explosive."

"Yikes." I thought back to the classes I'd had when I was learning to drive the forklift. I didn't remember the instructor specifically addressing potassium cyanide or hydrogen cyanide gas. "They told us in training a lot of the stuff we use, especially in plating, was dangerous, but I didn't realize it was that bad."

"Yeah. I was on the crew that handled it last time they had a bad spill of that stuff. Dumb. They tried to keep from making an environmental protection report, so they didn't call anybody to find out how to handle it. If they had hazmat books back then, they didn't bother to look it up."

"What did they do?"

"This was years ago, when I first started working here. They tried to wash it away. Fire hoses. A couple of people ended up with permanent lung damage. Come to think of it, Steb may have been one of them."

"I take it that fire hoses didn't work too well."

"No. It got washed into the drains and out in the river. There was a major fish kill, and the company had to pay thousands in fines." Kelly shook her head. "Both environmental violations and work safety issues."

"How do we clean it up, then?"

She shrugged. "Now they'll check the hazmat manual. John'll follow the directions in it. If he has to, he'll call in an outside hazmat team. They won't be happy, but it sure as hell beats the trouble they'll get into if they try to cover it up again and get caught."

"No wonder they're so careful with that stuff."

"Yeah. No matter how you're exposed to it, it's dangerous. If you ate even a tiny little bit, it could kill you. You'd turn bright red."

I remembered the odd reddish tinge to Steb's complexion and how red the blood from his nose had been. "Why would you eat something like that?" I asked.

"I don't think you would, on purpose. But you might get some in your mouth. And it's supposed to look like sugar."

"There was a pile of it on the floor, and you're right, it did look like sugar. But still…"

"You better get back there and see what they need you to do," she said, glancing down the shipping room at the rows of pallets that still needed to be loaded. "You still planning on coming over to watch the kids for me tonight?"

I grinned. "I'm looking forward to it."

When I pulled up by the storage room, Hank and another worker were putting on hazmat suits and respirators. Hank's bulk strained the seams of his suit. He picked up a large shop vac, nodded at John, and waddled around the corner toward the spill.

John gripped the hazmat binder, reading and rereading the instructions and cautions. I parked the lift and went over to him.

"Victor and Steb on their way to the emergency room?" he asked me.

"Yeah. Steb didn't want to go outside in his stocking feet, but Kelly jollied him into it, and Victor got him in the car."

"Good. The plant manager's on his way in. It'll be his decision, but I think we got a handle on this now. Vacuum up the loose stuff. Dump it in a clean drum. Then vacuum up the rest still in the drum and put that in the clean drum, too. Then seal the drum and wash down the area. Call a company for hazardous waste disposal. Probably the shop vac goes, too. And the suits."

"What do you want me to do?" I asked.

"How much of it did you breathe in?"

"Not a whole lot. Probably a lot less than Hank. I was behind him."

John glanced at the pallet with the filled drums that was still by the side of the hallway. "You didn't get any on yourself? Or your clothes?"

"No."

"Or on your boots, like Steb?"

"No. I didn't go near the spilled stuff."

"Then tell me." John drew himself to his full height of well over six feet and looked down at me from under his busy eyebrows. "How the hell did you manage to spill that stuff all over and not get any on you?"

CHAPTER 6

I stared at John. "What?"

"How did you manage to spill that potassium cyanide all over the place and avoid any contact yourself?" John repeated.

"You think *I* spilled it?"

"Had to have been you, Jesse. You were the one who was moving the shipment. One of the drums got knocked over. There's a hole in the side. Probably punctured by one of the forks. Some of the potassium cyanide spilled out. A simple accident."

"But..." I couldn't think of anything to say.

"These things happen. I wish you'd reported it right away," John said, "instead of leaving it for the watchman to find. Could have kept poor Steb from breathing it in and getting some on his boots. And maybe saved him a trip to the hospital."

"The gate was locked when I got there with the pallet. I had to go find Hank to unlock it for me. You can ask him."

"Then how'd Steb get in there?"

I thought for a minute. "He's got a key. He has to, so he can punch in on the clock in there. He must have unlocked it himself."

John raised his busy eyebrows and looked down at me. "Are you trying to tell me you think *Steb* knocked over the drum?"

"No." That didn't make sense. "But he ought to be able to tell you if it was spilled when he first went in there."

John spoke slowly and deliberately, like he was explaining something to a not particularly bright child. "Those drums are pretty sturdy. Looks to me like someone must have drove into it with a forklift. One of the forks must have punctured it. *You* were driving the forklift, weren't you?"

"Yeah, but I never even got inside the storeroom with the load. Isn't there some way you can check the forks of my lift? See if there's any residue on either one of them?"

John scratched the side of his neck with his pencil stub. "I don't know if that would be helpful. I didn't see any residue, and you've driven it all over the place already. But I'll mention it to the plant manager. When he gets here."

* * * *

When I returned my forklift at the end of the shift, no one I spoke to knew if the problem had been resolved. Or at least no one would tell me. I avoided Bucky, the day shift foreman. He would have no doubt that I was the culprit, and he'd be pretty loud about sharing that opinion with anybody who'd listen. Only he'd make it sound like proven fact, not opinion.

Pulling the clipboard off its hook, I went over the end of shift checklist carefully. I was pretty shaken, and now was not the time to mess up. Then I punched out and walked across town to the carriage house.

I let myself in quietly. Eileen's suitcase was still open on the chair, but she and Abigail were nowhere to be seen. Probably upstairs in the bedroom. I didn't want to wake her if I could help it. Might be the first restful sleep she'd gotten in days.

The problem was that the only way to the bathroom was upstairs through the bedroom. I liked to take a shower as soon as I could after work. I usually smelled of oil and sweat. And the clothes I could change into were up there. Despite my assurances to John that I hadn't been exposed, I was concerned that I somehow had some traces of potassium cyanide on my clothes. I'd hate for a baby to breathe any of that.

Maybe I could go check the main house now instead of after I showered. After all, that was the whole reason Mandy had asked me to stay in here in the carriage house.

There were a whole slew of bathrooms in the house—I'd never really counted—and I routinely flushed every toilet as I made my rounds, just to make sure there were no problems. I could use one of them if I needed.

After taking the back door key from its hiding place in a kitchen cabinet, I listened at the foot of the stairs for any indication that Eileen was stirring, but I didn't hear anything. I crossed the fenced yard toward the house, looking around to see if anything was amiss. Some of the flowers were faded and could maybe use deadheading, but they'd been like that the whole time I'd been here, so I didn't concern myself with them. Otherwise, everything in the yard was neat and the way it should be.

Using the key, I let myself in the back door of the house and then stopped and looked down at my boots. Were there traces of potassium cyanide on the soles? I tried to look and couldn't see any, but there was a big greasy blob on one side of the left boot. Mandy's house had some gorgeous rugs. I sat on the top step and took the boot off and turned it over. The greasy blob oozed down between the tread, all over the sole.

I took off the other boot and put them on the doormat outside the back door.

The house was quiet, its ornate flowered drapes and spindly Victorian furniture giving the impression that the whole place was suspended in time. Until I opened any of the bathroom doors. I padded through the maze of small rooms on the first floor and slipped through the door in the kitchen that led to the back stairs to the second floor.

I made the rounds of all the bedrooms and bathrooms, plus a few rooms whose purpose I couldn't identify. Everything seemed to be in place. I went down the main stairs into the entry foyer and opened the front door to check the porch.

One of those free advertising newspapers lay on the walk just inside the hedges. In this tidy neighborhood, if it was left for any length to time, it would be a dead giveaway that no one was home.

I wasn't wearing my boots. But the newspaper couldn't stay there. How dirty would my socks get if I dashed to the end of the walk to retrieve it? I'd swept the walk a few days ago.

Taking an elephant's foot umbrella stand from a corner of the foyer and propping the door open with it so it couldn't close and lock behind me, I went across the porch, down the steps, and onto the slate walkway.

Maybe it wasn't all that dirty out there, but it sure was wet. The bottoms of my socks were soaked and my feet were freezing.

Since I didn't want to go back into the house with the wet socks and I had the back door key in my pocket, I went back up on the porch, moved the umbrella stand out of the way, and shut the door. Then I circled around the house, stopping to check on the garage where Eileen's car was parked, and retrieved my boots from the back doormat, carrying them rather than putting them on over the wet socks. The floor in the carriage house was some kind of ceramic tile. Wet socks wouldn't hurt that permanently. Neither would dirty boots.

When I opened the door to the carriage house, Eileen was standing at the stove. She was dressed in a pair of blue jeans and a thin sweater.

"I hope you like pancakes," she said. "I found a box of mix and a bottle of syrup."

"That sounds really good. But it's not *my* pancake mix. Or syrup."

"Then it's got to be Aunt Nicole's. She won't mind if we use it."

I wasn't about to argue with that. "Let me run up and take a quick shower," I said, mindful of how I probably smelled and the possibility of traces of potassium cyanide powder on my clothes.

I hurried upstairs, showered quickly, and got dressed. I thought about shaving, but decided it would take too much time.

When I got downstairs, Mandy was pouring another spoonful of batter into the frying pan.

"Want coffee?" I asked her.

"Yes, please." With an expert flick of her wrist, she flipped another pancake.

Getting down a pair of coffee mugs, I heated water in the microwave. I got out the coffee, milk, and sugar. Frowning, I shook the milk jug. It was almost empty. I'd have to get some more soon. Or mix up some powdered milk.

"Where's the baby?" I asked.

"She's lying on her blanket behind the sofa." Eileen gestured in that direction with the pancake turner. "I already fed her, but I don't think she went back to sleep."

I went around the sofa. Sure enough, Abigail was lying on her blanket, her eyes wide open. When she saw me, she grinned, waving her hands and feet in the air.

It was impossible not to grin back. I got down on one knee and held a finger out toward her. She batted at it with a closed fist.

Eileen put two plates on the table. "Pancakes are ready."

I got up and sat at the table.

"I'm sorry there was no bacon or sausages or anything." Eileen handed me the bottle of syrup. She'd heated it up.

"Hey, pancakes is a treat," I said. "Usually I'd just have another bowl of ramen noodles. Or some peanut butter on toast."

"What kind of a breakfast is that?" She wrinkled her nose. "But I guess it's not really breakfast for you, is it? Not after you'd worked all night. How did work go?"

I chose my words carefully. "Interesting. There was a chemical spill that we had to deal with. But they had it under control by the time I left."

"Chemical spill? In a steel fabrication factory? What kind of chemicals do they use?"

Cutting into the stack of pancakes with the side of my fork, I said, "They use some pretty caustic stuff, both for cleaning steel and in the finishing processes. Some of the parts finish up with a nickel plating, and some of them get a powder paint coat. The chemicals they use for both of them can be pretty nasty."

"Was it a big spill?"

"Not really. One ruptured fifty-five-gallon drum, and not all of it spilled out."

"Liquid?"

I shook my head. "Granules. But they would dissolve in water, which could create a gas, and if any of it got washed into the sewer system and made it out to the river, it wouldn't be good for the fish. Or anything else that lives in the river."

"Did they manage to keep it out of the sewers?"

"I'm pretty sure they did." I decided not to tell her about Steb. "So, what are you planning to do today?"

Eileen smiled, but her eyes were grim. "I thought I'd go to the library and try to e-mail Aunt Nicole. She's got to check her e-mail sooner or later, right? Then maybe she can tell me when they're going to be back. How far away is the library? I'd just as soon not have to drive the car if I can help it."

"Not far. Mandy works there, and she walks most of the time."

"Can you tell me how to get there? And give me the e-mail address you have?"

"Tell you what." I drained the last of my coffee. "Let me shave, and I'll take you there."

"You've been so kind. I hate to put you to any more trouble."

"I was gonna go to the store anyhow," I said, thinking of the almost empty milk jug and my dwindling supply of cash. "That's right on the way."

Eileen cleaned up from breakfast while I shaved. Remembering her thin coat, I pulled out a heavy sweater I'd bought at Goodwill. I brought it downstairs in case she wanted to put it on.

But she opened the door to the coat closet next to the front door, took out a warm parka, and slipped it on. "I know Aunt Nicole won't mind if I use some of her clothes," she said.

I didn't know about that, but I didn't say anything. It didn't make any sense for her to be cold if there were warm clothes to wear. And since Nicole had been living in the house with Mandy, she probably had her best clothes over there.

Eileen must have caught the expression on my face. "If there are any problems from it," she said, "I'll tell Nicole it was my idea to borrow some of her clothes. You had nothing to do with it."

I nodded and held up the warm sweater. "It's cold out there. Is the baby gonna be warm enough?"

Taking the sweater, Eileen said, "If I can borrow this, she should be. I have a warm hat for her, and I can wrap her in your sweater, thanks. I'll put the blanket over that. She'll be okay."

The wind was cold as we made our way down the alley, but at least it wasn't raining. Eileen kept switching the baby from one arm to the other. Finally, I just took her and carried her.

The public library wasn't overly crowded on this weekday morning. A row of computers stood against a wall. Three of them were not in use.

"I don't really know how to use a computer," I admitted to Eileen. "Do you?"

She shook her head. "I mean, I used one when I was in school, and Gary had one in the house, but we didn't have an Internet connection, so we never got an e-mail account. But I can figure out how to send one anyhow."

"That's a lot more'n me. All I know how to do is print out stuff at work. And that don't always work." We went up to the main desk, and I asked the employee, "How do I get to use a computer?"

"You got a library card?" he asked.

"Yeah." I handed Abigail back to her mother and pulled out my wallet. Two IDs, one from Quality Steel Fabrications and one from prison, and a library card. I pulled out the library card.

The guy took it and wrote something down. He handed it back to me and said, "Computer number four. You have thirty minutes. After that, you can sign up again if you want to and there's nobody waiting for it."

"Are there instructions on how to use it?" I asked.

"On the desk next to it is a sheet with log-in instructions. You need your library card number. After you're logged in, though, it's just like any other computer."

I felt like saying that was the problem, that I didn't know how to use any computer, but decided maybe we should give it a try first. "Here." I handed my library card to Eileen. "Let me hold the baby. You take the card and see if you can figure it out."

Eileen slipped into the chair and peered at the instructions. She starting punching keys, and the screen changed. "Read me your library card number," she said, shoving it across the table so I could see it.

I did so, and all of a sudden, she was on the Internet. Or that's what it looked like to me.

Abigail stirred in my arms. She started making a happy babbling noise, growing louder and louder. Uneasily, I looked around at the other people using the computers. One man's eyebrows drew close together over his nose, and he frowned, shaking his head.

The guy who worked at the desk across the room looked at us.

"We're disturbing other people," I whispered to Eileen. "I can take Abigail outside if you want, but…" Was she really going to trust a convicted murderer with her baby, out of her sight? I couldn't blame her if she didn't.

Eileen hesitated a minute. "Go ahead. I'll try to get this done quickly."

I carried the baby outside and moved to the side of the wide steps, standing so the building blocked the sharp wind. Abigail continued her babbling, interspersed with loud, sharp squawks. She seemed quite pleased with herself and the loud noises she could make, so I just rocked her a little and turned so my back shielded her from any sudden gusts.

After a few minutes, Eileen came out the front door and joined us on the steps. "I got it sent. Now it'll just be a matter of when she looks at her e-mail and responds." She sighed. "I guess I'll have to come back here and check tomorrow. If we had a phone, I could have given her that number, but as it is…"

I nodded. "Seems like everybody but us got phones, don't it?"

She smiled.

"I got to stop at the store," I said. "I could give you the key and you could go on ahead if you wanted."

"I have a few things I need to get, too," Eileen said.

As we reached the sidewalk at the bottom of the stairs, a battered station wagon pulled up to the stoplight at the corner.

"I think that's Kelly, somebody I work with," I said, clutching the baby more closely to me and increasing my pace. "I bet she'd give us a ride."

Eileen frowned, but she hurried to keep up with me.

The light changed. With the morning sun in my eyes, I couldn't see the driver clearly. I pulled one hand out from under Abigail and waved at the station wagon. It paused for a minute. The car behind it honked, and it darted through the intersection. I expected the car to pull over into one of the parking spaces on the next block, but it kept going.

I slowed down and watched until I lost sight of the car in the next couple of blocks.

"I must of been wrong." I shook my head. "It must be somebody else with a car like that." Not too many cars like Kelly's around, especially that banged up, but there were probably a few. And in the bright sunlight, I couldn't even be sure it was the right color. If it had been Kelly, she would have stopped for us.

We went the couple of blocks to the Best Deals for Your Dollar store, which is where people like me shop. That and Goodwill. Wal-Mart is too rich for my blood, and it's way out on the edge of town. I don't have a way to get out there anyhow.

Eileen held the door for me, and we went in.

I knew there were a whole bunch of stores fancier even than Wal-Mart, but the only time I could remember being in one was just before I was released from prison, when staff from the prison took me and a few other guys to a shoe store to get boots for work.

Taking a cart from near the front door, I laid Abigail down in the basket. She couldn't sit up well enough yet for the child seat. I got a gallon of milk and a loaf of the cheapest bread, tucking them around the baby. I hesitated in front of the tuna fish before I moved to the dollar food shelf and got a couple of cans of beans and soup. I added a jar of peanut butter. Mentally, I added it all up. I would need to pay my parole expenses later in the week, and I wanted to get some stuff to cook at Kelly's place tonight with the kids. I had a small emergency stash, but I should be adding to that, not taking anything out.

Eileen was standing in the baby supplies section, which was only a few shelves. She had a tube of generic diaper rash ointment in her hand. As I watched, she took a small "travel pack" of disposable diapers off the shelf. It only had five diapers in it.

I looked at the shelf prices. "That's not that much cheaper than this bigger one," I said, indicating a package of fifteen. "And they're even cheaper in the packages of fifty—you only pay about a third each as much in that size. You're gonna be using them eventually."

"Yes. But…" Eileen looked around to see if anyone could overhear us. She leaned closer to me. "That's about all I can afford. Gary doesn't give me any money, and all I could stash away was a little bit of change here and there." She opened her hand, and sure enough, what she had was a handful of coins.

I took the package of fifty off the shelf and put it in child seat of the cart. "Maybe this'll hold us until Nicole gets back. Or at least until I get paid again." Which would be on Friday.

She held onto the small package of diapers and lifted her chin. Her eyes glistened with tears. "There's no reason why you should be paying for Abigail's diapers. You've fed me and let me stay in the carriage house with you. I can't ask you to do anything else."

I took the travel pack out of her hands and put it back on the shelf. "The baby needs diapers, don't she?"

Eileen nodded.

"End of discussion. If you want, you can pay me back when you get some money."

I turned and pushed the cart toward the checkout line. Eileen hurried to catch up with me. She put her purchases on the counter along with her coins. When the cashier ran it up, I paid the rest from my meager cash supply and paid for my own purchases. I'd make it until Friday without hitting the emergency stash if I was careful and nothing happened that I needed to spend money for.

We divvied up the stuff so we could carry it. She took the big bag with diapers and the milk. I juggled the baby and the other bag.

When we got back to the carriage house, I said, "I got to make some lunch and get some sleep."

"I'm not hungry yet," she said.

Since it was just me eating, I made myself that sloppy but filling old standby, a bean sandwich, and washed it down with water. The instant coffee had to last until Friday. For two of us.

"I promised a friend I'd go over her house for supper tonight. I'll head straight to work from there. You okay with that?"

"Yes," she said. "I'm going to do some laundry. Give me your dirty clothes."

"You shouldn't wash my stuff with yours and Abigail's," I said. "It's got oil and grease all on it, and it might have some chemicals." Like potassium cyanide, but I didn't say that.

"So I'll wash them separately," she said. "It's the least I can do."

I was still a bit hesitant. What with the stuff from work and the sweat I worked up every night, my dirty clothes were pretty funky. But I got my laundry bag and handed it to her and then went back upstairs to sleep.

CHAPTER 7

I rang the doorbell at Kelly's house with my elbow since my hands were full of bulging grocery bags.

Kelly's eight-year-old son, Chris, opened the door and grinned. "Jesse!"

Grinning back, I stepped inside. Brianna, age six, sat on the floor watching cartoons on TV. She looked up long enough to give me a shy smile and a wave.

Kelly came out of the kitchen. Her glossy dark hair was swept up smoothly on top of her head. Gold bands with twinkly stones dangled from her ears. The shirt she was wearing was tight and cut low enough that it showed the cleavage between her ample breasts.

She looked good.

I put the grocery bags down and pulled her to me, burying my nose in her neck. She smelled of soap and bath powder and something else. Perfume.

She returned the hug, but then pulled away. "Don't mess up my makeup! It took forever to get it right."

Kelly didn't usually wear makeup. I looked. Sure enough, her lips were a luscious red and her eyes were ringed with some kind of eyeliner.

"It sure looks good," I said, still holding her around the waist.

She smiled. "I'm trying. I figure if I look better, maybe I'll start to feel better."

"You look fabulous."

"Thank you." She stepped back and frowned at the grocery bags. "What do you have there?"

"Just something to fix for supper. If I'm gonna stay with the kids while you go to your AA meeting, you shouldn't have to cook for us."

She nodded toward the kitchen. "I left some frozen pizzas for you guys."

"You can save the frozen pizzas. I've got stuff to make chili. And cornbread. You can have some when you get home."

She laughed. "All they serve at the AA meetings are coffee and stale donuts."

"Yeah, I know. And you're lucky to get the donuts. Any meeting I ever been to, all they had was the coffee." I reached up to stroke her cheek fondly, but remembered the makeup and laid my hand on her shoulder instead, giving it a little squeeze.

Frowning, she said, "I didn't know you ever had an alcohol problem."

"Well, not really. It was really Narcotics Anonymous meetings. In prison. I didn't have a problem, but it passed the time some. More interesting than lying there on my bunk staring at the ceiling. Got me out of the cell for a little while. I never went to the closed meetings—those were only for people who were serious about it. But the lectures and classes and things, they were open to anyone who signed up for them."

"So you were a druggie wannabe." She bent over to pick up two of the grocery bags.

I laughed. "I hadn't thought of it like that, but I guess you could put it that way." Her tight jeans clung to her shapely rear. I resisted the urge to run my hand over the curves and instead picked up the other two grocery bags. We carried them into the kitchen.

Eying a gallon of milk and a dozen eggs, she asked, "What did you say you were fixing?"

"Chili and cornbread."

"With a gallon of milk and a dozen eggs?"

I shrugged. "I need a little bit for the cornbread mix. I wasn't sure you'd have any. And it's so much cheaper to buy the big packages than just a quart of milk or a couple of eggs. With the kids, I figured it'll never go to waste."

"That's true."

When she opened the refrigerator to put them in, I could see that the milk jug she had in there was almost empty.

"You know, I can feed my own kids," she said, an edge to her voice.

I knew she was a little touchy about that. But last month, the city had experienced a lot of flooding and the electric power had been out for a while. She hadn't worked for two weeks. Like everybody else who'd worked there long enough, she'd gotten unemployment compensation payments, but they were nowhere near as much as a paycheck would have been. And they were giving out emergency SNAP benefits to families that needed food. I think she refused to apply for them.

Since I hadn't been out of prison for long and didn't have enough work credit to collect any benefits, I'd taken all the work I could get when they called people in to retool the shop and otherwise get it ready to open again. It hadn't been anything like full-time, but it was some income.

Now we were back to work full-time, but I was still feeling the pinch. What with the house and the kids and the car and the lawyer, I knew Kelly had to be struggling, too.

"I don't got a good place to cook right now," I said. "Fixing chili here will be a nice change from ramen noodles and peanut butter sandwiches."

She pulled two big cans of kidney beans out of a bag. "How much chili did you plan to make?"

I shrugged. "A crockpot full. Enough so you can have some when you get back. If you're hungry." I'd actually planned to leave some in the refrigerator for another meal or two.

A car horn sounded from the street.

Kelly straightened up. "I got to go."

"Someone picking you up?" She should go, of course, but I really wished she could stay and have supper with us.

"Yeah. You know the car's been giving me grief. That clutch is gonna go completely one day soon. So when somebody offered me a ride, I said sure. Save the car for when I got no other way to get someplace."

That made sense. "Somebody from AA giving you a ride?"

"Yeah. Someone I met at the last meeting."

That was a good sign. A support system helped. "Your sponsor?" I asked.

"Maybe. Something like that. It's early days, so it's not official yet."

"Okay. I'll feed the kids and put them to bed if you're too late."

"Thank you." She gave me a quick peck on the cheek. "I appreciate you coming over and keeping an eye on them for me."

"Anytime."

"And when I get back…" She gave me a meaningful grin and squeezed my arm.

I started to lean in for a hug and a good smooch, but she put her hand up between us. "My lipstick!"

Instead, I contented myself with wrapping my arm around her shoulders and said, "I'll be waiting." We should have a few hours before the college girl who stayed overnight with the kids showed up and we had to report to work.

She went into the living room, me trailing behind, and said to the kids, "You be good, now. Do what Jesse says and don't give him a hard time."

"Yes, ma'am," Chris said, getting off the sofa to give her a hug.

Brianna hardly looked up from her TV show. "Okay," she said and then stuck her fingers in her mouth.

Walking over to the door with Kelly, I glanced out.

Her ride was a little red sports car. Cute. And expensive. The driver was standing next to it and opened the passenger door for Kelly, taking her elbow to help her into it. He leaned in close, and I would have sworn his arm brushed her bosom.

He was a well-dressed, middle-aged man with a mane of silver hair.

Slamming the door behind her, he went around the car and got in the driver's seat.

He didn't exactly peel rubber as he took off, but he gave that impression.

I stared out the front door. I thought usually AA sponsors were the same sex.

All kinds of people were AA members, I assured myself. Some of them were doing well financially, especially if they managed to keep their demons under control. It would do Kelly a world of good to be around people who handled the financial aspects of their lives well. I had encouraged her to join. She would get a lot of support, but everyone would expect her to stand on her own two feet. No bleeding heart types survived for long there.

So why was I concerned that a handsome middle-aged man with a sports car was picking her up for a meeting?

People often formed close relationships, born of mutual understanding and similar experiences, with other members. Usually platonic. It could be almost a cult type thing, and outsiders didn't have to understand.

And it made no sense to waste gas if someone else was going in the same direction. So what if it was a good-looking guy who drove a sports car?

Arguing with myself didn't make me stop feeling a lot of discomfort at the situation. But so what? That was my problem to deal with.

I tried to put the tales I'd heard of predators hanging around the meetings and taking advantage of vulnerable newcomers. Vulnerable was not a word that came to mind when I thought about Kelly.

"You guys wanna help fix supper?" I asked the kids. "We're making chili."

Chris got up and headed toward the kitchen, but Brianna just shook her head no without taking her eyes off the TV.

Surveying the ingredients spread out on the counter, Chris said, "Can I cut up the onions and the peppers? I'll be real careful."

I almost said no, that he could stir everything together, but when I saw his shining eager eyes, I said, "Sure."

I gave him the smallest sharp knife I could find and a cutting board. The onions made him tear up, so I moved the cutting board near the stovetop and turned the exhaust fan to high to blow away the fumes.

That worked. While I browned the ground beef, I deliberately didn't look toward him until I needed to ask for the onions to toss into the frying pan. If he cut himself, I'd find out soon enough. And Kelly would be furious with me.

The pieces of pepper he cut were uneven and ragged, but none of them were too big, so I added them. We added the beans and the seasoning, stirred everything together in the crock pot liner, and stuck that in the microwave to give it a head start on heating it up. We mixed up the cornbread mix, adding some sugar and a small can of creamed corn to the batter.

While that baked, we put the crock pot back together and let that simmer. Then we made a pan of brownies, again from a mix.

Lifting the lid of the crock pot and taking a good sniff, Chris said, "That sure smells good."

I nodded. "Yep. And we made it."

He beamed.

Without being asked, Chris set the kitchen table and poured glasses of milk.

When the cornbread was done, I went into the living room to get Brianna. She didn't look like she'd moved an inch.

"Suppertime, sweetheart," I said.

She didn't respond.

"Come on and have some supper."

"I'm not hungry," she said, her eyes still on the TV.

I went over and switched it off. "At least come sit with us. We fixed brownies for dessert."

She stuck out her chin. "I don't like brownies. I want to watch TV."

"Well," I said, "we're not gonna have the TV on during supper. And afterwards, we're gonna do homework."

"Mom lets me watch TV at suppertime."

"We're gonna leave the TV off. We can turn it back on when the homework's done."

She made no move to get off the floor. "Mom never makes me do my homework."

That was probably true. Since Kelly couldn't really read, she had trouble helping the kids with their homework. She was embarrassed about it, and one way she coped was by acting like homework wasn't all that important anyhow. Which was an unfortunate idea to give the kids.

I reached down and scooped her up off the floor. She stiffened up and then snuggled in against my chest. "Come on, sweetheart. Just try a little chili. Chris and I worked hard to make it."

She laid her head on my shoulder. "I don't like chili," she said.

I deposited her in a chair at the kitchen table. "Then have a little cornbread and drink your milk."

She folded her arms in front of her narrow chest and set her jaw stubbornly.

Chris cut a few squares of cornbread and put margarine on them. I put one in front of Brianna and put a big spoonful of chili in her bowl. "Just eat what you feel like," I said.

Scrunching up her face, she looked away from us as Chris and I dove into the chili.

"This is really good," he said, taking another serving and another piece of cornbread.

Brianna just sat there.

"Are the brownies done yet?" Chris asked when he was finished.

"They take a long time," I said, removing our bowls from the table. "Why don't you go get your homework? And bring Brianna's book bag, too. The brownies will have to cool off when they're done anyhow before we can eat them."

"Can I have another glass of milk with the brownies?" he asked.

"Sure. That's why I brought a whole gallon."

He slid off his chair and went to get his book bag. The crock pot was still three quarters full. I turned it down to warm so it would be ready when Kelly came home and wrapped the leftover cornbread so it wouldn't go stale. I started rinsing the dishes and putting them in the dishwasher.

When I turned back to the table to get Brianna's bowl, it was empty. So was the milk glass, and the cornbread was gone.

Wordlessly, I put another spoonful of chili in her bowl and cut her another piece of cornbread. This time, she picked up her spoon and ate.

Chris spread his books on the table and got to work.

"You want any more?" I asked Brianna when she'd finished.

She shook her head. "I'm not going to do any homework."

I took her dishes and wiped the cornbread crumbs from the table. "Just get your things out of your book bag so we can have a look," I said.

Reluctantly, she opened the book bag and dumped the contents on the table. It was a tangled mess of cards, papers, pens, and pencils.

"What do you have for homework?" I asked.

"I have to do continents," she said. "Not from my regular class. From the resource room."

Geography wasn't my strong point. But weren't there only, like, seven continents? "What do you have to do with continents?"

"Flash cards. I hate going to the resource room."

"Why is that?"

Tears filled her eyes. "Only dummies have to go to the resource room."

"I don't think that's true," I said.

Chris looked up from his math worksheet, pencil poised. "The resource room is for anybody who needs some extra help. Lots of people go there. Some of them are really smart."

"The smart kids from my class don't have to go to the resource room. They get to stay in the classroom and play games while the dummies like me go to the resource room. They don't have to do continents."

Chewing on the eraser of his pencil, Chris said, "I think she means *consonants*, not continents."

I scratched my chin. "Consonants?"

"Yeah. You know, like vowels and consonants. She's still working on her consonants." Chris returned to his math problems.

Sure enough, when I sorted through the cards in the pile of stuff from her book bag, I found alphabet cards. No vowels. "What do you have to do with these?" I asked.

"Match up capitals and smalls," she said, "and tell what they sound like."

I stacked the cards. Wasn't that *kindergarten* work? Or even preschool? Brianna was in first grade. And it was the second semester already. She should already know this.

Maybe that's why she had to go to the resource room.

I laid the capital letters out on the table and gave her the rest of the stack. "Can you put these where they belong?" I asked.

"You mean, like a small B on a capital one?"

"Yeah."

She wasn't bad at it, but predictably had trouble with small b, d, q, and p.

When the oven timer went off, Chris took the brownies out and set them to cool. "I'm done," he said. "Can you read us a book while the brownies cool?"

"Sure," I said. "Just let Brianna do the flash cards one more time."

She still couldn't get those four letters. I hoped the teachers knew some way to help her learn the difference. I couldn't figure out a good way.

"Go put your jammies on," I told the kids, "and bring the books you want me to read."

They scrambled upstairs, returning in their pajamas and carrying books. We snuggled on the sofa, Chris pressed up against my side and Brianna practically in my lap.

I read Brianna's book to them, stopping to discuss the pictures. Chris wanted to read his own book to us, so I let him.

"I bet the brownies are cool enough to cut," I said. "How about we go find out?"

They were still a little warm and gooey in the middle, but they tasted great. I made myself a cup of instant coffee, and the kids had milk.

"Okay," I said when they were done. "Brush those teeth and climb into bed."

"Are you gonna come up and kiss us good night?" Brianna asked.

I was a little uneasy with that, but I said, "I'll be up to tuck you in. Just let me clean up here."

They were both in bed when I got upstairs. Chris was stretched out on top of the covers, reading one last book. While he finished, I went to Brianna's room.

She was huddled in a little ball, the blankets drawn up over her head.

I took a teddy bear from the dresser and tucked it in beside her. She reached out a hand and snatched it to her, pulling it under the covers. I pulled the bedding down away from her face and tucked it in. Then I kissed the top of her head. "Good night, sweetheart," I said. "Sleep tight."

She nodded and buried her face in the teddy bear.

Chris was under his blankets. I tucked them in for him, too, and we bumped fists. "Good night, dude."

"Good night, Jesse," he said.

"Thanks for helping make the chili."

He grinned. "We did a good job, didn't we?"

"We sure did."

I turned out the light and went downstairs.

It was getting late. Shouldn't this meeting of Kelly's be over by now? Maybe some of them had gone out to get some supper. She had a right to splurge a little on that if she wanted to. And since she wasn't driving herself, she couldn't leave when she wanted. Maybe the guy with the red sports car was footing the bill. Sure looked like he could afford it.

I went to the kitchen and unplugged the crock pot, pulling out the liner and putting that in the refrigerator. If Kelly was hungry when she got home, we could heat some in the microwave.

Back in the living room, I turned on the TV. Like I'd told Eileen, I'd never had the money to buy a TV when I was in prison. The one in the common area of the cellblock was usually tuned to cartoons, except when there was a major sporting event. Unless I was at work in the prison laundry or we had yard, I spent most of my time in my cell. Less chance of getting in trouble there. I read a lot.

I flicked through what seemed like hundreds of channels, but nothing seemed interesting enough to bother watching. Where was Kelly?

Finally, I heard a car pull up outside. Going to the window, I pulled the drape aside just enough to see.

It was the little red sports car again. Kelly seemed to be in no hurry to get out. I stayed glued to the window. Was that spying or something?

The same good-looking guy got out, went around, and opened the door for Kelly. She climbed out and turned to face him. He put his hand under her chin, lifting it and placing a gentle kiss on her lips.

Wasn't that messing with her lipstick? She didn't push him away.

I stepped back from the window, my stomach twisted in a knot. We didn't have an exclusive relationship—Kelly insisted she wasn't ready for one—but I didn't think she'd been seeing anyone else.

I sure wasn't seeing anybody else. Nor did I want to.

She could have been, though. It would really be none of my business. She wouldn't have had to tell me. She kept her options open.

Realistically, what did I have to offer her? I could have my parole violated any time and be on my way back to prison in a heartbeat. I had almost another twenty years backup time. Not the best foundation for a future.

And while I made okay money at Quality Steel Fabrications, I'd never be anything like rich. When I was released, I just had the clothes on my back and a little start-up money I'd managed to save from my prison job. Plus the fifty dollars gate money they gave everyone on the way out. I was trying to save up some money to get my driver's license and maybe buy a pickup truck someday. But I had my regular living expenses, and the parole costs I had to pay ate up a fair chunk of what I made. That wasn't anything to take lightly.

The reward money, if I ever got it, would help a lot. But I knew better than to count on it. And while five thousand dollars was a fortune to me, I was realistic enough to know it wasn't really that much money to build a future with a woman who had a family.

If Kelly could find somebody stable, somebody who could take care of her and the kids, I shouldn't stand in her way. If I really cared about her, I should be happy for her.

If it came down to that, though, I might tell her I was happy for her, but deep down inside, I'd be hurting.

The front door opened, and Kelly came in. She still looked fantastic, and she had this kind of a glow about her.

My guts froze. Post sex? I tried to put that idea out of my mind.

"You hungry?" I wiped my hands on the sides of my jeans to keep from reaching out to touch her. "There's plenty of the chili left. And some cornbread. I can heat you up some."

She smiled and shook her head. "We stopped for a bite to eat after the meeting, thanks."

It was hard not to ask who "we" was, but I was pretty sure I already knew. "How'd the meeting go?"

"Okay, I guess. How do these meetings usually go?"

No answer came to mind, so I didn't say anything.

Stepping up to me, she gave me a kiss on the cheek.

Her perfume was still strong, and she smelled fantastic.

I put my arm around her and tried to pull her close to plant a kiss on her mouth, but she stepped back. That couldn't be a whiff of *alcohol* on her breath, could it? Not on the way home from an AA meeting, especially not with another member. Maybe mouthwash.

"Kids okay?" she asked.

"Yeah. We worked on their homework after supper."

"Thank you," she said, but she yawned and turned away. "We have to be at work in a few hours. I need to get at least a little sleep."

I waited for the invitation up to her warm, soft bed. We could be quick about it and then sleep until it was time to get ready for work. I could think of nothing better than holding her in my arms as she drifted off to sleep after we made love.

She slipped her feet out of her shoes. "You gonna stay here and catch a ride to work?"

That didn't sound like what I wanted to hear. "I guess," I said. I knew I should keep my mouth shut, but I couldn't help myself. "That guy, he's gonna be your sponsor?"

A soft smile played over Kelly's lips. "Sydney? Maybe."

"He's an active member, is he?"

"Yes. Long-term. Says he's been sober for over ten years now."

I scratched the side of my neck. "And he still goes to meetings?"

"Yeah. He says it keeps him on the straight and narrow. And he can help other people who are just starting out and still struggling."

That appeared to be Kelly right now. "Nice car he drives," I said.

"Isn't it? He's got his own business, a check cashing place over on Green Street. He says that's another way he helps people."

Given the fees most of those check cashing services charged, I wouldn't call such a business exactly a way of helping people. The only ones who used it were people who couldn't cash checks any other way, though, so maybe it *was* helping.

"He's divorced," Kelly said, a slight smile playing on her lips. "He's got four children, but they live with their mother and she won't let them see him. Even though he pays child support."

"Can't he get a court order?" I asked. Kelly should know all about that. She didn't like Chris and Brianna going to visit their father, but she knew she'd better follow the court orders.

"I suppose he could," she said, "but he wants what's best for them. He figures they'll come around some when they're older, realize he cares about them."

"How old are they?"

"In their teens and early twenties."

That seemed plenty old enough to me for them to be making up their own minds about seeing him. But if he'd been drinking when they were younger, maybe they had terrible memories of him. And maybe legitimate gripes. "He can't be still paying child support for kids in their *twenties*," I said.

A cloud crossed her face. "Maybe they're going to college and he helps out."

"Maybe," I agreed. "Still, you'd think if they wanted to see him…"

My voice trailed off. Kelly had turned away completely and was headed toward the kitchen.

"I got to fix lunches," she said. "For me at work and for the kids at school tomorrow."

I noticed I was nowhere in that plan. "You know," I said, "those AA meetings can get kind of intense."

"That's the whole idea. It's what makes them effective." She opened the refrigerator and got out some cold cuts and cheese.

"Yeah. It can mess up your mind a bit. Especially when you're new."

She swung around to face me. "And your point is?"

I should have kept my mouth shut, but it was a little late now. "You know how the AA program is a twelve-step program?"

"Yeah?"

"You ever hear of 'the thirteenth step'?"

"What's that?"

"That's when some of the old heads troll the new members, looking for sex and stuff."

"Are you insinuating that's what's going on with Sydney?" she demanded.

It was, but I backpedalled a little. "I just wanted you to be aware…"

"I'm plenty aware, thank you very much." She grabbed a jar of mustard and plunked it down on the counter with a resounding thud. "And I'm perfectly capable of taking care of myself."

I stood there silently as she opened a loaf of bread and spread six pieces out.

A sandwich for each of the kids. And one for her. None for me.

"Maybe I ought to be going," I said, hoping she'd ask me to stay.

"Okay."

"See you at work later," I said.

"Okay."

CHAPTER 8

If I didn't have anything for lunch, I'd be very sorry at four a.m.

Even if I thought I could make it back to the carriage house and then to work in time, which was doubtful, I'd already told Eileen I wouldn't be back until sometime in the morning. I really didn't want to have to explain to her what had happened. Or make something up.

On the way to work, right where the residential neighborhoods turned into commercial strip malls, there was an all-night gas station and convenience store. Not my first choice for picking up something to eat, but it would do.

Pulling the door open, I went in. At this late hour, I was the only customer. A young female clerk stood behind the counter, a big nametag on her uniform shirt announcing her as "Sadie." She leaned against the cash register, loudly chewing gum and keeping an eye on me via the mirrors in the corners. That kind of gave me the creeps, but I couldn't blame her. I'd want to keep an eye on me, too, if I were her and working alone in a store like this at night.

I picked up a can of iced tea and looked at the sandwiches in the cooler. They looked good, but they were pretty much out of my price range. Maybe I could find something cheaper. Peanut butter crackers or something. I went down one of the back aisles.

The front door flew open and banged hard against the door stop. Two kids, one tall and heavy, the other tiny, swaggered in and straight up to the counter.

"Gimme a pack of Marlboro lights," the tiny kid demanded. He looked like he was about fourteen.

"I need to see your ID," Sadie said.

"No, you don't," the kid said.

She shook her head. "Company rules. And state law. They find out I haven't been checking IDs, I'll get fired."

"Ain't nobody gonna find out," he said.

The big kid was wandering around in front of the counter. He stopped at the end. "Go on," he said. "Give Kiddo the smokes." Despite the chilly night, he was just wearing a T-shirt. And his arms glistened, like he was sweating.

Sadie took a step back and tried to watch both of them. "I need this job. I can't take that kind of chance," she said. "I need to see an ID."

"Yeah?" Kiddo sneered and took a step closer to the counter, putting his palms on it and bouncing on the balls of his feet. He acted like he was high on something, like meth.

"What about spice?" he asked. "You got to see an ID to sell that, too?"

"No." Sadie moved so her back was shielded by the cigarette shelves. "We don't carry spice no more. We got raided, and they took it. Said it might be artificial, but it was a drug."

"Yeah?" Kiddo said. "Me and Jazz, here, we don't really believe that. Some kinds of it are legal. I bet you got some stashed under there somewheres. If you're nice, we might even pay for it. And the smokes."

Sadie's face paled and she backed up against the cigarette shelves, but she said, "I done told you. We don't have it no more."

He bounced harder on the balls of his feet again, bracing himself on his hands. "Maybe I best just hop over there and take a look, huh?"

"No. I'm not allowed to let anybody back here." Her eyes darted from Kiddo to Jazz, who was moving toward a gap where the counter didn't quite reach the wall.

"You'd best give me that pack of cigarettes, then. You know what? Better make it a carton. Don't want to make trouble for you."

Jazz slid through the opening and behind the counter.

They didn't pay me any mind. Either they didn't see me back among the shelves, or they figured I wasn't any kind of threat to them. I stepped up to the counter, put my can of iced tea down, and said to the Kiddo, "You heard the lady. You got an ID that shows that you're eighteen, get it out and show it to her. Then take your cigarettes—and pay for them— and get going. If you don't got an ID, just get going."

"Yeah?" He seemed to be stuck on that word. "And who's gonna make me?" He turned and sneered at me, taking in the hair drawn back into a ponytail, the work clothes, the steeled-toed boots. A look of uncertainty flickered over his face.

"And you…" I nodded toward Jazz. "You best be getting out from behind that counter."

He shook his head. The pupils of his pale eyes were dilated. "I know she's got spice under that counter," he said, bending down and beginning to rummage around on the shelf. "I'm not leaving without it."

I squared my shoulders and narrowed my eyes into the big yard stare that had served me well for years in prison. "Yes, you are. She says she don't have any, she don't have any."

Sadie's gaze flickered from me to the kids and back to me. She pressed herself farther back against the cigarette shelves.

Kiddo's face flushed and he inched toward the door, keeping a close eye on me. "Come on, Jazz," he said. "We don't need no trouble."

"Trouble ain't nothing new to me," Jazz said. He swept the contents of the shelf under the counter onto the floor and kicked at something. Then he braced on the counter, leapt over, and faced me square. He raised his fists.

I didn't move a muscle.

"You afraid to fight?" he sneered.

I narrowed my eyes further and kept staring at him. My hands hung loosely by my sides. I was trying to look as non-threatening as possible, but I was ready to spring into action if he swung at me.

He took another step toward me, waving his fists back and forth. He had his thumbs tucked down inside his curled fingers, where they would get broken if he connected with a solid punch. Obviously he had no real experience fighting.

I didn't really want to get into a fight if I could help it. There'd be a lot of explaining to do, probably to cops who wouldn't want to listen to me. I'd also have to explain to Mr. Ramirez at my next parole appointment. I might be late for work. Or worse, dragged down to the police station. I just wanted these punks to leave. Then I'd pay for my iced tea and get to work.

If they were ignorant of how to fight, and high, they might fall for a stupid bluff. Keeping my eyes on Jazz, I raised my leg and reached toward my ankle.

"He's got a gun!" Kiddo yelled, making a dash for the door.

His eyes wild, Jazz shoved past me and followed him.

Sadie screamed and ducked down behind the counter.

The urgent sound of a siren reached us, screaming down the street and into the parking lot.

I leaned over the counter and said, "They're gone. You okay there?"

"Yes." Her breath was coming in gasps. "You got a gun?"

"Nah. They just got overly active imaginations."

She crept out from under the counter and stood up. "Are you okay?"

"Well, right now I am." I probably wouldn't be in a few seconds when the cops came in, but there wasn't much I could do about that. "How about you?"

"I'm okay." She didn't look okay, though. She was pale and she was hugging herself.

"How'd the cops get here so fast?" I asked. I didn't see any way to slip out of here now without having to talk to them.

Sadie brushed her hair back. Her hand was trembling. "I got a panic button on the floor here. Goes to 9-1-1 dispatch. Most people who come in here know about it, so I don't get too many people giving me a hard time. But those punks…" Her voice trailed off as the door burst open and a cop came in, gun in his hand.

The parking lot was filled with flashing emergency lights and the wail of sirens winding down.

When the cop looked at me, raising the gun in my direction, I stood still and put my hands on the back of my head, fingers interlaced.

"Somebody in here got a gun?" the cop asked, his gaze darting from me to Sadie.

"No, sir." My ruse had worked too well. "Leastways, I don't have one."

"Put your hands on the counter and spread your feet," he ordered.

I did as he said.

"Do you have a gun, ma'am?" he asked Sadie. "Somewhere there under the counter?"

"No. The owner wanted to put one there, but I'm scared of guns. I figure I'd have more of a chance of getting shot myself than of scaring anybody off."

"That might very well be true," he said, moving up behind me.

To me, he said, "I'm going to frisk you. You got anything on you I should know about?"

"No, sir." I looked down at the counter surface.

"No guns? Knives? Needles I'm gonna stick myself with?"

"No, sir."

He pulled my wallet and keychain out of my pocket and laid them on the counter. He must have holstered his gun since he used both hands to run under my jacket, between my legs, down my arms. He squatted down and paid particular attention to my ankles, loosening my boot laces and feeling around.

Taking one of my hands from the counter, he pulled it behind my back. I felt the familiar cold metal of handcuffs encircling my wrist. He repeated it with my other hand.

"You're not under arrest," he said. "At least not now. I'm doing this for everyone's safety until we figure out what's going on."

I noticed he didn't feel he had to cuff Sadie for everyone's safety, but I used some good sense and kept my mouth shut.

He tossed my wallet to another cop who came through the door. "You wanna run this ID?" he asked.

"Okay. Any gun?"

"I didn't find one," the first cop said. "Better search him again better before we put him in a car."

So much for getting to work on time. And when they ran my ID, I was going to come back "armed and dangerous."

"He was *helping* me," Sadie said. "Why are you going to arrest him?"

The cop looked at her. "I said he wasn't under arrest. Yet. Someone will be here in a minute to take your statement, though, ma'am. Then you can explain how what happened."

The door opened yet again and another cop came through the door, a notebook in his hand.

The first cop said, "I didn't find a gun on him. But I'm not taking any chances."

The newcomer nodded. "So there wasn't a gun? Both the suspects say the guy in here has a gun in an ankle holster." He turned to face me and looked me up and down. "Why did they say that?" he asked.

I tried to look clueless. "I don't know why they'd say that," I said.

Chuckling, he said, "They swear they saw it. A little black automatic. In an ankle holster."

"Well," the first cop said, "he definitely don't have an ankle holster. And he might have been able to kick a gun under some of the shelving or something, but he didn't have time to unbuckle an ankle holster."

He turned to Sadie. "Did you see a gun?"

"No. That guy was *helping* me. Why did you put him in handcuffs?"

Shaking his head, he said, "Just for everybody's safety."

I spoke up. "It's okay. They don't know much about me, and they thought I might have a gun. It's standard procedure."

"Oh." Sadie looked doubtful. "But now that they know you don't have a gun, why don't they take the handcuffs off?"

"They're not in any hurry until they figure out what happened. Besides, I'm on parole. As soon as they run my ID, they'll find that out. And then they'd just put the cuffs right back on."

The cop chuckled and checked the cuffs. "Parole, eh?"

"Yes, sir."

"Violent conviction? Gun charges?"

"Yes, sir."

A police supervisor came in. How many cops had they sent? He looked me over and asked the two cops, "What've you got here?"

"Parolee," one said, nodding toward me. "Violent conviction."

Turning toward Sadie, the supervisor said, "Are you okay?"

"Yes," she said.

"No one hit you or anything? Don't need a medic?"

"No, I'll be fine." She gestured toward me. "This guy wasn't part of it. Even if he is on parole, he was helping me."

The supervisor frowned. "Are you sure? Sometimes, these guys work together. Send one person in to distract the clerk while the others carry out the robbery."

"You can look at the security tape if you want to. I can rewind it. It doesn't have audio, but you can see what happened."

"Where's the monitor?" he asked.

"Back in the office."

Sadie took him through a door.

Some shouting erupted in the parking lot. One of the two cops went outside.

The other cop and I waited. He turned to me. "What are you doing here this time of night?"

I shrugged as well as I could with my hands cuffed behind my back. "I was on my way to work. Just stopped in to get something for lunch."

"On your way to work?"

"Yeah. I work midnight to eight at Quality Steel Fabrications. Drive a forklift."

He grinned. "Sometimes we forget other people work nights, too."

We watched out the window. Two of the patrol cars switched off their flashing lights and pulled out of the parking lot.

"Come on," he said, tugging on my arm. "Let's either get you transported downtown or cut loose. One or the other."

Of course I was hoping they'd cut me loose, but I doubted it would work out that way.

We stepped out the door. "You got a cage car I can put this guy in?" he asked a cop who was standing with his back to us.

Only it was a her, not a him. A female cop I knew from a previous encounter. Officer Richards. She'd hauled me in before. But she'd always been professional. I wondered if she'd remember me.

She looked me over, a smile playing on her lips. "Well, Jesse, what have you gotten yourself involved in this time?"

She remembered me.

I shook my head.

"You know this guy?" the cop said.

"Yeah." Richards pushed her hat back a bit on her head. "He's on parole. And he manages to turn up in the oddest places."

"Should we put him in your car?"

"Let's wait. If past performance is any indication, he won't give us any problems." I had no intention of giving anyone any problems. I debated whether it would annoy her if I asked a question that was on my mind. She'd never given me a break—never had any reason to—but she'd treated me fair before. I took a deep breath and asked. "You think there's any chance I can make it to work on time? Or get a call if I'm not gonna make it? It's a good job, and I don't want to lose it if I can help it." I was in enough trouble at work without not showing up or calling.

She glanced at her watch. "Not my decision when—or if—you'll be released. Partly depends on what they found on you. The report was a man with a gun. That'd make you a convicted felon in possession of a gun. If that's the situation, then you best believe you're headed downtown."

"I didn't have no gun. I mean, I may not be the sharpest tack in the box, but I know better than to violate my parole like that"

"So no gun, eh?" She grinned. "Despite two eyewitnesses claiming they saw it."

"Eyewitnesses see what they want to see," I said. "They're notoriously unreliable." I should know. If the eyewitnesses who had seen the murder that resulted in my conviction had been anything like accurate, the sentencing judge would have at least realized I wasn't the triggerman. Too late to worry about that, though.

Richards raised her eyebrows. "Do you know why they thought they saw a gun?"

I just shrugged again.

Sadie and the supervisor came into the parking lot. He was carrying a small black case that was probably a video cassette.

He said to Sadie. "I'm leaving one car in the parking lot until your manager shows up." Then he turned to Richards. "I got the clerk's statement." Nodding toward me, he said, "Take a statement from this guy. Have him sign it and make sure you know how to get in touch with him in case he's subpoenaed as a witness. Store manager says he's gonna want to press charges against those kids. Then you can cut him loose." He went back into the store.

I gulped in some air. I hadn't even realized I'd been holding my breath.

Richards flipped open her notebook. She asked me some questions and wrote down what I said. "You willing to sign this?" she asked.

"Yeah. But first you got to uncuff my hands."

She smiled. "That's right. Turn around."

I did so, and she unlocked them. Then I signed the statement.

Putting the cuffs on her belt with her own pair and tucking the notebook into the breast pocket of her shirt, she looked at me and pursed her lips. "You do manage to end up in the damnedest places, Jesse. You better be careful, or you're gonna find yourself locked up again."

"True, that." I sighed. "Trouble just seems to keep finding me."

She laughed and checked to make sure her holster was snapped. Then she nodded at Sadie. "You gonna be okay til your manager gets here?"

"Yeah. He should be here in a few minutes."

"I think my wallet and keychain are still on the counter," I said. "Can I go get them?"

"I guess," Richards said.

Sadie and I went into the store. I retrieved my things. "I got to pay for that can of iced tea," I said, "and see if I can find something cheap for lunch. Maybe a pack of crackers or something."

"Look." Sadie glanced at the door, which was now closed. "You go ahead and take a couple of those sandwiches with today's date on them. They should be good for a while yet, but I'm gonna have to throw them out at midnight anyhow."

"Really?" I asked.

"Yeah. I'm not supposed to give them away—they say it just encourages the street people to hang around waiting for them to get thrown out. So we put them in a trash bag and toss it in the dumpster in the morning. But I don't imagine you'll come back to rummage through the trash. And I owe you…"

"You don't owe me nothing," I said.

"Take a few of the sandwiches."

They were mostly subs, with meats and cheeses and lettuce and tomatoes and who knows what else tucked into substantial sub rolls. All sealed in plastic wrap. I eyed them hungrily. "You sure?" I asked.

"Yeah. Just take them before my manager gets here and I have to explain to him and get him to okay it."

At least a dozen of the sandwiches had dates that would expire at midnight. I took two for lunch. It'd be the best lunch I'd had in a while.

"That all you want? They should be fine for at least another day."

"If it's okay…" I picked up two more, for when I got out of work in the morning. One for me and one for Eileen.

"Sure." She rang up the can of iced tea and put it and the sandwiches in a bag. "Have a good night at work."

"Thanks," I said, clutching the bag.

If I didn't hurry, I was going to be late for work. I started to leave.

"What are you on parole for, anyhow?" she called.

Reluctantly, I paused. "Murder."

CHAPTER 9

I slipped into work seconds before the midnight whistle, glad to have made it. Without taking off my jacket, I grabbed my timecard and punched in. Then I put my lunch on one of the battered picnic tables between the time clock and the aging vending machines. I shrugged off the jacket, hung it on a hook, and grabbed my hard hat and work gloves off their shelf.

The whistle blew. The thundering of the machinery stopped. The second shift workers crowded around the time clock to punch out. I moved out their way.

"There you are, Jesse." John, the foreman, frowned at me. "I was a little worried that you weren't going to show up."

I'd been more than a little worried about that myself. But I didn't say anything. Usually, I showed up at least fifteen minutes early.

"The inspector from MOSH, the state occupational safety and health folks, wanted to talk to you," he said. "He talked to Hank, but when you didn't show up, he left. Said he'd be back again in the morning, and he'd talk to you then if you showed up, so don't leave without seeing him."

"Will do." I wasn't about to ask if I was going to get paid for the time.

"He wants to get all the info he needs before the weekend so he doesn't have to come back on Monday."

Nodding, I said, "Is that watchman going to be okay?"

"Steb? Yeah, seems like it. They didn't keep him at the hospital. He's off for a few days, though. And he was pissed about his boots. They kept them, and I don't know when they're gonna let him have them back. Or if."

I pulled on my work gloves and adjusted my hard hat, waiting to see if John had anything more to say.

He checked his clipboard. "You'd better go pick up your lift and get to work."

"Yes, sir." At least he hadn't taken me off the forklift and given me another assignment. Or, worse yet, told me to punch out and go home. But then, I had to see the guy from MOSH.

I was so late that everyone else had already cleared out of the charging station, so I didn't run into either of the second shift drivers. Or Kelly. I ran through the checklist as fast as I reasonably could and still do a decent job. Then I unplugged the lift and swung up into the seat.

Despite the reduced workload we ran on the overnight shift, the air was filled with showers of sparks, the smell of hot steel and oil, the thunder of presses and forming machinery, and the hiss of compressed air hoses. Not easy to carry on any kind of casual conversations to ask anyone if they knew anything, even if they'd heard about the chemical spill yesterday. Or were willing to talk to me.

Hank had been involved in the whole incident, so if anybody knew something, it would be him. And he would tell me anything he knew, even if what he had to say was that I was in big trouble.

Anxious to talk to him, I did a quick check of the work stations that were operating to see if I needed to bring any supplies or move any loads. The work was proceeding on schedule, and everybody seemed to have what they needed. Making a quick round by the shipping room, I craned my neck looking for Kelly.

She was way down the end of the loading dock, shuttling a load onto a truck. Her hair was pulled back into its usual ponytail.

Of course. Did I really think she'd show up for work with her hair done up? For one thing, it wouldn't fit under her hard hat. She'd probably scrubbed the makeup off, too.

I swung around back to the plating room and stopped next to the office.

Stack of papers in his hand, Hank opened the door and gestured for me to come in.

I left the lift running right next to the office, where I could see it through the smudged window in the heavy door.

"I think I got this stuff together," Hank said, beaming proudly. "Check it over."

Taking the papers from his hand, I riffled through them quickly. He'd stapled each set together and circled the relevant stock numbers and production goals. "Yeah, Hank. Looks to me like you got it." I handed the papers back to him.

He grinned and tapped them into a neat stack.

"So what'd you find out about that spill last night?" I asked.

Shrugging, he put the papers on the desk and pulled on a pair of work gloves. "They're not telling me a whole lot. There was an injury, though—Steb—so they had to call in MOSH. So far, I haven't heard about the environmental folks. Or OSHA—that's the feds. I think maybe we got it cleaned up before it got into the drains or anything."

"You're okay, though? You and the other guy I saw suiting up?"

"Yeah. They sent us to the doctor for a checkup, but we're okay. We vacuumed up all the powder and dumped it in another drum. That got sealed, and we put it aside. Said they were gonna call some kind of hazardous waste company to come pick it up. I don't know how they're gonna clean the shop vacuum, though. Maybe just toss it."

"That might be the best bet. John said Steb's off for a few days, but he's gonna be all right."

Hank chuckled. "Yeah. If they're smart, though, they're gonna buy him a new pair of boots. If he files a complaint, he can cause a lot of problems. And he's obsessing about them damn boots. New pair'd probably make him happy and shut him up."

"Them boots can cost a pretty penny."

"Yeah. But still one whole hell of a lot cheaper than what they'll have to put out if Steb goes to one of them 'you don't pay me one penny unless I collect for you'-type lawyers."

"True, that." I rubbed my cheek. For once, it felt reasonably smooth. I'd showered and shaved before I went over to Kelly's last night. Waste of effort. "Did they ever figure out how that potassium cyanide got spilled?"

"Not that they're telling me. But I know they pulled the security tapes. And Diffy was called in to talk to the MOSH guy and never showed up in the plant again."

"Do you think he started to move the chemical pallets, had an accident with the one, and didn't report it?" I asked.

Hank riffled through his stack of papers. "Possible, I guess. If I had my druthers, they'd blame it on the last shift and leave us alone. Except for Steb, a course." He shrugged his massive shoulders. "But it is what it is." He grabbed the clipboard from his desk and secured the papers. "And we got work to get done tonight."

The night's shift was blessedly uneventful, with no major break-downs or disruptions. And no chemical spills. Most of the workers got their three-tenths of an hour lunch from four to four eighteen, but lift drivers and workers on continuous operations went when the foreman or group leader told them to. I asked John if I could go about four thirty, which I knew was about when Kelly usually took hers, but when I pulled up at the picnic table out in the back of the shipping, she was just finishing up. I didn't see any trace of her makeup left. If she was still wearing perfume, the smells of the factory overshadowed them.

She looked fine to me, though.

I had no idea what I wanted to say to her.

"Were you late?" she asked as she swept the wrappings from her lunch into a trash barrel.

"Just made it." I debated telling her about the convenience store, but decided that could wait until we had more time. If she showed an interest.

"Look," she said. "Sorry if I was short with you. I should have at least fixed you a lunch. Let you catch some sleep and given you a ride."

"Not a problem." I held up the bag with the iced tea and the sandwiches. "I picked up something on my way over."

"Good," she said. "I was afraid when I didn't see you before the shift started that you weren't coming."

"Why would I not come?" I didn't add, "Besides the police holding me."

"I dunno." She shrugged. "I thought maybe you fell asleep and didn't wake up in time." She drained her can of soda and tossed the empty into the recycling barrel. "Or maybe you were upset with me and decided not to come."

It was my turn to shrug. "I wasn't real happy, but no reason you got to let me stay at your place if you don't want to."

She looked at my lunch bag. "I know money's tight. I shouldn't have made you have to buy your lunch."

"Not a problem." I seemed to be stuck on that not entirely truthful phrase. I didn't tell her I didn't have to pay for the sandwiches. "But even if I was mad—which I wasn't, really, and I had no good reason to be if I was—this is too good a job to skip out on just 'cause I was upset. With you or anything else. I know I'm never gonna get another job this good. Not in this economy."

She smiled. "You may be right about that. Jobs are hard to come by, period."

"And when you got a violent felony conviction…" I let the thought trail off.

"How about we meet after the shift breaks?" she said. "Breakfast at the diner. My treat."

I bit my lip. "Uh…" I'd told Eileen I'd be back right after work. And now I had to see the MOSH guy, which would make me late. I couldn't take even more time to go to breakfast with Kelly. Which, with any luck, would end up back in Kelly's bed. And the babysitter would have gotten the kids off to school and left for her own classes. "I got a few things I have to handle first. But it's my turn to treat." She was right that money was tight all around, but I had my emergency stash. As far as I was concerned, this qualified as an emergency.

"We got a few things we got to talk about," Kelly said.

"Okay." I wasn't entirely sure I'd want to talk about the Sydney person, but any conversation was a start.

"I got an appointment with my lawyer at nine thirty," she said.

"Oh." So much for ending up back in her bed.

"So we have to get out of here fast."

My heart sank. "I got to stick around and talk to the guy from MOSH. I don't know how long that'll take."

At least Kelly had the decency to look disappointed. "Oh. Another time, then."

"How about lunch? After the meeting with the MOSH guy, I got to check on something. I could meet you at the diner."

Her eyes narrowed. "You got to check in on something? Or somebody?"

"Well…" I hadn't told her about Eileen showing up. I should explain, but we didn't have much time right now.

"That's all right." She backed away. "You take care of what you got to take care of. Maybe later this week."

"Okay." My heart sank. "And do you want I should come keep an eye on the kids one night soon so's you can go to another meeting?"

Her eyes clouded over. "I'll have to see about that. I mean, I appreciate you doing that and all, but…"

But what? She wanted to see Sydney again?

"Well." She straightened up and pulled on her gloves. "I got to get back to work. And you have your lunch to eat."

She climbed on her lift. "One other thing."

I looked up at her. "Yeah?"

"Don't you be following me no more. I don't appreciate it." She drove off.

Follow her? What was that supposed to mean?

Two of the sandwiches, I ate, and then packed the other two back into the bag. They tasted every bit as good as I'd thought they would.

The two that were left should still be fine in the morning. One for me and one for Eileen. Not a traditional breakfast, but a lot better than we might do. And the price was right.

Maybe because I was a little worried about the interview with the guy from MOSH, the rest of the shift seemed to rush past. By the time I got the lift plugged in again and gone over the checklist, Kelly was gone. I didn't punch out, in case they decided they would pay me for the time with the inspector, and went to find John.

He was talking to a tall thin man in a wrinkled gray suit, who wore a scuffed hard hat and carried a battered briefcase.

When I approached, John said, "Ah, here's Jesse Damon. He was the lift driver on midnight to eight who you wanted to talk to. Jesse, this is Mr. Ziraldo. He's with MOSH."

Mr. Ziraldo offered his hand. Mine was dirty and oily. I wiped it on my jeans leg before I took his.

He didn't seem bothered by the possibility that he'd get dirty and gave my hand a hearty shake. "May we use the same office upstairs?" he asked John.

"I imagine, but it's not up to me," John said. "Why don't you go ahead up there, and I'll check with the security guard."

We went through the plant to the plating room, where a staircase led up to a hallway to the offices that overlooked the production floor. Mr. Ziraldo went first, with me following.

I smiled to myself. That was one of my private little pleasures. Prison staff and police officers always stepped back to let me precede them. It was a sensible, standard security procedure, followed with all prisoners. To me, it was a constant reminder that no one trusted me enough to let me out of their sight or get behind them.

A security guard met us at the door to one of the offices and unlocked it. After the thunderous roar of the shop floor, the well-insulated hallway and offices were eerily quiet.

We went into the office. Mr. Ziraldo moved behind the desk and gestured toward another chair for me to sit in.

"As Mr. Bigham told you, Mr. Damon, I'm with MOSH."

I was momentarily confused. I wasn't used to being called "Mr." Damon. And I had no idea who Mr. Bigham was. "Mr. Bigham?" I asked.

He looked up from opening his briefcase on the desk. "John Bigham. Your foreman."

"Oh, yeah." I didn't know if I'd ever heard John's last name before.

Mr. Ziraldo sighed and settled himself in the desk chair. I had a feeling he'd decided he was dealing with a total moron. That was okay with me.

"Now, Mr. Damon," he started. "Do you know what MOSH is?"

"Maryland Occupational Safety and Health?" I ventured.

"Very good, Mr. Damon. Do you know why you've been asked to speak to me?"

"Because of the potassium cyanide spill?"

"Very good again, Mr. Damon," he said.

"Do you know what happened?" I asked.

His face tightened and he tapped the papers in front of him with a gold-colored pen. "I'm the one asking the questions here, Mr. Damon."

That put me in my place. "Yes, sir. Sorry."

He relented a bit. "After the investigation is completed, I will submit a report. It will be reviewed and then released. Quality Steel, of course, will get a copy. You could ask them to let you read it." At least he didn't question whether I could read.

"Okay." All I really cared about was that they didn't blame it on me.

"Or you ask for a copy yourself. File a Freedom of Information Act request if you had to."

"Oh." I had no intention of doing that unless there was a real reason to do so.

"But it will contain a lot of technical language, and you may find it difficult to understand."

I nodded.

"Let me ask you a few questions about what you saw and your actions yesterday."

Since he didn't seem to think I was all that bright, I realized I could get away with giving very sketchy answers. I didn't lie at all, but I didn't explain any more than I had to.

He did ask me the same thing several times in different ways, especially about whether I had moved the barrel that had ended up with the hole in it. I could truthfully assure him I hadn't. If he was trying to trip me up, he'd have to be a whole lot more sophisticated with his techniques. Montgomery could have given him numerous pointers.

The whole thing took more than an hour. Kelly would be well on her way to the appointment with her lawyer.

Mr. Ziraldo put most of the papers in his briefcase and shoved a form across the desk to me. "Please sign here," he said, pointing at a place at the bottom of the page.

"What am I signing?" I asked.

He sighed. "Just that you've given me your statement about the incident."

"Can I see the statement before I sign it?" I asked. Heaven only knew what he'd written down.

He said, "If you wish," with a pained expression on his face. He pulled some of the papers back out of his briefcase and handed them to me. Two of them dropped to the desk surface. He scooped them up and put them on top.

I shuffled them, trying to figure out what order they went in.

He closed his eyes and sighed yet again. "Do you need me to read it to you?" he asked.

"That's okay. I think I can make them out," I said. "Thanks, though." His handwriting was easy to read. I skimmed the papers. He'd pretty much written down what I'd said. I handed them back to him.

He probably didn't think I'd really read them through. But I had.

"Ready to sign now?" he asked.

"Yes, sir." I took the gold pen and wrote my name on the blank and dated it.

Mr. Ziraldo took the paper back and held out his hand for the pen. I gave it back to him, and he put everything back in the briefcase, latching it firmly. Then he stood up.

"I understand you're on parole," he said.

"Yes, sir." I didn't see what that had to do with anything, although I suppose if a question arose, it might make somebody say I was a less-than-credible witness.

"For murder," he continued.

"Yes, sir." I wondered who had told him that. Not that it mattered.

He nodded knowingly, settled back into the desk chair, and spread the paperwork out on the desk. "Thank you for cooperating."

I wasn't sure if it was appropriate to say, "You're welcome," but I said it anyhow.

"You can go now," he said, reaching for the phone.

"Yes, sir. Thank you." I wasted no time getting out of the office.

Several people were in the hallway. None of them wore blue jeans or boots or hard hats. Administrative employees of some sort.

"Excuse me," I said, trying to make my way past them to the stairs down to the plating room.

"Damon," a man said. He was very tall and wearing a gray business suit with a maroon tie. Somehow, he didn't look as spiffy as Montgomery did. I recognized him as one of the company executives. The one who'd seen me when Belkins and Montgomery had detained me the other morning.

"Yes, sir?"

"You're the one the cops picked up the other day, right after the midnight shift ended?"

What was he getting at? "Yes, sir."

"And you were involved in that chemical spill?"

I didn't think it would do any good to try to explain, so I just said, "Yes, sir," again.

"You know, that potassium cyanide is pretty deadly stuff."

"Yes, sir."

"And you've had unfettered access to it."

Unfettered? My guess was that meant unrestricted. Me and about a dozen other people. But I saw nothing to be gained by pointing that out.

"Just let me tell you that the symptoms of cyanide poisoning are easy to detect if you know what to look for."

I thought about Steb, confused and with a bloody nose. "Yeah."

"And lab tests can confirm exposure beyond reasonable doubt."

He certainly was making a big deal out of something that was pretty obvious to anyone who thought about it. Why was he pointing this out to me?

He answered that with his next breath. "I understand you're working here under that state program that we use to hire convicts on parole."

"True, that."

"And that you have a history of violence."

I nodded.

"A conviction for murder."

"Yeah."

"If anybody turns up poisoned anytime soon, we'll know exactly who to look for."

CHAPTER 10

Clutching the bag with the remaining sandwiches, I hurried back to the carriage house. I hadn't given her an exact time, but based on yesterday, Eileen would have expected me by now. I didn't want her to worry, and I'd hoped to get her the sandwich before she fixed something else for breakfast so we could save the food we did have for later. It would taste pretty good, even if it was an unusual breakfast.

Probably too late for that, though.

When I turned into the alley, I had to step aside to let a trash truck lumber by. I gave myself a mental pat on the back for remembering to get the garbage cans out in the alley yesterday afternoon before I left for Kelly's.

Down the alley, a car was parked at a careless angle near the gate to the backyard. It had run into the trash cans. They were scattered around, some of them lying on their sides and dented. There was no garbage strewn around, so they must have been empty when they were hit.

The car had Ohio license plates.

The car Eileen drove here, still in the garage, had Ohio license plates.

My stomach clenched. I picked up my pace, running the half-block to the backyard gate. It was swinging open.

Dashing through the gate, I could hear the baby wailing inside. I couldn't imagine Eileen letting her cry like that. The door to the carriage house was closed, but it had scratches around the doorknob and lock. And the doorframe was splintered.

I tried to push the door open. When it stuck, I dropped the bag with the sandwiches and put my shoulder to it, shoving hard. It flew open.

A man, his back to me, had seized Eileen and held her tight. His fingers clenched white on her thin arms as he shook her. He held his face inches from hers.

Tears were streaming down her cheeks. "Please, Gary, let me get Abigail." She glanced toward a corner of the room, where the baby lay face down, the pink blanket half covering her. "She might stop crying if I pick her up."

They didn't seem to notice me.

Between clenched teeth, I said, "Let her go!"

Gary loosened his grip on Eileen a bit and swung around to face me. Then he stepped behind her and grabbed her tight again, holding her in front of him. He pulled her up against his chest and slammed one arm over her throat.

I stopped dead. He could really hurt her like that. Crush her windpipe, whether he meant to or not. Or even break her neck.

"So this is the guy you ran off to be with, huh, bitch? 'Aunt Nicole,' my ass," he said.

Gagging, she raised her free hand, trying to claw at his elbow.

He tightened his hold on her throat and leaned back, lifting her feet off the ground.

She coughed and struggled frantically for a few seconds, and her body went limp, her toes just barely touching the floor. Her breath was coming in harsh gasps, and her eyes were still open, but her face was turning red.

From where she lay on the floor, Abigail continued to wail.

I didn't know Eileen all that well, but I was pretty sure she hadn't been the one who'd left the baby on the floor like that.

Gary's eyes were wild, and his nostrils flared as his breathe came in sharp gasps. He might be high on something. Or just furious.

I had to do something.

Focusing my eyes on the floor next to them, I tried to appear as non-threatening and non-confrontational as possible. With an effort to keep my voice low and steady, I said, "Eileen came to see her Aunt Nicole. She didn't have no way of knowing I'd be here."

"Yeah? What are you doing here, then?"

"I'm keeping an eye on the place while her aunt's out of town. Eileen's been trying to get a hold of Nicole since she got here."

"Yeah? So you just happened to be here? Like I'm supposed to believe that. When I find the two of you shacked up together?"

Eileen's breath was ragged and her body looked limp, but she was moaning softly. That meant she was still breathing.

"I wasn't here when you got here," I pointed out. "So we weren't 'shacked up.'"

His eyes shot wild looks around the room. "You just went out to get something."

"I just got here. I was at work," I said, struggling to keep my voice calm and steady. "She and the baby were here by themselves. All night."

"What, you work nights?"

"Yeah. Midnight shift. I don't get out til morning."

His eyes narrowed and focused on me. "So you were coming here to meet her?"

"I wouldn't really call it 'coming to meet her.'"

"I would." His gaze flashed from me to the crying baby. "I *knew* that damn kid didn't look anything like me. Are you the daddy?"

Yikes. He really was irrational. And dangerous. Could I distract him enough so Eileen could catch her breath? Then she had to get away from him, grab the baby, and slip out the door. A tall order.

I said, "No. I never laid eyes on Eileen until two days ago."

"Kid's got the same brown hair like you."

I tried to think of something reassuring to say that he might actually listen to. "We can get DNA testing done if you want to."

He looked at me like I was crazy. I tended to agree with him on that.

"Why the hell would I want to do that?"

"To prove you're the baby's daddy." I couldn't see it coming down to that, but if it ever did, I sincerely hoped he really was the baby's father. But that wasn't the immediate problem. "You give a sample. Eileen gives a sample. If you want, I'll give a sample. It's easy. They'll be able to tell who's the daddy."

He frowned. "I hate it when they have to draw blood."

"They don't use blood. They just take a swab from the inside of your cheek. Don't hurt or nothing."

"You ever have it done?"

"Yeah. It don't hurt at all."

He smirked "Yeah? You involved in a lot of paternity suits, I guess?"

"Not for that. The cops took it. They keep a bank. Like they keep fingerprints."

"You some kind of sex offender or something?"

I struggled to keep my voice calm. If we were discussing DNA and my criminal record, he wouldn't be thinking about doing anything to Eileen. At least for the moment. "No. It's just routine."

He looked thoughtful. Eileen coughed and her eyes opened wide. A bit of color came back into her face.

"How long did it take?" he asked.

"Not long. You let Eileen go, we can go find a lab right away." Now I was just babbling. I had no idea if this were even possible, but if he would move away from her, even a little, I would tackle him and hope she had enough sense to grab the baby and make a run for it.

Instead, he tightened his grip again. Eileen gagged. "You're lying. Eileen's *my* wife. If I find out she's been messing around with you, I'll kill both of you."

"That don't make no sense. You'd go to prison."

"No, I wouldn't."

"What makes you think that?"

He smirked. "I'd kill myself, too, before I let them catch me."

I had no doubt he was perfectly capable of doing that. I struggled to think of something to say that might make him rethink his ill-considered plan. "Then your poor little baby won't have no one. No mommy or daddy. She'll go into foster care. And she'll never have a family to call her own." Not that I thought he would make a reasonable parent, but we weren't talking reason here.

He shifted his weight and glanced at the baby. "Damn kid's prob'ly not mine anyhow."

When he moved, Eileen's breath came a little easier.

"I bet she is. Your little girl. You gonna let her just lie there and cry? Don't it hurt your heart to hear your little girl cry like that? Don't it hurt your head?"

An uncertain look flashed over his face. "I *do* have a headache. Do you think it's the baby crying?"

"I bet it is. All you got to do is let Eileen pick her up. She'll be able to stop the crying."

He shook his head. "All that baby does is cry. Gives me a headache all the time."

"That's only when her mama can't take care of her. If you let Eileen pick her up and feed her, she'll stop crying."

He spat on the floor. "I done told Eileen I don't want that kid sucking on her boobs. Make 'em all swollen up and disgusting."

"It's only for a little while." Once again, I had no real idea what I was talking about, but he was listening to me, and that was all I could ask for. "It's one whole lot cheaper than buying all that baby formula, and it's better for the baby."

"I don't give a damn about what's better for a baby that ain't mine."

"And it helps Eileen get her body get back in shape." For sure I didn't know much about that, but I'd heard something like that. Probably from one of the crazy would-be studs in prison who were always bragging about how many women he'd gotten pregnant.

"Really?" Gary looked interested. "Tighten her up again? Down there, y'know?" He leaned forward a bit. Eileen was able to put her feet flat on the floor and maybe even support her weight on them.

That was a little progress.

She made a little mewling noise.

He jerked her head back. "Why'd you take off, bitch? I done told you you couldn't get away from me. Ever. And what I'd do to you if you tried."

"She can't answer if you don't let her catch her breath," I said, trying to sound reasonable.

Loosening his arm a bit, he said, "Well?"

She could breathe enough now to sob. After a few labored breaths, she said, "You said you didn't think the baby was yours. She is, but you said you weren't going to support a baby that wasn't yours. I was afraid you were going to hurt her."

"So what were you planning to do?"

Looking at me with frightened eyes, Eileen said, "Like Jesse said. Get DNA testing to prove she is yours."

"Without telling me?"

"I was afraid you wouldn't listen. So I figured I'd just do it and then tell you. I thought I could get it done before you got back from that out of town job." She'd picked up on what I was saying quick. If she got a chance, I hoped she'd be as good at grabbing the baby and getting the hell out of here.

"So why did you come all the way here?"

"I thought Aunt Nicole would help me get it set up. And lend me the money. But she wasn't here."

"And how," Gary said, "were you going to do all that testing without me being there?"

"I was going to find out how to do it. Get me and Abigail tested. And then ask you to go get tested, too."

He tightened his arm against her neck again. "And suppose the test showed the baby wasn't mine?"

Eileen was choking again, but she managed to say, "That wouldn't happen, Gary. I swear."

The baby let out a particularly piercing screech.

"Go make it stop that noise," Gary said, removing his arm from her neck and giving her a shove in toward the corner where Abigail lay. "Or I just might shut it up myself. Permanently."

As soon as Eileen moved away from him, I launched myself at Gary's legs, knocking him to the floor.

"Grab the baby and run!" I shouted to Eileen. Would she have enough sense to do it?

"I'll kill you both!" Gary snarled, grabbing me by the hair and pounding his fist into my face.

I was trying to hang onto his legs to keep him from scrambling to his feet, so I couldn't use my hands to shield my face from his clawing. He kicked at my chest and tried again to smash his fist into my nose. All I could do was tuck my face against his knees to minimize the damage he was doing. It wasn't a particularly effective tactic.

My hair came loose from its ponytail and tangled with the blood in my eyes. I heard rather than saw Eileen skitter across the floor. The door slammed, I hoped behind her. Now I just had to keep Gary from following her long enough for her to get some help. Not an easy task.

He gouged his fingers into my eyes and tried to flip us over. I ducked my head down against him and held on, managing to stay more or less on top of him. I didn't know where Eileen could go, but for now, away from here was enough. I had to give her enough time to put some distance between her and the carriage house.

It was probably just a few seconds, but it felt like forever, with us rolling around on the floor and Gary beating on my head. My ears were ringing and I ached all over. How much longer could I hang on like this? How much time did Eileen need to get away?

Gary was cussing up a storm, but my ears were ringing and I couldn't really hear what he said.

I felt strong arms grabbing me from behind. How was he doing that? I held on tighter.

"Let go. Stop resisting."

"*Stop resisting*." That was cop talk.

I relaxed my hold on Gary's legs and felt myself being dragged away from him. My head and chest were slammed into the floor, a sharp knee pressing down between my shoulder blades.

My hands were roughly yanked behind me, the palms turned outward. I felt the all-too-familiar bite of steel handcuffs on my wrists.

Definitely cops.

Second time in less than twenty-four hours. Somehow, I didn't live right.

I lay still, trying to breathe with the weight on my back. I could only hope Gary was getting the same treatment. If he was, Eileen would be all right. For now.

A voice somewhere above me commanded, "We're gonna stand you up. Cooperate."

The pressure on my back was removed.

I felt my arms grasped, and I was pulled up. I made an effort to get my feet under me, but my legs felt too weak to hold me up and my knees buckled. Strong hands held my arms as I managed to get first one, then the other, boot flat on the floor and straightened up my legs. The room spun and my head pounded.

When they loosened their grip, I swayed, and they tightened it again. I would have bruises where they grabbed me, but that was the least of my worries. And the least of my injuries.

I brushed my eyes against my shoulder, trying to wipe some of the blood and hair out of the way so I could see. I was marginally successful.

Gary was standing across the room, two burly cops holding onto his arms. His arms were pulled behind him, too. Handcuffs. He didn't look anywhere near as battered as I felt.

He shook his head and sputtered. "Thank goodness you came when you did, Officer. I thought he was going to kill me."

"Oh?" A female cop took a notepad out and started writing on it.

"Yes. He kidnapped my wife. He was holding her captive."

"Is that right?" She turned her head in my direction. Officer Richards again.

How could she still be on duty?

She pulled a card out of her shirt pocket. "Let me read you both your Miranda rights."

If it was just me, she probably wouldn't have bothered to read them, so at least they weren't automatically assuming Gary was a total innocent.

He tried to dissuade her of that notion. "You don't have to read them to me. I was just trying to rescue them."

"Them?"

"Yes. My wife Eileen and our baby."

"Just let me get these read to both of you anyhow. To be on the safe side." She droned through the familiar recital and turned to Gary. "You understand your rights?"

"Of course. Ask me anything you want. I've got nothing to hide."

"So you still want to talk to me?" she asked.

"I said yes. Why am I in these handcuffs?"

"For everyone's safety, until we figure out what's going on here." She looked at me. "How about you, Jesse? You understand your rights?"

"Yes, ma'am," I said.

"Do you want a lawyer before you answer any questions?"

"No, ma'am." I knew it wouldn't do any practical good anyhow.

"I'll tell you what's going on," Gary said. He'd calmed down amazingly and no longer looked or sounded like the raging maniac I'd originally encountered.

"You have a right to a lawyer," Richards reminded him.

Was she concerned that he'd claim later that he hadn't known he could talk to a lawyer? If so, she couldn't be buying the innocent, wronged husband act.

He ignored what she said. "Look, this guy was the instigator. He attacked me."

Richards glanced at me. "That true, Jesse? You hit him first?"

I shrugged. "Well, I wasn't the instigator. But yeah, I was the one who threw the first punch, so to speak." That was going to come out no matter what, so I didn't see any point in not admitting it.

She wrote something down. Maybe I should have kept my mouth shut. "So what started all this?"

Gary frowned and said, "He kidnapped my wife. Probably raped her. A sex pervert."

"Is that right?" Richards said, her pen busy. But thank goodness she didn't sound convinced.

"Yes. You don't have to worry about me, Officer," Gary said, trying to shake the restraining hands off his arms. The cops just gripped harder. "Everything will be okay now. He isn't holding Eileen and the baby anymore, and rescuing them was what I set out to do. Now I can just take them home. They'll be fine. We'll all be fine."

She tapped her pencil on the top of the notepad. "You were planning to rescue them all by yourself? From somebody you thought was a sex offender? And who'd kidnapped them? That could be pretty dangerous. You didn't call the police and report it?"

"I wasn't sure at first, really, whether she'd gone with him willingly or he'd forced her."

"That's something I'll find out when I talk to her," Richards said.

"Oh, you don't need to do that. That'll just upset her more. She'll let me talk for her. I'm her husband."

He was her husband, true enough, but it hardly told the whole story. Richards narrowed her eyes and looked him over. She was no dummy. "I'll decide who I need to talk to."

"Okay. But I need to know if she's all right. Let me see her."

Richards had dealt with enough domestic situations to know better than that. "You can see her later. If she wants to see you."

His nostrils flared in indignation. "What? Of course she wants to see me. She's my wife."

"So you said. Like I say, you can see her later. Maybe. Meanwhile, the medics are on their way to check her out." She turned to me. "You're a mess. You need to go to the hospital?"

"No."

"I'll ask the medics to take a look at you, too."

"Just some scratches and bruises. I'll be okay." I had pretty good insurance through work, but the copay for an emergency room visit was pretty stiff.

If I ended up in the county lockup, and it looked like that was going to happen, the nurse on duty would give me a good checkup at intake.

"Meanwhile, let's get both of you down to the station where we can figure this out."

"What?" Gary was indignant. "Me? Aren't you going to take the handcuffs off?"

Richards shook her head. "Not yet. Like I said, for everyone's safety."

She gestured to the cops, who still had a firm grip on both of us. "Frisk them. And keep them separate."

"Run the IDs?" one of the cops asked.

"Yeah. And run the car out in the alley. I don't know about that guy—" she nodded toward Gary "—but I know this other one, Jesse Damon, is on parole for a violent conviction. Murder, if I recall correctly."

Gary's eyes opened wide.

CHAPTER 11

Since we had to be kept separate at the police station, they left Gary handcuffed to the bench outside control, where people are usually kept waiting, while I was hauled back into the secure area of the jail.

The disinterested nurse on duty checked me over none too gently, scrubbing the blood and dirt from my face. He had to be used to cleaning up the physical aftermath of fights. "When they arrested you, did they ask if you wanted to go to the hospital?" he asked me.

"Yeah, but I said no."

"Okay. Just so's you had the opportunity." He scribbled a note before he poked at my nose and the sore spots on my head. Shining a light into my eyes, he turned my head at various angles and peered.

When he was done, he stripped off his gloves and scrubbed his hands thoroughly. He glanced at the paperwork that accompanied me. "You're not being processed. Odd."

"Keep-away order," I said. He would know that meant I needed to be isolated from someone else. "Fight." He wouldn't be interested in any of the details.

The nurse smiled. "The other guy in as bad shape as you?"

"Nah. I got the worse of it."

"What, he attacked you?"

I grinned sheepishly. I'd already told Officer Richards what had happened, so I saw no reason not to say, "Actually, I attacked him."

He laughed. "And got the worst of it? Not smart. You got a possible concussion. What have you been using?"

"Nothing."

"Alcohol?"

"No."

"Really? Then why'd you attack him?"

I just shook my head. Mistake. It made me feel like I was going to throw up. "Seemed like a good idea at the time."

"Other guy arrested at the same time as you?"

"Yeah. They got him out front."

"Okay." He picked up a pen and started writing. "If they do decide to process you, I'm going to recommend that you be transported to the emergency room. I don't think that nose is broken, but it might be. It'd take an X-ray to tell for sure. And with those wounds on your head, I wouldn't want to take a chance on a more serious head injury."

I winced. Visiting hospital emergency rooms was one of my least favorite things in the best of circumstances. All shackled down and escorted by a couple of COs from the jail was far from the best of circumstances. "And they'll go along with that suggestion?" I asked.

He shrugged. "I don't know. Or really care. I get off duty in—" he checked his watch "—forty minutes. I just don't want you going into a coma on *my* shift. After that, it's someone else's problem. You might be able to talk them out of it. You know what they're going to do with you now?"

"Holding cage somewhere, I imagine."

He tapped the pen on his teeth. "I'll tell them to keep an eye on you, make sure you aren't throwing up. Or passed out."

I grinned ruefully. "That's okay. If I pass out, I'll be sure to holler for a CO."

He laughed again. "You just do that. But maybe I should put a formal watch on you to make sure you're okay."

I froze. "Like, suicide watch?"

Shrugging, he said, "Something like that. I don't have a whole lot of options. If I put you on suicide watch, someone will check on you every ten minutes, so if you did pass out, you'd get medical attention right away."

"Yeah. And they'll take away my clothes and put me in an observation cell. Without a blanket or anything. And I'll get meal loaf if I'm there long enough to be fed. They'll maybe ask for a psych eval. And hold me until it was done. Then it'll all go in a report that my PO gets."

"Probably." He raised his eyebrows in amusement.

"Please don't."

"Okay." He nodded. "But don't go dying on me or anything, okay?"

"You got my word on that."

Next stop for me was a holding cell just inside the sally port. The walls were painted detox pink over cinderblock. I had a steel shelf for a bed, if I wanted to lie down, and a standard one-piece-serves-all-needs plumbing unit. They let me keep my own clothes, minus the boots and belt.

The way I looked at it, the holding cell might be depressing, but it was a lot more comfortable than being out front where Gary was. My wallet and key were already in a property bag, and my jacket, boots, and belt should have been added to it. They had been confiscated when I'd arrived. The floor was cold through my socks, and my feet felt pretty vulnerable. I had to keep hitching my jeans up. But I could move around, and I was likely to be fed when meal time came around.

Gary had not only been relieved of his belt and the laces out of his shoes, but he was probably shackled to an eyebolt in the wall so he couldn't move around much, and no one would think about getting him fed.

Somebody would be by sooner or later to interrogate me. Probably later. All I could do was hope Eileen had told the truth and that they'd believed her. If that happened, I might be released with just a report to Mr. Ramirez, my parole officer. Or if I were really unlucky, I might be held while he made a decision on whether to schedule a parole violation hearing.

On the other hand, if Eileen told them what Gary wanted her to say, I was totally screwed. Not only a parole violation, but new charges. Maybe kidnapping. With a presumption of some kind of perverted sex offenses. Plus the assault on Gary. And who knows what else. Between a conviction on new charges that serious and the backup time I still had on the original murder bit, I'd spend the rest of my life in prison.

Totally out of my hands now. Back at the carriage house, Officer Richards seemed to be in charge of the situation, and she seemed familiar with the abused spouse syndrome. Although she took it seriously, I knew a lot of cops either had never been properly trained to identify it or they discounted the training they were required to attend as a bunch of psychobabble.

Richards would never put Eileen in a position where Gary could intimidate her prior to giving her side of the story, but it was likely she'd just write a report and someone else would take over. I wondered if the department was big enough and sophisticated enough to have a domestic violence team. I could always hope.

Whatever was going to happen, I would need to be well-rested. I'd worked all night and was tired. I'd need my wits about me when they finally did come to interrogate me, and being exhausted would work against that. The steel shelf wasn't exactly comfortable, but I'd slept on worse surfaces. I lay down and closed my eyes, trying to clear my mind of all the worrying things I couldn't control.

The message from the nurse to make sure I didn't pass out apparently didn't get through to the staff supervising the holding cell, and I slept fitfully until the port on the cell door clanged open. Someone shoved a brown paper bag through the port without saying anything, so it landed on the floor of the cell. I retrieved it.

It was a standard bag lunch. Bologna and cheese sandwich on whole grain bread, an apple, carrot and celery sticks, and a carton of milk.

Tasted better than I would have fixed for myself, and a lot more nutritious, but not as good as the two subs I'd abandoned back at the carriage house. By the time I got back to them, they'd probably be no good at all. If I got back to them. I scarfed the lunch down and lay back down to get whatever sleep I could to face the ordeal ahead.

The door slid open with a metallic clang, and I jerked awake. It seemed like I'd been sleeping for a long time, but since no supper had arrived, it had to be still early afternoon. As soon as the evening shift came on at four, they'd do a head count and get the feed up out of the way.

I sat up, blinking.

A CO stood there, his expressionless face reflecting the tedium of his job. "Somebody wants to see you."

Rubbing a sore spot on the back of my head, I said, "Who?"

He shrugged. "How the hell do I know?" Then he grinned. "But it ain't no social visit."

Since he wasn't carrying handcuffs or leg irons, I could be pretty sure I would be remaining in the secure area of the jail. He stepped away from the door to let me precede him down the dismal gray hallway.

"The trash from lunch is still in there," I told him. "Nobody came by to pick it up."

He nodded. "I'll make sure somebody on sanitation duty gets it."

His boot steps and the jangle of his keys echoed off the cinderblock, but my unshod feet in their wool socks made no noise at all. We turned a few corners, stopped to wait for a grille to be opened remotely, and then proceeded down a short hallway with solid metal doors on one side.

The CO lifted his radio to his mouth. "Pop the door on C3." When the door buzzed, he pulled it open and stood back. "In you go."

I stepped inside.

Detective Montgomery was perched on the edge of the table, swinging his lanky legs clad in well-creased trousers. He looked up at my face. "Wow. How does the other guy look?"

"Prob'ly a whole lot better than I do."

"How'd that happen?"

I shrugged. "How much you know about the whole thing?"

"Some. But I want to hear your side of it. Sit down and tell me about it."

Of course he'd want me to sit down. Much safer for him. I slid into one of the chairs placed on either side of the battered table.

"Now." He got up and walked behind me. "Who was this guy you got into it with?"

"His name is Gary. I don't know his last name. He came looking for his wife, who was at the carriage house where I'm staying at right now."

"And his wife is…"

I shifted in my seat. "Eileen's her name."

"No last name for her, either?"

"She prob'ly told me her last name, but I forget it. And she's got a baby. A little girl. Abigail."

He circled around into my line of vision, shaking his head. "And you know this Eileen how?"

"Well, she showed up at the carriage house looking for her aunt. Nicole somebody. She actually lives in the main house with Mandy Radman."

"What were you doing at the carriage house behind Mandy Radman's house?"

Awkward. I hadn't told anyone I was staying there for a while, and I didn't want it to look like I'd been withholding information from my parole officer. "I told Mandy I'd go by and keep an eye on it. Maybe stay there a night or so."

"And where is she?"

I wasn't sure what I should tell him, but I was better off sticking fairly close to the truth. He wouldn't be likely to judge them. If he did, so what? "They got married. And went on a honeymoon."

He raised his eyebrows. "Married?"

"Yeah. You know, now that same-sex marriage is okay, they decided to tie the knot."

"And how do you come into it?"

I looked down at a stain on the table. Was that coffee? Or blood? "I kind of know Mandy. She asked me to keep an eye on the house for them while they're away."

Montgomery laughed. "Isn't that like asking the fox to guard the henhouse?"

No good reason for me to be surprised by that statement, but coming from Montgomery, it stung. "I'm not a thief."

"No? We still haven't settled that ATM break-in, have we?"

I didn't have any answer for that, so I just kept quiet.

"And how come we didn't know about the house-sitting gig? Did you tell Mr. Ramirez?"

"I may not have mentioned it." I knew I hadn't said anything to him. "It's just a temp thing. Till they get back. I got some other places I can stay at, too. Until I find some place permanent." I didn't really, but it shouldn't make that much difference.

"But back to this fight, or whatever it was. You know the guy Gary claims you kidnapped his wife?"

"Yeah, right. Why would I want to do that? And how the hell would I go about doing it if I did want to do it?"

"You tell me."

I shrugged. "What does Eileen say?"

"What do you think she said?"

"I dunno. She's scared of him, for sure. She ran away from him, came where she thought her Aunt Nicole was and would take her in."

Montgomery sat on the edge of the table again, adjusting his trousers leg so the sharp crease was straight. "Why do you think she would have done that?"

"It sure ain't none of my business, so I didn't ask too many questions, but sounded to me like she should have left him a long time ago."

"Why do you think she left him *now*?"

I started to rub my nose, but the minute I touched it, I remembered how sore it was. "Prob'ly because of the baby."

"What about the baby?"

"Gary, he claimed the baby wasn't his. Jeez, he thought the baby was *mine*. I never seen Eileen before two days ago."

"And if I do the math correctly," Montgomery said, "you were still in prison when the baby must have been conceived."

"True, that."

"But when was the first time you met Eileen?"

That was him trying to trip me up. "Day before yesterday. She was sitting on the doorstep when I got there after work."

He leaned forward and said, "Let's get back to the actual altercation with this Gary. How'd it start?"

Maybe I shouldn't have admitted to Officer Richards that I'd been the one to attack Gary, but it was too late to take it back now.

"Well?" he said.

Sighing, I said, "I was coming from work, down the alley. I seen that car with Ohio plates in the alley by the carriage house. I knew Eileen was afraid that her old man would be looking for her."

Montgomery straightened up and looked at the ceiling. "Why were the Ohio plates significant?"

"The car Eileen drove here in had Ohio plates. I figured that was where she was from."

"You didn't go pick her up?"

"Hell, no. I didn't even know her."

"She lives out of state?"

"I guess. I can't just go leave the state whenever I feel like it. I don't got no driver's license. And where'm I gonna find a car to use if I did decide to go?"

"You tell me."

"I don't know nobody I could borrow a car from."

"How about the girlfriend?"

"Not likely. She's gonna need a new clutch. You can smell it burning. Even if I was gonna drive it—which I'm not, since I don't have a license—I wouldn't take it out of town."

"I wouldn't put it past you to boost a car if you needed one bad enough."

"Well, I didn't."

He paused and gazed at his perfectly manicured fingernails. "You say she came in a car. She drive?"

"I guess."

"And where is that car?"

"In the garage back at the house." I hoped it was still there.

He leaned back. "So you're coming from work to look in on this house you're supposed to be looking after. Given the time of the call, you must have been running late. You see this car with Ohio plates parked in the alley near the carriage house. What did you do?"

"I started running toward the yard. When I got to the gate, it was open. The doorframe to the front door was busted. And it wasn't locked." I was talking a lot more than I liked to, but I didn't see any other way to explain. And he wanted an explanation. How deep a hole was I digging for myself?

"And then?" he prompted.

"He was holding her real tight by the arms, hurting her. She was crying."

"How about the baby?"

"She was there, too."

"Where?"

"Lying on the floor in the corner. She was crying, too."

"On the floor like somebody laid her down on a blanket or something?"

"No. On the floor facedown, like somebody threw her there."

He got up and walked behind me again. "Who would have done that?"

"Not Eileen, I don't imagine. And for sure not me. I wasn't there. So if somebody did throw her down, it had to have been Gary."

He stopped right behind me. "Are you sure it wasn't you?"

My throat tightened. "I would never do that to a baby. And I told you, I wasn't even there yet."

"Are you sure of that? You get off work at eight, and this was around ten. You were really just getting there?"

At least I had a reason for that he could check on. "Yeah. I had to stay late at work."

"Why is that?"

I looked down at my socks. My feet were cold. "There was this accident at work."

"Last night?"

"No. The night before."

"What kind of accident?"

"A chemical spill."

"Do you know what the chemical was?"

"Potassium cyanide."

He started pacing again. "Potassium cyanide? Isn't that some pretty toxic stuff?"

"Yeah. And if it mixes with water, it's supposed to be explosive. And not good to breathe."

"So you were the one who spilled it?"

"No! But I was moving chemicals in when they discovered it."

"What do you mean, moving chemicals?"

"You know. They came in fifty-five gallon drums on pallets. They was in the shipping room and had to get moved back to the locked storage area by the plating room."

"With the forklift?"

"Yeah."

"And they think you had something to do with it?"

I shrugged. "I donno. But I was there. So they wanted to question me."

"Somebody from MOSH?"

"Yeah. Some guy named Ziraldo. You can check and see what time he got done talking to me."

"I'll do that. Now, as to how the baby ended up on the floor." He came around in front of me and perched on the edge of the table again. "You sure you didn't toss it yourself? Maybe just to get it out of the way in case there was a fight."

"Is that what Eileen told you? That I threw the baby down?" I said bitterly. If it was, I was totally screwed.

"Why would she tell me that if it wasn't true?"

I was screwed. "I guess because that's what Gary told her to say. She's scared of him."

Montgomery swung his long leg. "They're married. Don't you think she might love him? And be upset that you attacked him?"

My stomach cramped. "I wouldn't know about all that. If I was her and married to him, I'd think this was a good time to get rid of him once and for all."

"If that was what she wanted to do."

I wiped the corner of my mouth with my hand. It was sore. "I don't see how she could want to stay with him. That poor kid's not gonna have a chance. He's gonna kill one or both of them sooner or later. Prob'ly sooner."

Montgomery resumed pacing. "Maybe she does really love him. You never know how anyone else's relationship works."

"Maybe I don't know a whole hell of a lot about how relationships work, but that sure ain't nothing I'd call *love*."

"So if I'm going to believe you, you burst into the house where this guy was being threatening toward his wife. Probably broke down the door—the doorframe was splintered. What makes you think that was any of your business? Maybe that's just the way their marriage works."

My head was aching. "I couldn't just stand by and let him hurt her."

"Why didn't you call the police?" he asked.

"No phone."

"No phone?"

"Nah. I don't got a cell phone. Far as I know, neither does Eileen. And there's no landline into the carriage house. Or even the main house, I don't think. Anyhow, he could have really hurt her. There weren't nobody else to help her. Or the baby."

"It's my understanding the police were on their way. If you'd held off for a few minutes, you wouldn't have had to get so involved."

"How the hell was I supposed to know anyone was coming? Who called them?"

Montgomery considered whether to answer me or leave me in the dark. Finally, he said, "Trash truck crew. They said this guy almost drove into their truck. Then crashed into a bunch of garbage cans they'd just emptied, jumped out of the car, and ran into the yard. They said he seemed kind of irrational, so they talked about whether they should call 9-1-1. When they swung around at the end of the alley and drove back past where he'd left his car, they heard a woman scream."

"So they called?"

"Yes. *They* have cell phones."

I didn't doubt that. Everybody seemed to have cell phones. Except me and Eileen. And Kelly.

Montgomery checked his watch. "Okay. So you get there and you think he's threatening her."

"Not think. And not just threatening her. He was hurting her."

He corrected himself. "You thought he was hurting her."

"Think, hell. He *was* hurting her. He got behind her and he was choking her."

"With his hands?"

"He had his arm around her neck, and he'd lifted her up so only her tiptoes were on the ground. She was making choking noises."

"So you tackled him?"

"Not right away. I was afraid he'd crush her windpipe. Or break her neck. So I tried to talk to him. Calm him down a bit."

Montgomery looked up and cocked his head. "You? Talk somebody down?"

I shook my head. "Yeah. Not my territory, actually, talking somebody down. But I didn't know help was on the way."

"Did it work, this talking him down?" he asked.

"Not really. That's when he accused me of being the baby's daddy."

He laughed. "That would have been a good trick. Long-distance conception. What did you say?"

"I tried to tell him that Eileen wouldn't do that to him. The baby had to be his. The poor kid was crying real loud, and it was making us all a little crazy. I told him he shouldn't let his little girl cry like that and that Eileen could calm her down if he'd let her."

"Did that work?"

"Better than anything else. He let go of Eileen, and she went to pick up the baby."

"Did she try to leave with the baby?"

"I guess so."

"You don't know? What were you doing?"

"That's when I tackled him and shouted for her to get out of there."

He smiled. "And that's how you got all beat up?"

"Yeah."

"And he hardly has a mark on him."

"I grabbed his legs and held on. He was beating on my head."

"You didn't hit him back?"

"Not really. We was rolling around on the floor. All I was trying to do was keep him from following Eileen. I kept my head tucked in, but he kept hitting me."

Montgomery stood up straighter and glanced at his watch again. "So do you think we should be charging you?"

What I thought didn't matter, but I asked, "With what?"

"Oh, I don't know. At least assault and battery. Kidnapping. Maybe, after we finish talking to Eileen and get the rape kit results back, sexual assault."

"I didn't touch that woman."

"Really?"

"No, sir."

"Come on, now. She's a pretty girl. You're in the same place. Maybe even slept there. I know you're on the outs with your girlfriend now." He smiled. "Seems like you usually are. What would any man do in the circumstances?"

I took a deep breath. "I don't know about 'any man.' I didn't touch her."

He shrugged. "Whatever you say. I got some other things to look into. Both with this and ATMs."

"What's gonna happen to me?"

"You can stay put. I'll contact Mr. Ramirez and tell him where you are."

Telling my parole officer I was locked up wasn't going to be a big help. At least Montgomery couldn't tell him I'd been uncooperative.

He stepped over to the door on the far side of the room. "Officer?" he called.

As we waited, he looked back at me. "Should we consider child abuse charges, too?"

Angrily, I swiped away tears that were gathering in my eyes. "I didn't touch that baby, either. Not to hurt her. Is she okay?"

Montgomery raised his eyebrows. "Just a broken arm and a few cracked ribs."

CHAPTER 12

I ended up back in the same holding cell. The lunch bag was still in the corner. How long could they hold me without charging me?

Actually, I already knew the answer to that. Indefinitely. Maybe not officially, but I'd pretty much signed away all my rights when I was granted parole. They could do whatever they wanted, and even if I could get someone to listen to me if I complained, it wouldn't make any difference. Or if it did, it would just make things harder on me.

The image of Abigail lying on the floor, wailing pitifully, made me sick to my stomach. She must have been hurting bad. I couldn't put it out of my mind. How could anybody do that to a baby?

Lying down on the steel shelf again, I tried to doze. I didn't want to fall completely asleep, since when someone delivered my supper, I had to see if I couldn't get somebody to let me call in to work. Union regs said I couldn't be fired unless I was absent without notice for four days, but I wanted to let John know that he might have to find a replacement lift driver for the shift.

The door slid open. Not likely food—they'd pass that through the port in the door. Another CO, his eyes blank and emotionless. My heart sank. Was I going to be booked and processed into the jail population?

I stood up. "Can I get a phone call?" I asked.

The CO just looked at me.

"Can I talk to a lieutenant on duty?"

"What do you want to talk to a lieutenant for?"

"He—or she—'ll be able to get me a phone call."

He shrugged. "Fill out a request form." He fished one out of the breast pocket of his uniform shirt. "Here you go."

I didn't have any way to fill it out right now, but I stuck it in my jeans pocket. Somewhere along the line, I'd be able to get somebody to give me use of a pencil. Or fill out the form for me.

"Meanwhile," he said, "they want you up front."

"Booking?"

"I suppose that could be it. I was just told to bring you up front."

We passed through the sally port in reverse, but the CO didn't go through the last door. It slid closed after me, leaving me in my sock feet, standing there confused in the visitor's entryway, outside the secure area of the jail. Through a plexiglass information window, I could see several COs in the control room. None of them looked at me. Beneath the window was a dirty phone receiver half off its hook.

I was tempted to just walk out the front door, but that would get me in worse trouble if I wasn't supposed to leave. I was sure they could make it look like it was my fault and conjure up some kind of escape charge. Besides, they still had my boots and the rest of my stuff.

When no one paid me any mind after a few minutes, I went up to the information window and picked up the phone receiver. I waited until the CO in the control booth acknowledged me. Feeling like a total idiot, I said, "Uh, I'm not sure what I'm supposed to be doing."

He looked bored. "Oh? Visiting hours are morning only during the week. You'll have to come back."

"I'm not here to visit anyone," I said. "I was being held."

A flicker of interest showed on his face. "Where'd you come from?"

"I was in a holding cell, the one just beyond the sally port."

"How'd you get out there?"

"A CO escorted me."

"Let me check." He tapped on his computer keyboard. "Nobody assigned to that cell right now. What's your name?"

"Jesse Damon."

He checked the computer again, got up, and went to the board that held pictures of all the inmates and their cell assignments. "Don't see you on the board here. When were you processed? Or did you get transferred here from another lockup?"

"Neither, really. I was just brought in and seen by the nurse. Put in the holding cell."

"Huh. Wasn't this shift, was it?"

"I'm not sure. I lost track of time."

"Were you booked?"

I must have looked as confused as I felt. He said, "You know, did they take your fingerprints and a picture and all that?"

"No."

"But you were arrested?"

"I'm not sure about that. Held, yeah. But nobody ever told me I was under arrest."

He shook his head. "I can check the arrest records. But if I can't find anything…" his voice trailed off. "What exactly do you want me to do about it? You *want* to be locked back up?"

"It's not that. I don't want to get in any worse trouble if I leave when I'm not supposed to. But if I can, I'd like my property back." I didn't really want to walk outside in my sock feet, and I couldn't go to work without my steel-toed boots.

"Did you check the property room?"

"No. I thought that was back in the booking area."

"Well, the one for the jail is. Let me ask 'em if they have your stuff." He picked up another phone and made a call.

"Nope," he said. "They don't have your stuff."

"So any idea where my stuff might be? I mean, it's my boots and belt and wallet and things."

He stood up to get a closer look at my feet, which of course were covered only by my socks.

"You got a receipt?" he asked.

"Uh, I don't think so." Of course they should have given me a receipt. I didn't remember getting one.

I checked my pockets. "No."

"There's another property room, down in the police station," he said. "You could check that. But they're not supposed to keep your stuff down there if you been moved up here."

"How do I get there?" I asked.

"It's down these outside stairs and just go in the front door. Maybe they can help you there."

I thanked him and limped out the door, down the steps, and through the door to the police station. The sidewalk was damp, and the moisture soaked through the socks.

A woman sat at the front desk.

"I was wondering about retrieving some property…" I said.

She snapped her gum and didn't look up. "Was it confiscated?"

"Yes, ma'am."

"You got a court order to get it returned?"

"No, ma'am."

She rolled her eyes. "Search warrant or what?"

"I was arrested. Or at least brought down here for questioning."

She looked at me like I was crazy. Maybe I was. "You didn't come from back there." She jerked her head toward the hallway behind her. "So where were you?"

"Up in the jail. In a holding cell."

"Well, they got a separate property room. All we keep here is stuff taken off people when they're brought in. And stuff seized in searches."

"Yes, ma'am. That's what it is—stuff taken off me when I was brought in. My wallet and my keychain. And my boots and belt and jacket."

She glanced down at my sock feet, closed her eyes, and sighed. "And you think we have your boots and things down here?"

"I sure hope so. They say they don't have them up in the jail."

She took a pencil and scratched her scalp through several inches of bouffant hair. "Give me your name and have a seat. I'll see if I can find anything out."

"Jesse Damon," I said and then spelled it. Then I plunked myself down on a bench. I was surprised to see the clock on the wall said "Two thirty." It seemed much later.

Several uniformed police officers came through the door. One of them peeled off from the group and approached me. My muscles tensed, but I forced myself to sit still, not looking in their direction.

"Jesse Damon?" It was Officer Richards.

I raised my head. "Yes, ma'am?"

"What are you doing still here?" she asked.

I didn't know if she thought I should have been released earlier or if she thought I should be up in the jail. "Trying to find out what's going on. And get my stuff, if I can."

"Your stuff?" She looked at my feet and grinned. "You mean, like your shoes?"

"Yes, ma'am. Boots. And my belt. Jacket. And wallet and keychain."

She went over to the woman at the desk and said something to her. Then she came back to where I sat. "Somebody talk to you about this morning?"

"Detective Montgomery. But it wasn't what you'd call a real interrogation."

She nodded. "I think we got a pretty good idea of what happened. I can see somebody did a fair job of beating you up. You see a doctor?"

"No, ma'am. But the nurse in the jail took a look at me."

"You thinking about filing charges?" she asked.

The idea startled me. "Me? Against that guy Gary?"

She laughed. "He's the one who beat you up, isn't he?"

"Well, yeah. But…" I thought for a few seconds. "Charges? No, ma'am. I figure he would say I attacked him first and he was just trying to defend himself. In a way, I guess he'd be right. I did tackle him."

"Why?" she asked.

"I was trying to give Eileen a chance to grab the baby and get away."

"Uh-huh."

I looked Richards straight in the eye. Hers were a startling shade of green. I bit my lip and asked her, "Did Eileen get away?"

"She's safe."

"What does that mean?"

"That means I'm not going to discuss her condition or whereabouts with anyone involved in the altercations this morning."

I shifted uncomfortably on the hard bench. "Montgomery told me the baby was hurt. Is she gonna be okay?"

"She's gotten appropriate medical attention. So has the mother."

That was a relief. "Where's Gary?"

Richards raised her eyebrows. "That's the husband, is it? That's not something I'm at liberty to discuss. Especially with you. Eventually, it may be a matter of public record, but not yet. You could try getting a copy of the newspaper tomorrow."

I didn't exactly trust the newspaper to give an accurate description of anything, not after they published some of the stuff Carissa had written about me. "You didn't let Eileen leave with him, did you? He's gonna really hurt her someday. Maybe kill her."

"What business is that of yours?" Richards asked.

Shrugging, I said, "I dunno. I'd just hate to see her back with him."

"You familiar with domestic violence shelters for women?"

"Yeah." I knew Mandy had stayed in one until her husband Sterling was jailed. By now, though, he had to be a former husband. If she had gotten married to Nicole.

"So you can stop worrying about her, at least for now."

"Should I bring her stuff somewhere?"

Richards shook her head. "They have everything she needs where she is. How secure would a facility be if I could tell you where to bring her stuff?"

I had to concede that she had a point.

The woman at the desk raised her voice. "Here's his property bag. He has to come over and sign for it."

Getting to my feet, I padded over. The woman shoved a form in front of me to sign. She was annoyed that I opened the property bag to check the contents and counted the meager supply of money in the wallet to make sure everything was there before I signed the paper. I stuck the wallet and the keys in my pocket and slipped the belt through my belt loops. I took the jacket and the boots back to the bench.

Officer Richards was still standing there. She watched while I put the boots on and tightened the laces. When I stood up and put the jacket on, she held the outside door open for me.

I went out, and she followed me.

Turning to her, I said, "Thank you."

"For what?"

"If you hadn't of checked with that lady, I might never of gotten my stuff back."

She laughed. "You probably would have. Eventually."

"Mind if I ask you a question?" I asked.

She raised her eyebrows. "Ask away. But I don't guarantee I'll answer."

"How the hell long is your shift? You was at the convenience store last night, and you was at the house this morning, and you're *still* here? In your uniform?"

She laughed again. "I worked a double. Then I had to fill out some paperwork about both those incidents, plus some other stuff. I got off less than a half hour ago. Now I'm going home to get some sleep. You probably ought to do the same thing."

I nodded. "True, that."

"And," she said, "I got almost a whole week off now. I don't want to come back and find you locked up again. Or in any kind of trouble at all. Hear me?"

"Yes, ma'am," I said. "Not if I can help it." But trouble had a way of finding me.

CHAPTER 13

Zipping up my jacket against the wind, I turned in the direction of the carriage house. Officer Richards was right. I did need to get some sleep.

As I was walking by the courthouse, I heard somebody call me.

"Jesse! Oh, Jesse! I need to talk to you!"

Looking in that direction, I saw a woman trying to hurry down the courthouse steps toward me. She teetered on high heels, her unbuttoned bright red coat flying out to either side of her.

Carissa. The newspaper reporter.

I grimaced. She was one of the last people I wanted to talk to. I ducked my head down and continued to walk, trying to ignore her.

I had to stop at the corner to wait for the light to change. Carissa caught up with me.

She pulled out the camera that she always carried, ready to go, and started snapping pictures of me. Conscious of my bruised face, I tried to turn so she couldn't get a good shot, but she just moved around to my other side and kept taking pictures.

"Oooo, Jesse," she said, her bright red, overly full bottom lip sticking out. "Are you mad at me or something? I just wanted to talk to you."

Conversations with Carissa eventually ended up in the newspaper, everything I said totally distorted. "Makes a better story," Carissa would say if I pointed that out. "More colorful. People like it better that way. And if they like it, they're going to buy the newspaper. And if enough people buy the newspaper to read what I've written, I'll still have a job. You know, it's tough keeping a job as a newspaper journalist these days."

I didn't doubt that, but her articles always made me sound like some kind of depraved criminal. I suppose the criminal part was valid, but I didn't need it all over the paper.

And she'd use the worst of the pictures she could get hold of, ones where I looked at least partially demented.

She called it feature writing.

I called it harassment.

The light changed, but a patrol car, siren screaming, tore out of the parking lot next to the courthouse and down the one-way street toward the intersection where we were standing. I considered making a dash in front of it, figuring Carissa, in her heels, wouldn't attempt it, but I decided against it. With my luck, I'd probably get hit. Or she would, and I'd be detained as a witness.

I heard a few other people come up to the corner, waiting for the street to clear. I kept my head down and my hands in my pockets, not saying anything to anybody.

Carissa swung around, the coat brushing against me. "Jesse won't talk to me," she whined. "I asked him all nice and everything."

"Is that so?" a familiar voice growled behind me.

The hairs on the back of my neck stood up. Detective Belkins, who was convinced that I belonged behind bars. And Carissa's unlikely boy-friend.

Hastily, I pulled my hands out of my pockets. I didn't want to give him any excuse for doing anything and saying I'd gone for a weapon.

"What's the problem, Damon?" he asked me.

The other people stepped into the crosswalk. I didn't dare move.

"Look at me," he ordered.

Reluctantly, I lifted my head and focused my gaze somewhere around that red bulbous nose. In the cold, it was even redder, and it stood out all the more against his pasty white face.

"You got a problem with the little lady?" he demanded.

"No, sir. But I don't got nothing to say," I said.

He put an unlit cigar in his mouth and chewed on it. Without taking it out of his mouth, he said, "You can't just answer her questions?"

I shrugged.

"Oh, Roger," she simpered, giving her head a toss that sent her multi-colored shaggy blond hair cascading around her head and settling back into place.

Belkins's first name was Roger?

The corners of Carissa's mouth turned down. The corners of her eyes followed suit. Her lower lip stuck out. "He's just come out of the police station! And look at those bruises! A real shiner, if ever I saw one. I'm sure there's a story there. But he won't talk to me."

He took the cigar out of his mouth. "Now, snookums, you can get that information from the police blotter. You know I don't like you hang-ing around low-lifes like Damon."

She tossed her head again and said, "You know I can take care of myself. Remember how I managed to get away from those bikers who kidnapped me and wanted to hold me at their clubhouse."

Even Belkins raised his eyebrows at that. We both knew she'd gone to the clubhouse, way out in the country, voluntarily, thinking she was on the trail of a feature story. And it was me who got her out of there, although Belkins would always be sure I had an ulterior motive.

A black Lincoln Continental slid up to the curb. The driver's window rolled down. Detective Montgomery. When he needed backup, he often got Belkins as a partner. They were an unlikely duo, but they seemed to make the best of it. And they were very effective.

"We got work to do, Belkins," he said. "Unless you really got something going with him, leave Damon alone and get in this car."

"Oooo, can I come, too?" Carissa asked.

Please take her, I thought.

"No can do," Montgomery said.

"Aw. I never get to go interesting places!"

"Now, that's not entirely true," Belkins said, wiping his mouth. "I take you lots of nice places."

"Nice, yes. Interesting, no." She folded her arms over her almost non-existent breasts and frowned.

"Snookums, I'm sorry. I'll make it up to you when I get off duty."

"You always say that." She stuck out her bottom lip even farther.

Belkins reached out, drew her up against his protruding stomach, and leaned his face down to her. He gave her a big smooch on the mouth.

His breath always smelled of stale whiskey and cheap cigars. I imagined it tasted that way, too. And I couldn't imagine how being pressed up against his unwieldy bulk could be desirable, especially not when it looked like he might fracture her fragile spine.

But she snuggled up against him and giggled.

He let her go. "I got to leave now, snookums."

I turned to cross the street, but the light changed again. Even if there hadn't been a steady stream of traffic, jaywalking in front of the courthouse with Belkins and Montgomery right there probably wasn't a good idea.

Belkins stepped around to the passenger side of the car and got in. The car pulled off.

Carissa looked at me and grinned. "Now we can talk," she said. "Wanna go get a cup of coffee?"

I didn't answer or look at her. When the light changed yet again, I stepped off the curb and into the crosswalk.

Carissa kept right up, jabbering away. "We could go get lunch at the trendy soup and sandwich place over by the courthouse," she said. "Or McDonald's, if you'd rather. My treat. Actually, on my expense account…"

I tried to tune her out and kept walking.

She kept teetering along beside me.

All I wanted to do was go back to the carriage house, take a shower, and get some sleep. But I didn't want Carissa to know where I was staying, and if I went there now, she would follow me and know for sure. I'd never be able to go out the door without being afraid she was lying in wait.

So I turned toward the library. It was a public building, so she could go in as easily as I could, but most people were respectful enough of the quiet atmosphere to keep their voices down in the adult reading room and the stacks. If I sat down in the reading room and picked up a newspaper, she'd most likely have enough sense to be reasonably quiet. If not, they would ask her to be. Or kick her out.

I took the wide stairs up to the entrance two at a time, Carissa trailing behind, and stepped up to the heavy front door. I pulled it open and went in, not even bothering to hold it for her to catch it.

She didn't seem to notice. She grabbed onto it and minced in behind me.

"The library!" she said, although she did lower her voice. "What a good idea! Maybe we can get one of those little meeting rooms or something and have a good talk there. Then I'd even have a table to take notes on. Let me go see if there's one available."

She headed off to the circulation desk, pushing ahead of some people waiting in line.

I didn't wait to see how that would play out. I slipped through the reading room and into the stacks. There had to be a fire exit of some sort at the back. It might have an alarm or something if it was opened, but this wasn't a new building, and security didn't seem to be a major concern. The alarm would probably stop when the door was closed again.

Following the red "Emergency Exit" signs with their arrows pointing toward the rear of the building, I glanced behind me. No Carissa in sight. I opened the door. An alarm did sound. I slipped through the door and pulled it shut firmly behind me. The alarm stopped.

Carissa didn't give up easily. When she realized I was gone, she would go looking for me. She'd most likely go out the front door and look around. If I went out to the street, she might see me.

I crept next to the wall behind the dumpster and then wove my way around cars parked in the lot between the library and an office building. I had to climb over a waist-high barrier to get to a narrow pedestrian alley that ran next to the office building. I could see that beyond a collection of trash cans the alley opened on the next street, so I sprinted through it.

Still worried that Carissa would catch up with me, I ducked through a tiny park and past an upscale clothing store with a striped awning shading its front windows. The word "Boutique" was emblazoned on the awning. I glanced into the window. A trio of nearly featureless and handless mannequins stood there, their suggestions of noses lifted haughtily in the air and their arms raised in elegant, helpless poses. The scraps of fabric draped on the mannequins were also more like suggestions of dresses than real pieces of clothing. A price tag caught my eye. $750. I almost stopped. That was a lot more than I made in a week. Surely no one would ever pay that kind of money for a dress that consisted of a flimsy scrap of fabric?

Not a good time for me to window shop. And the price people were willing to pay for scraps of fabric, or dresses, was nothing I needed to be worried about. I slipped down another alley that I thought might intersect with the one that eventually ran behind Mandy's house. As I turned that corner, I glanced over my shoulder for the first time.

Clarissa was nowhere in sight.

Relieved, I dodged into the next pedestrian walkway between two buildings and headed through the alleys toward the carriage house.

Gary's car was still parked at the crazy angle, but traffic could get by. The garbage cans were still scattered all over, so I retrieved them, sticking my fist inside and bashing out the dents as well as I could. One was underneath the car. I pulled that out and tried to straighten that one out, but it was smashed beyond reasonable hope.

Should I do anything about the car? I decided no. It was in a public alleyway, and the police certainly knew where it was. They could decide to tow it, or leave it where it was. I hoped Gary wouldn't come to pick it up himself, or if he did, that he wouldn't bother with me.

The police had closed the door to the carriage house as well as they could. It kept out the weather, but it wouldn't keep out anyone who wanted to get in. With the doorframe splintered, there was no reasonable way to secure it. Tomorrow after work, I'd have to see if I could make a temporary fix. Maybe pick up a padlock and one of those security latches.

The bag with the sandwiches was tossed against the wall. I retrieved it.

Inside was a bit of a mess. The floor was covered with splotches of blood. Undoubtedly my blood. Fortunately, none of it seemed to be on the rug. Chairs and the dining table were knocked over. The sweater I'd lent Eileen to wrap the baby in and some of the baby's things were scattered around.

I righted the furniture. None of it looked like it was any the worse for wear. I tossed the sweater and the baby clothes in the washing machine and got a roll of paper towels and a spray bottle of cleaner to tackle the floor. The blood came up easily.

I pried open the soggy sandwich rolls and picked the meat and the cheese out from the limp lettuce and disintegrating tomato. The cheese ought to still be good. I rinsed the slices off. How about the meat? I sniffed it. The salami was heavily spiced and maybe would be okay. It and the bologna were probably so full of artificial ingredients and preservatives that they shouldn't spoil easily. I rinsed them off, too, and made two big sandwiches with my own bread, which I stuck in the refrigerator. It would be a welcome change from peanut butter. If I didn't die of food poisoning.

The big package of diapers I'd bought was almost full. Looked like that was a total waste of money. I folded down the top and put it in the coat closet. If, when they got back, Nicole arranged for Eileen to move into the carriage house, diapers would come in handy then.

A hot shower eased my aching muscles. I glanced in the mirror—no point really looking to see just how bad my face was. I'd skip shaving, at least for tonight. If I lay down now, I could catch a good six hours' sleep. I set the alarm and climbed into bed, closing my eyes and trying to will my brain to stop thinking.

Instead of settling down, my mind raced.

Was I in trouble at work? Enough to get fired? The union would go to bat for me, but even they couldn't save my job if an infraction was serious enough and I got blamed. I had a feeling a potassium cyanide spill, especially one that wasn't reported immediately, was serious enough.

I knew Kelly was seeing that Sydney guy. Was it just AA business, or were they settling in for a fling? Or something more serious?

My stomach curled when I thought about Kelly sleeping with him. Much as I hated that idea, I had to acknowledge that Kelly could sleep with whoever she wanted to, and she wasn't exactly a virgin.

And what was that video Montgomery kept talking about of me breaking into an ATM? Couldn't be me. Was the story totally fabricated? Or did they have someone that *looked* like me breaking into an ATM?

I couldn't go to work exhausted. What was happening to my old trick of emptying my mind and willing myself to sleep? It was a trick I'd learned when I was a kid, living in foster homes. If nothing I did was going to have any effect on what happened to me, why worry about it?

But I was an adult now. For now, at least, I wasn't locked up. Maybe it was time for me to realize that, while I didn't have any control over what other people did, I did have total control over what I did. Act like an adult. And stop messing up.

CHAPTER 14

The alarm pulled me from a restless sleep. I got dressed and stumbled downstairs. I made enough instant coffee to drink a cup and fill the battered thermos, which I stuffed into the lunchbox along with the recycled sandwiches.

I hesitated about eating something right now. My gut was still churning—I hadn't exactly spent a restful day, and my mind was so crowded with the mass of concerns that I couldn't even pull just one out to think about. In the end, I toasted two pieces of bread and spread them with peanut butter. Better to have something in my stomach.

Since I left plenty early, I got to work with time to spare, intending to punch in and get the pre-shift checklist done before Diffy's shift finished up. I didn't want to hear what he'd have to say about the spill. If he had shown up for the shift.

I wasn't particularly anxious to see Kelly, either, and hear what she'd have to say about my bruises.

After I hung up my jacket and got my hard hat and gloves, I punched my timecard and shoved it back into its place on the rack.

"Jesse."

John's voice. I stopped in my tracks and turned to face him.

He was standing there, his clipboard in his hand, with a man wearing a business suit and hard hat and carrying a briefcase.

"Yes, sir?" I said.

"Glad you're here a little early," John said. He peered at my bruised and cut face. "You look kind of rough. Again. Are you okay?"

"Uh, yeah. But it's just superficial. A few scrapes and bruises." I didn't want to go into the whole thing about the fight with Gary if I could help it.

"This is Howard Mannings, chief safety officer for Quality Steel Fabrications."

I definitely didn't want to go into the whole thing about the fight. Not in front of a safety officer. For sure I didn't want him to start thinking I had violent tendencies. Not with all the workplace shootings that been in the news. And not with my murder conviction.

"He's here to take a look at our operations, especially the chemical storage area. If he has any questions, I want you to answer them as completely as you can."

I swallowed. "Yes, sir."

"He wants to see the procedure you use for signing out a forklift. Take him with you."

"Yes, sir."

Mr. Mannings made no attempt at small talk as we proceeded to the charging stations. It would have been difficult as we walked through the noisy shop, but once we were in the more isolated area where we kept the forklifts, he still didn't say anything.

I took the clipboard off its hook on the wall and pulled out my stubby pencil.

The clipboard had only a stack of brand new sheets on it. All the old lists were gone. Usually they stayed until the end of the month. I glanced at the clipboard for the next lift in line. It still had its messy stack of filled-out papers held tight by the clip. I couldn't see the clipboards farther on down without stepping out in the aisle and being obvious about it.

Had I messed it up in the last few days? I didn't think I'd missed anything, but now I wished I'd gone over what I'd put down for the last couple of shifts.

"You want to see the list?" I held out the clipboard toward Mr. Mannings.

He moved way back against the wall, out of the way, and got a notebook out of his briefcase. "No. I have a copy. Just go ahead and run through it like you usually do."

Pencil in my hand, I started the checklist.

"Hey, Jesse! You beat me tonight," Kelly called as she went by, heading toward her bigger lift at the end of the line. She didn't look closely, and I didn't think she saw Mr. Mannings right away.

"Yeah," I shouted back to her.

"We got to talk," she said.

"Okay." I glanced at Mr. Mannings, but his face was expressionless. "Maybe lunch, if we get it the same time. Or when the shift breaks."

"Or how about now?" she shouted from next to her lift. "We got a few minutes before the whistle blows."

I grimaced. "Kelly, have you met Mr. Mannings? He's the plant safety officer."

Her clipboard in her hand, she came back to where I was. "What? Whoa, what happened to you? And who's Mr. Mannings...?" Her voice trailed off when she saw him.

"Mr. Mannings, this is Kelly Mathais. She's the other lift driver on the shift. She mostly works in shipping. I mostly work on the shop floor and in the warehouse."

He glanced at her and scribbled something in his notebook. "You work in shipping?" he said. "Did you handle the chemical shipment the other night at all?"

Kelly cast a nervous look at me and licked her lips. "No. The shipment was unloaded before I started the shift. It was all off to the side, with that yellow caution tape on it. I had a couple of trucks lined up waiting to be loaded, so I didn't have a chance to even go look at it."

He nodded, scribbling away in his notebook. "And is that normal procedure? The shipment of chemicals is just left by the side of the shipping dock?"

She frowned. "With caution tape around it," she pointed out.

"With caution tape," he said, continuing to write. "Is that the way it's usually left?"

"Usually it's all put away before we start our shift," Kelly said. "Sometimes supplies—wire, sheet metal, things like that—are left for us to put in the warehouse, but I think that's the first time I've ever seen the chemicals left like that."

"I see." He flipped to a new page in his notebook. "And do you ever put these supplies away?"

"Not usually. I'd unload them off the truck, of course, if they came during our shift. But moving stuff into the warehouse is pretty much Jesse's job. Or, in the case of the chemicals, into the storeroom."

"So you never move supplies into the warehouse or the storeroom."

She sighed. "I wouldn't say 'never.' Jesse and I help each other out when we need to."

"Would the foreman order you to do that?"

"He might. But Jesse and me, we keep an eye on things. Sometimes, he'll load a truck or move shipments around if I'm getting behind. And I'd put stuff away if he needed help. He's pretty much on top of things, though, so I don't do much of that."

"Would he be aware that you were moving things into a storage area? Or would no one tell him?"

Kelly frowned. "Well, it wouldn't be like we were keeping it a secret or anything. But unless he came by and happened to notice, he might not find out. We wouldn't stop work to go find him and tell him, for sure."

Mr. Mannings continued to scribble away in his notebook.

Kelly made a face at me and rolled her eyes. I shrugged.

"I got to get my checklist done," she said and then went back to her lift.

I noticed the clipboard in her hand had its usual stack of papers on it.

"Do you find the flashing lights, turn signals, and backup warnings to be adequate?" he asked me.

"Yeah," I said. "But it can be noisy. And people are busy. So that don't mean I expect anybody to get out of my way."

The lifts are electric and don't make much noise. They do beep when they're backed up, but generally, it's hard to hear them coming. That, in itself, is a safety issue, and I knew to be very careful in the plant, especially on the crowded shop floor. If he asked, would I admit I often didn't bother with the turn signals?

The end of the shift was approaching, and Diffy came careening in on his lift. Somehow, he managed to make the tires squeal as he roared into the charging area. He veered toward where I was standing, clipboard in my hand. I stepped back closer to the lift.

He laughed and stopped next to me. "Hey, dude," he shouted. "They still think you must've dumped all that potassium cyanide?" He laughed. "And what the hell happened to your face? You look like you done run into a windmill. Another fight? Don't you ever win 'em?"

He laughed again and swung his lift into its slot halfway down the line. He hadn't even noticed Mr. Mannings, who had opened his note-book again and was writing furiously.

"And who was that?" he asked.

I shrugged. I wasn't about to roll over on a fellow employee. Even Diffy. "One of the second-shift lift drivers. I'm not sure of his name, though."

He could find out easily enough if he really wanted to know.

I hung up the clipboard and unplugged the lift. The whistle for shift change sounded. "You got any more questions, or should I get to work?" I asked.

"Go ahead," he said. "I'll be looking round for a while. If I need to ask you anything else, I'll find you."

"Okay." I waited while Kelly drove past and then guided my lift out into the shop to begin my rounds.

Anxious to see if Hank had heard anything, I swung by the plating room office a few times, but Mr. Mannings seemed to be hanging around the area, especially the hallway by the storage room. That made a certain amount of sense, since that was where the problem had occurred, but when I got close to him, I could see sweat beading on Hank's forehead. He clung tightly to the clipboard with his paperwork, rather than leaving it in the office. When I looked at him inquisitively, he shook his shaggy head and continued on his way.

Finally, Mr. Mannings strode off down the hallway toward the shipping room. I pulled up by the plating room office door and climbed off the lift, but I didn't step away from it. We weren't supposed to leave them running when we weren't right there with them.

Hank stepped out of the plating room office, the paperwork still in his hand.

"I don't want that guy to report that I left the lift running and unattended," I shouted above the din of the machinery. "So I don't think I ought to go into the office."

Hank nodded and handed the clipboard to me. I riffled through the papers. It was all organized and stapled, with the relevant quantities and part numbers highlighted.

"You're getting good at this," I said, raising my voice to be heard.

Hank grinned and scratched his neck under his beard.

"How's Steb?"

"Better," Hank answered.

"You hear anything else about anything?"

He looked around, opened the office door, and tossed the clipboard onto the desk. Then he gestured down the hallway toward the lacquer line. "Meet me down there in a few minutes," he shouted. "It's quieter. We can maybe talk for a minute."

I gave him a thumbs up.

"First, I got to check on plater three. It's been running rough tonight. And we don't have a mechanic on this shift who can work on it."

Swinging the lift past the platers and through the shop, I kept an eye out to see if I could find out where Mr. Mannings was. I caught a glimpse of him walking with John. They were headed toward the dispatcher's office, which was usually locked tight on this shift. Mr. Mannings, though, probably had keys to get in wherever he wanted to go.

The plater operators took the parts off the overhead conveyors on the platers and hung them on another overhead conveyor, where they dried. They then headed toward a lacquer tank. Before they got to the tank, they went by a work station, where someone was assigned to remove any parts that weren't supposed to be lacquered. He would also quickly inspect the remaining parts before they reached the lacquer tank, removing any with obvious plating defects. It was much easier to remove the plating and replate them before they hit the lacquer. Once they were lacquered, the stripping process was expensive and the chemicals used were toxic. They only ran the stripping tank after dark, when the smelly gray clouds of vapor at least weren't visible to anyone in the neighboring plants or houses.

Tonight, all four platers were running shelves that needed to be lacquered, so the guy assigned to that work station was having an easy night. A pallet was three quarters full of shelves that had been pulled for defects, but it had been half full when the shift started.

I eased my forks under the pallet so that it would look like I was getting ready to remove it if Mr. Mannings happened by.

Hank trudged in from the plating room, shouting a greeting to the guy who was inspecting the shelves on the line, who shouted back but never took his eyes off the shelves on the moving line.

"So what do you hear?" I asked him.

"About the chemical spill?"

I started to say something sarcastic, but Hank was a very literal man, so I bit my tongue and said, "Yeah."

He sighed, his entire chest heaving. "Steb's gonna be okay, I think. Victor, the union steward, said they finally did wise up and bought him a new pair of boots, so he's happy. I guess he's not got any permanent damage, at least from this spill."

"That's good to hear. Did they ever figure out what happened?"

"More or less. They pulled the surveillance tapes and talked to everybody who could have handled the shipment. It came in around four thirty, and they wasn't all that busy, so there was really no reason for it not to get put away on second shift."

I adjusted my hard hat. "So why was it left for us to move?"

Hank wiped his gloved hands against his thigh. "You ask me, it's cause Diffy started to move the stuff and he wasn't careful enough. So one drum fell off the pallet. And then, instead of reporting that and getting some help to set it back on the pallet, he tried to shove it back up with his forks. And ended up puncturing the side."

I could see how that could happen, although if I dropped a drum, especially a drum of potassium cyanide, I sure as hell wouldn't try to use the forks to move it. I might try to right it myself before I reported it, or seen if I could get some help from Hank or Kelly, but I wouldn't take a chance on puncturing the drum. "They know that for sure?" I asked.

"Nah. Diffy ain't saying nothing. He clammed up when they asked him about it. I think he got a letter of reprimand, and he was suspended for part of a shift, but then he went to the union. They started to file a grievance. So they rescinded the suspension, at least for now. And they gotta pay him for the time he was off."

"But that's the official version of what happened, Diffy did it?"

"I don't know about official, but as far as I can tell, yeah."

I heard him, but I could hardly believe I was off the hook. I had to make sure. "So they're not saying it was me who dumped the drum and punctured it?"

"Nope. I think you got off scot free on that one."

Muscles I didn't know I had relaxed. I took a deep breath.

"I wish that damn safety guy would leave," Hank said. "He asked me about the hazmat sheets. I showed him the binder. Thank goodness he took it and went to the pages he wanted by himself. What if he'd asked me to show him?"

"Maybe we could put some sticky notes on the potassium cyanide pages, kind of like book marks," I said. "Then you could just flip to them if you needed them."

"We could do that for now," he agreed. "But next time, it'll be something else." He frowned. "I'm too old to find another job. What if they realize I can't read and fire me?"

I wasn't the only one who worried about my job. "Well, you got through this fine," I reminded him. "And you're handling the work orders better all the time. I think you'll be okay."

He nodded glumly. "But I almost puked the other night when John asked me to read him stuff from the hazmat sheets. I thought he was gonna tell me to punch out and go home. If you hadn't of been there and grabbed the book from me..."

"They'd be stupid to let you go; John knows there's nobody better to handle the platers. Nobody's irreplaceable, but you're as close as they come. It's not a job a lot of people want, to begin with. And not too many could do it."

Hank rubbed his nose with his glove. "You might be right about that. But it ain't John making the decisions all the time. If the bosses decide they don't want people who can't read in jobs where they might have to, I'm fried."

"Look, Hank," I said. "The absolute worst they'd do is demote you and put you operating a plater. So you'd still have a job."

He brightened. "That's true. The union would never let them fire me over not being able to read when there's lots of stuff I could do."

"True, that."

"But I think my best bet is if nobody finds out I can't read. I'm much obliged, Jesse. You showed me how to get all the stuff organized so it looks like I know what I'm doing."

"Hey, you gave me a break when I first started working here, before I got in the union. You and John."

He shrugged. "No big deal."

"It was a big deal. I'd been locked up for twenty years. If I hadn't been able to keep this job, I would have been totally screwed."

"You're a good worker, Jesse. You deserved a chance to show what you can do."

"Not everybody feels that way."

* * * *

I didn't see Mr. Mannings after about two o'clock. I asked John if I could take my lunch about four fifteen, which was just about when most of the workers would be settled back at their workstations. I was hoping to overlap with Kelly's lunch.

He had a load he wanted moved first, so it was more like 4:25 when I got to the rough-hewn picnic table back in a corner of the shipping room. Kelly was still eating.

She looked up when I parked nearby. "That guy, that Mr. Mannings, he been talking to you?"

"Yeah. Beginning of the shift." I got out my recycled sandwiches and sniffed one to make sure it didn't smell too funky. Kind of spicy, but not too bad. "He asked a lot of questions. How about you?"

"Uh-huh. A whole bunch of questions about that chemical shipment. Same shit he'd asked me before the shift started. If I knew when it had arrived, if I tried to move any of it. Stuff like that. I don't know why he did that—waste of time. All I could do was give him the same answers."

"Standard interrogation techniques," I told her. "Ask the same questions different ways and different times. See if they can get you to give contradictory answers."

"He didn't even bother to ask them in different ways. He just asked the same damn thing again."

"What did you tell him?"

"Just that the shipment was sitting there when the shift started, with that caution tape draped around it. And that I didn't go near it." She stuffed a cookie in her mouth and took a swig of her can of soda.

"So then did he leave you alone?"

"Not completely. He wanted to know why I didn't move the load, since I was a forklift driver, and if I would ever move stuff like that if it was in the way. That kind of thing."

"Then what?" I took a tentative bite of my sandwich. It tasted fine. Good, in fact.

"I told him I was pretty busy that night—in fact, you had to help me load a truck—and that, generally speaking, I would stick to the work in the shipping room and you would move anything that needed to be moved in and out. But that if John told me to move something, I'd move it, whether it was my usual job or not. But I might have to go switch for a smaller lift if I was gonna move pallets into the chemical storage area. It'd be kind of a tight fit, making it through the gate and around some of those corners."

Pondering the fact that what she told him did contradict what she'd told him before the shift started, that she might move some stuff without John being aware of it, I nodded. No point in worrying her.

She finished her can of soda and started gathering her trash together.

I swallowed. "Look, you said you wanted to talk to me. Want to go out for breakfast when the shift breaks? Unless one of us got to stay to answer more questions."

She didn't look at me. "I can't. But I can stay for a few minutes if you want. I could drive you home. If the damn clutch doesn't decide to give up completely."

"I can walk. That's not a problem. What did you want to talk about?"

"A couple of things."

About Sydney? My stomach twisted. "Anything important?"

"Partly that I want you to stop stalking me."

"Stalking you?"

"Yeah. You know, following me. I told you I didn't appreciate that."

"I haven't been stalking you. Or following you. What's giving you that idea?"

"Couple of times, when I've gone into a store or something, I've seen you hanging around on the corner. Pretending not to be watching me."

"Like when?"

"Like yesterday afternoon."

I started to say that couldn't have been me, I'd been locked up, but an alarm went off in my head. An alarm that had nothing with me stalking her or with me being locked up. "Like, around the liquor store?"

Her nostrils flared. "I'm in AA. That's an insult."

I didn't say anything, but I did note that she didn't deny it. "That couldn't have been me there."

"Then how did you know where it was? And by the library the other day, middle of the morning. You were on foot, but you tried to follow me."

"Well, yeah, I was by the library. But I was trying to flag you down. That's a big difference from stalking you."

She snorted. "Trying to flag me down? I don't think so. And I suppose if I tell you I saw you with that other woman, carrying her baby, you'd say I was wrong about that, too."

"No." I hadn't told her about Eileen. Now I wished I had.

"Your baby?" she asked.

"Aw, Kelly. Do the math. I was locked up when that baby was conceived. I may even have still been locked up when she was born. Not my baby."

"So what were you doing with that woman?"

"Helping her use the computers at the library."

Kelly's laugh wasn't particularly amused. "You? Helping her use a computer?"

"Well, she needed my library card to use one. Of course I can't really help her actually use the damn thing."

"Where did she come from?"

"Ohio somewhere, I think."

Kelly shook her head in disgust. "I mean, how did you hook up with her?"

"She's Nicole's niece. She's probably gonna move into the carriage house when they get back from their trip. I'm just s'posed to be staying there while they're away."

"So is she staying in the main house?"

"No. Mandy specifically told me not to let anybody stay there. I don't think she was thinking about Eileen, but I don't know that for sure. And I haven't heard from Mandy. That's what Eileen was trying to do on the computer, get in touch with Nicole. Or Mandy."

"So where'd she stay at?"

"Well, that first day, she stayed in the carriage house."

"With you stayed there, too? Like, slept there?" Kelly wrinkled up her nose.

I sighed. This was going nowhere fast. "Well, more or less. I mean, we work nights. So it wasn't like we were sleeping together or anything."

"By anything, you mean sex?"

"Well, yeah."

"And you expect me to believe that?" That was the second time she'd said that. But if she wasn't being honest with herself about her alcohol use, why would she think I was being honest with her?

"Yes, I do. But you don't have to if you don't want to. You and me, we're not an exclusive item here. I admit I'd like to be, but we're not. And you're seeing this Sydney fellow."

She squared her shoulders. "He's in AA."

"I know that. I hope he's doing you some good." It didn't seem like that to me, but what it seemed like to me wasn't important. "Especially if he's your sponsor."

"None of your business, is it?" She wouldn't look at me.

"Not if you don't want it to be."

Kelly threw her trash in the can and climbed on her forklift. Her movements were stiff and jerky.

I watched her. "You still want to meet for a few minutes when the shift breaks?"

She looked over her shoulder, but again avoided looking directly at me. "I don't think that's necessary. We've said all we need to for now, haven't we?"

She drove away.

CHAPTER 15

At the end of the shift, nobody said anything to me about any more questions or staying late, so I punched out a few minutes after eight. It was Friday morning, and I had a paycheck in my pocket.

Leaving the door to the carriage house unsecured wasn't a good idea, and I didn't want to let it go any longer than I had to. I stopped at an Ace Hardware and looked for latches.

Back before I'd been locked up, hardware stores used to have bins of loose stuff, bolts and nails and washers. Now everything was secured to cardboard with plastic bubble packaging and hung from hooks on some type of pegboard. I guess that made it harder to pocket anything and walk out.

I took a sturdy-looking shed latch and hasp off the display and examined it. It looked like what was needed. When it was closed, the latch pivoted on a post and covered the screws.

It was just under ten dollars, and it even had screws enclosed in the packaging.

A sturdy keyed padlock was another ten bucks. I paid for them out of my dwindling supply of money, confident that I could cash my paycheck later. I headed to the carriage house.

The car with Ohio plates was gone from the alley. Had Gary come for it? And had he decided to go look around in the carriage house?

I hurried to the door. To all appearances, it was like I had left it, closed securely in the splintered frame, but since the lock didn't catch any more, all it took was a good shove and it swung open.

Everything looked okay. Eileen's suitcase was still in the corner.

First priority was doing something about the door. There was a toolbox in the garage. I'd never looked in it, but I could probably find the stuff I needed to attach the latch.

Eileen's car was undisturbed. I slipped around it and took down the toolbox. Did the screws need a straight or a Phillips screwdriver? I hadn't checked, so I took one of each. I didn't see a drill to start pilot holes, so I took a small hammer and a good-sized nail.

It only took me a few minutes to get the door secured. I slipped the padlock through the hasp, put one of the keys on my keychain, and decided to put the other one in the kitchen in the house, where I could let Mandy know where it was. She'd have to get somebody to fix the door-frame better, but she used a local handyman for that type of work. He did a very good job, a lot better than I could ever do. When he got done, I doubted anyone could ever tell that the doorframe had been damaged.

I went on my rounds of the house. Once again, everything seemed to be in place.

Sorting through the mail before I put it on the table in the hall, I saw an envelope addressed to me.

In my whole life, I'd never gotten a piece of mail that wasn't bad news. Once, while I was first locked up, I got a personal letter from Mr. Coleman, my foster father. But it was to tell me what a disappointment I'd been to Mrs. Coleman and demand that I never try to contact them again.

All the other mail I'd ever received had been legal correspondence from the criminal justice system.

This envelope was different. It was business size, but it was ad-dressed by hand. And its return address, printed in the corner, was a bed and breakfast in New York State. A town up near Niagara.

My first impulse was to stick it in my pocket and deal with it later. Or maybe pretend I'd never gotten it.

That made no sense. It was probably from Mandy. Maybe it was even about what she wanted me to do about Eileen, but that was out of my hands at this point.

I tore it open. Sure enough, it was from Mandy.

She thanked me for taking Eileen in and seeing that she and the baby had a place to stay. I could let Eileen stay in the big house for now. And for sure, she—and me—could eat the food in the kitchen and the freezer.

They were cutting their trip short and would be back in another day or two. When they got back, I could move back to my own place, and Eileen would be moving into the carriage house.

Holding it with both hands, I stared at it as if the words might change. It said what I should have expected, really, but it was a shock nonethe-less.

I needed a new place to live. Very soon.

My old apartment wouldn't be ready for tenants for months, if ever. Because of the widespread damage to so many buildings, especially in the parts of town where I might possibly find some place, rentals were hard to come by.

Despite any wistful thinking on my part, Kelly's place was out, even for a short period.

I knew there were a few places with weekly rentals, usually rooming houses or such. As a rule, they weren't fussy about who they rented to, as long as the perspective tenant could produce the first and last week's rent along with a security deposit. I'd miss my own kitchen and bathroom, tiny as they had been, but I had to have somewhere to live.

Or Jumbo George. If he'd have me.

I'd met Jumbo George in the aftermath of the flooding, and he'd let me stay in his apartment, which was over a store he owned, in exchange for helping him with the cleanup he needed to reopen his store.

He used to live in the apartment himself, but as he put on more and more weight—he lived up to his name—he'd gotten to the point where he couldn't make it up the narrow stairs to the second floor, so he stayed in the back room of the store. His brother Nick, who was a long-haul truck driver, used to stay there when he was in town. But Nick was locked up now, facing a murder charge. And I'd had a hand in pointing the cops in his direction. I hadn't seen George since the arrest. I had no idea what kind of reception I'd get if I went over there.

Jumbo George's store was a head shop. There were two apartments over the store, one in the front, with its own entrance, and one in the back. The only way to get to the one in the back was through the head shop. That one, of course, was the one I might be able to get.

That was an arrangement Mr. Ramirez, my PO, would love. If I did move in, I could try to just fail to mention anything about the head shop, and if no one checked, he'd be none the wiser.

It would be a place to live, at least for now. And with his brother no longer staying there, Jumbo George might appreciate the extra income.

After I finished checking everything and made sure the house, the garage, and the carriage house were locked tight, I set out for Jumbo George's.

As I walked down toward the river from Mandy's neighborhood, I followed the descent from wealth to poverty that was obvious in the buildings. They weren't any older, but they had never been anywhere near as impressive as the ones downtown and in Mandy's neighborhood, and they weren't as well-kept. The streets and sidewalks showed more and bigger cracks. Even the trees looked discouraged and limp.

Jumbo George's shop was right down by the river, in an area that showed some signs of possibly gentrifying, if the newer residents could be convinced that the recent flooding was a fluke. They were calling it a hundred year's flood, but in a lot of places, those hundred years seemed to come around pretty frequently.

The shop stood in a row of stores that could be charmingly trendy and old-fashioned, or just plain old. A great spot for a head shop—near enough to the newer apartment buildings rising across the street from the river, in a block that headed back into the rundown section of town. Jumbo George was a crafty businessman, and his line of products was carefully selected to appeal to both segments of his potential customers.

The midday streets were almost deserted. A city bus lumbered up to a bus stop and paused, but no one got on or off. A whistle that could have been from a train or a river barge sounded in the distance. A small red sports car zipped by, splashing mud from a standing puddle onto the sidewalk and up its sides.

A small red sports car like the one I'd seen Kelly ride off in.

I looked at it with interest as it slowed and rounded a corner. Trying to keep it in sight, I picked up my pace.

The street it had turned down was even more desolate than most. The car slowed in front of the only building left standing on a block. The lots on either side of it were strewn with rubble and garbage bags.

The car angled across the sidewalk in front of the building, paused, and continued into it. Must be a garage with a remote control opener. Either that, or the car had vanished through a wall.

I voted for a garage. Curious, I turned the corner and went down that street.

The building where the car had turned was set squarely in the center of the block. It was made of solid brick, and all the windows on both floors were covered with sturdy burglar bars. A tall garage door was set in the front. I ambled along, my head down and my hands shoved in my pockets.

I could catch a glimpse of the red sports car in the dim interior. As I watched, a garage door slid down from the ceiling. When it was firmly closed, a security grill rattled down over it, the bottom slamming onto the sidewalk and bouncing up a few inches.

Most of the rest of the front of the building was bricked up. Two stone steps led up to a reinforced steel door with a tiny window set in the upper half. On either side of the door were small windows, covered by sturdy burglar bars set deep into the brick wall. Security cameras flanked a big sign that read, "Chillington's Financial Services. Check Cashing. Quick Loans. Bail Bonds."

I had no idea who Chillington was, but I had no doubt this was Sydney Jameson's place of business.

Whether the business helped people who had nowhere else to turn or took advantage of them might be open to question, but it was a legal business. Sydney seemed to be making a go of it, and if it was what he wanted to do, he was within his rights.

And if Kelly wanted to go out with a man who was making a good living at a questionably honest but legal business, she was within her rights.

Who was I to criticize either one of them?

I took a deep breath and picked up my pace. It's not like I could offer Kelly any reasonable alternative. She had the kids and the house she was trying to hang onto. Sydney had money and was willing to spend some of it on her. It made perfect sense for her to be seeing him. None of my business. And maybe she would be prepared to make a relationship with him that she wasn't willing to consider with me. I was really no worse off than I had been before I'd started seeing her.

So why did it hurt so much?

Angrily, I took a few deep breaths and swiped at my eyes, which seemed to have teared up. Maybe it was the wind blowing into them. I had better things to do than fret over my relationship with Kelly. When I came right down to it, what relationship? She was nice to me. We had sex, which was amazing and wonderful. Spending time at her place with her kids was my favorite thing to do, bar none. But she'd been perfectly clear from the beginning that she didn't want an exclusive relationship. At least with me.

My gut twisted. I'd probably read a lot more into the whole thing than she'd ever intended. My fists clenched in my pockets, I tried to concentrate on walking steadily, one foot in front of the other.

I'd covered the few blocks to Jumbo George's shop in record time. The row of storefronts looked fresher than they had last time I'd been here, and I realized they'd received a coat of paint. A new coffee shop had opened right next door to the head shop, and the enticing aroma of fresh-brewed coffee overpowered the smell of patchouli I remembered.

The front window to the head shop left no doubt as to what it sold. A hodgepodge of bongs and hookahs surrounded a display of rolling machines. Juicy Jay's rolling papers in a variety of flavors sprawled across the front. A few plastic gargoyles and a crooked, leering skeleton filled in the background.

When I opened the door and stepped in, though, the cloying scent of the patchouli hit me. I'd forgotten how strong that could be. I didn't remember it drifting upstairs to the apartment last time I stayed here, but that had been when the flooding had everything shut down. The dank smells that came with the flooding had permeated the air, and it had been a few days since I'd had a shower, so I might have missed it. Or forgotten. I wouldn't be thrilled to live with that smell constantly, but I was pretty desperate for a place to stay.

"Hey, there." Jumbo George was sitting on a stool at the counter toward the back of the store, painstakingly sorting through a box of plastic parts. In front of him was a type of a model or something, partially assembled. It looked like a medieval castle.

The project didn't seem to be going well. He had a piece that looked like the roof to a turret in his hand and was trying to fit it over one of the towers flanking the opening for the portcullis behind the moat, which was dry.

"How about here?" I said, indicating a round roofless structure sticking out from a wall on a back corner.

He glanced at me, moved his massive hand across the project, and perched the piece on the turret. It fit snuggly.

"Huh." He wiped his hand on his massive thigh and looked at the front where he'd been trying to place the piece. "Then what goes there?"

I shrugged. "More likely a flat roof piece. Something the defenders could stand on and shoot arrows from. Didn't this thing come with any instructions?"

"Yeah, it did," he admitted. "But they was hard to follow. I got frustrated and threw them away."

"That was smart. Now you can't check on anything."

He peered at a box on a stool next to him, which was full of unidentified parts. "True. But it's a little late to worry about that now."

"What is that thing, anyhow?"

"A castle."

"That much I figured out. But what are you going to do with it?"

"I was gonna put it in the window. What with the rich folks moving in down by the river, I figured I need a classier display than a bunch of bongs and rolling papers."

"That's probably true, if you're looking for them to be customers."

"I'm always looking for customers. Nobody comes in, nobody buys anything. Nobody buys anything, I don't make no money."

Nodding, I said, "I think that just about sums up retail business."

"I was thinking, this could be the centerpiece for a permanent display. You know, put flags and bunting on it for Memorial Day and the Fourth of July, Halloween stuff for the fall, Christmas lights. That kind of thing."

"That might look nice," I said, remembering the dingy, disorganized state of the present display. "And I bet it would appeal to all the yuppies moving in to the new apartments. They might be a little hesitant to come into a store with a bunch of bongs in the window."

He scratched his neck. "Yeah. I was thinking about adding some miniatures to the stock, too. You know, little knights on horses and soldiers and maybe eventually furniture and stuff. Like for dollhouses. A whole new line."

"You think that'd go over good with the new customers?"

"I dunno. Maybe. I'd like it. And maybe I could put some of the soldiers and things on the castle."

"But first you got to get it put together."

"Yeah. That is a problem. I'm looking at it like a puzzle. Do a little bit at a time."

I looked in the box of parts, extracted a grid thing with points on the ends, pointed at the front entrance and said, "Isn't this supposed to go inside the walls there?"

He scratched the straggly beard on his chin. "Does it?"

"Yeah. It's called the portcullis. In a real castle, you drop it down to seal off the entrance. Sometimes there's an inner one and an outer one. You drop the inner one first, then the outer one. Some of the attackers get caught in between. Then you shoot them."

"Shoot them? Did they have guns?"

"With arrows. Or sometimes they dropped hot sand or something on them."

He peered at the arched entry to the castle. "You sure seem to know a hell of a lot about castles."

"Yeah, well, they had this neat book in the prison library about castles. Lots of great pictures. I got it out a few times."

"And what? Studied it?"

I shrugged. "Kind of. After feed up, when you lock in, those evenings can get pretty long."

"I thought most guys watched TV."

"You got to have a TV. And you got to get it through the commissary. They're really expensive. I could never afford one."

Jumbo George sighed and shoved himself back from the counter. "You hear about my brother Nick?"

My throat closed. How much did he know about me steering the cops in his direction?

"Just a little. He get charged with killing your kid brother?"

"Yeah. Half-brother. I mean, we had different mamas and all, and he was a druggie snitch, but he was still our brother. Don't seem right."

I wasn't sure whether he meant that having a half-brother who was a druggie snitch that didn't seem right, or if it was killing him, so I just nodded. "Nick got a decent lawyer?" I knew what having to depend on a public defender could do to his chances in court. Public defenders figured most people were guilty anyway, so they specialized in getting the best plea bargain they could. That's what happened to me.

Jumbo George sighed. "Yeah. I put up the first retainer, but this is gonna be expensive. So I sold his rig. Got him to sign it over to me. He didn't want to, but I told him, what good would anything, much less his almost new Peterbilt cabover, do him when he was locked up?"

"Did they set bail?"

"They set it. But like his lawyer said, they always give credit for time served, so he might as well get started on it. Ain't gonna do him no good to be out on the street and get in any more trouble. And it's not like he could still work. He couldn't leave the state. Kind of interferes with working when you're a long-haul truck driver."

"Still, he probably wished he could hold onto that truck."

"Maybe. But it was likely to get vandalized, just sitting there. Tires slashed or something. I'da had to pay to put it in storage someplace. And if he picks up real time, it'd practically be antique by the time he got out. If he don't, he can buy another one."

I asked, "Look like he is gonna pick up real time?"

"'Fraid so. They're talking first degree murder. Life. Without parole. But the lawyer says he's looking to cop a plea down to negligent homicide. Or manslaughter. Even so, he'll be lucky to get off with anything under ten years."

Ten years sounded about right for that type of conviction. He'd be eligible for parole in two and a half, although hardly anybody made it that soon. Probably about seven, seven and a half.

Which really didn't seem all that long to me.

We sat there silently, Jumbo George's pale blue eyes blank above the folds of his cheeks.

Gently, I pried the parts that made up the castle entrance apart and inserted the portcullis grate in place.

"Say," George said. "You got some time, you wanna come by and work on this damn thing? You seem to got a knack for it."

"Yeah, maybe I could." I shifted uneasily on the stool. "You know, I wanted to ask you—you think I could maybe rent out your upstairs apartment for a bit? My place is wrecked, and where I'm staying now, I got to get out soon."

He scratched his cheek through his full beard. "Well, Nick sure as hell ain't using it right now, is he?"

"When I get paid next Friday, I could bring you a security deposit. And some of the first month's rent." This week's check was pretty much spoken for.

"You know there ain't no entrance but through the back of the store there," he said. "Prob'ly, if the fire marshal ever showed up, he'd tell me I can't rent it."

"Don't bother me none. And I sure ain't gonna say nothing to no fire marshal. Pay rent under the table, if you want."

"I sleep in the recliner in the back there. Can't make it up them stairs no more."

I looked toward the doorway that lead to the back room of the store. The door was propped open. A pile of empty pizza boxes lay on the floor. "Yeah, I know that."

"I don't want no partying or nothing going on up there."

I grinned. "No problem, there. No partying."

"And them biker buddies of yours—they'd scare away the new yuppie crowd if they started hanging around."

"Wouldn't exactly call them buddies," I said. But I knew who he meant. Members of Kelly's dad's bike club. "They won't be around. Besides, it'd just be temporary. I won't even tell nobody where I was staying."

"How about your PO?"

"Well, if he asks, I guess I got to tell him. But for sure he ain't gonna wanna party at my place."

George chuckled. "He gonna okay you staying over a head shop?"

That was a concern, especially since the apartment didn't have an outdoor access. "Don't know. But I got no intention of mentioning that to him. I ain't gonna lie, but unless he checks, or sends somebody by to check, I don't see how he's gonna find that out."

Jumbo George nodded. "When you wanna move in?"

"In a few days," I said. "I'm keeping an eye on somebody's house right now, while they're away. Soon as they get back, though, they'll want me gone." I didn't go into the whole bit about the carriage house and Eileen needing a place to stay.

"Okay," he said, turning back to the castle.

CHAPTER 16

"It gets a little lonesome here, with Nick not coming by no more. Customers ain't the same. You wanna go out and get some grub? It's kind of hard for me to get out, and I'm getting pretty tired of pizza and Chinese. Those're the only places that will deliver."

"Sure," I said. "What do you want me to go get?"

He pulled out his wallet and laid a fifty on the counter. "Fried chicken and mashed potatoes. And a couple of big bottles of root beer."

I knew him well enough to say, "Spend the whole thing?"

"Sure. If we don't eat it all tonight, it'll keep good in the fridge."

The two buckets of chicken came with biscuits and two sides. I got double mashed potatoes and made sure the guy working the counter put lots of gravy and butter and honey in the bags. Then I stopped at a small grocery store, where they didn't charge extra for taking the three-liter bottles of root beer out of the cooler instead of off the shelf. I had to toss in a dollar and change to the rest of Jumbo George's fifty, but I figured I'd be eating some of it, too. Cheap supper at that.

Dusk was falling as I headed back to the head shop, my arms full of bags of chicken buckets and root beer. Traffic was light, considering this was a commercial street, and I wondered how much business had fallen off since the flooding. It would probably pick up as the cleanup progressed and the yuppie types moved back into their expensive river-front apartments, and since Jumbo George owned the building, he could probably hang on until then. Rent coming in from the apartment would help, even if it wasn't much.

A car careened around the corner and screeched to a stop at the curb next to me. I ignored it and kept walking.

It was a new Toyota RAV4, bright red.

Kelly leapt out of the driver's seat. "Jesse! What are you doing here?" She was in her dress-up mode, her hair piled on top of her head, long sparkly earrings dangling from her ears and, under her jacket, a bright pink blouse that showed her ample cleavage.

Asking me what I was doing here struck me as an odd question, especially in light of how we'd been getting along lately. Or not. I said, "Visiting a friend. I just went out and got us some supper." It was a stretch to use the word "friend" for Jumbo George, but it did feel good to be able to say that about someone. "Where'd you get the car?"

She ignored the question about the car. "Thank goodness I found you." She turned around and looked down the empty street in the direction of the Chillington's Financial Services office. "Can you take the kids?"

"Well, I was heading back with supper here," I said, lifting the bags. "I was gonna eat with my friend. Where'd the car come from?" I was afraid I already knew.

"The clutch on my car finally gave out all the way. I'm prob'ly just using this one temporarily."

"It belong to Sydney?"

"Kind of." Her eyes teared up. "About the kids. It's an emergency. I have to get them someplace…safe. Can't you take them? It's just for a little while."

I peered into the back seat, straight at two pale, scared faces. "I guess. Let me drop off the food, and then you can give us a ride back to your place." Maybe Jumbo George would let me take a piece of chicken for each of us.

"No! You can't take them to my place," she said. "That's not safe!"

I shifted the bags in my arms. "Whad'ya mean, not safe?"

She shook her head. "I don't have time to explain now. Hop in, and I'll give you a ride to wherever you're going and drop you off with the kids. Then I got to go."

"I got to ask the guy whose place it is if he minds if the kids are there," I said. "I mean, it's his place. Maybe I could take them to the carriage house where I'm staying at for now."

"With that Eileen person? I don't think so."

So it was an emergency, but Kelly was going to be fussy about who was hanging around with the kids? But she was upset enough. I just said, "She's not staying there right now."

In spite of her urgency, Kelly smirked. "Had enough of each other already?"

I didn't dignify that with an answer.

She glanced at her wrist, where a jeweled watch caught the light. "I'm late. I haven't got enough time to take you over there and get back here." She pushed back a strand of long dark hair that had escaped from her upswept hairdo. "Please, Jesse? I'll make it up to you." She tried to smile, but her lips trembled.

Shaking my head, I said, "You don't got to 'make it up to me.' If the kids need a place to go, and I can help out, I will." I found that kind of offensive, but I didn't say so.

"I will, though," she said. "Get in."

Juggling the food, I climbed in the front seat. The car, which had that distinctive new car odor, filled up with a glorious aroma of hot fried chicken. I glanced back at the kids. "Hi, guys. You like fried chicken?"

"Do we," Chris said. "We haven't had any supper."

"Or lunch," Brianna added.

"Just let me check with the guy. Be sure it's okay with him. This ain't my place." Kelly had to understand that it was possible that Jumbo George wouldn't want them in the store, with all the breakable stuff. And it definitely carried stock that could be dubbed adult content.

Directing Kelly the couple of blocks to the head shop, I told the kids to stay in the car while I checked to see if we all could stay there.

Opening the door and putting the food on the counter, I said to Jumbo George, "Is it okay if a couple of kids stay with us for a little bit?"

He lurched out of his recliner in the rear of the store and lumbered toward where I'd put the fragrant bags, frowning. "Whad'ya mean, kids? Didn't I tell you I don't want no partying here?"

"Not that kind of kids. Little guys. My girlfriend's kids." Maybe at this point, I shouldn't be calling Kelly my girlfriend, but the whole situation was too hard to explain. "She says it's an emergency."

"How long?" he asked.

How would I know how long? But I just said, "I think it's only a little while."

He shrugged. "Sure. I guess. But you got to make sure they don't mess anything up."

"Thanks. I'll do that," I assured him and then headed back out to the sidewalk.

Kelly already had the kids out of the car, standing there. "You guys be good and do what Jesse tells you to," she said. "I'll be back for you as soon as I can."

She jumped in the car and sped off.

We all stood still, looking at the car fading off down the street.

"What the hell was that all about?" I said to no one in particular, not knowing if I would get any answer. Or if I wanted it if I did get it.

Chris took Brianna's hand. "I'm not real sure," he said, wiping his sleeve against his eyes. "But Mom said Sydney was looking for her, and she didn't want us with her when he found her. She didn't want to go home, 'cause Sydney knows where that is."

"Where'd she get the car?"

"Sydney. He took us to the dealership and let her pick it out. Anything she wanted, as long as it was red."

"You mean he bought it for her?"

He shrugged. "I guess."

"Who's gonna make the payments?"

"I dunno. Mom says it's too 'spensive for her."

She made the same kind of money I did. "I can imagine it would be. She been seeing a lot of Sydney?"

"Kind of. Our babysitter's been coming early, like when we go to bed, instead of when Mom has to leave for work. And then Sydney picks her up."

I felt like I'd been punched in the gut. "Yeah?" I didn't really want to hear any more.

"And," Brianna chimed in, "she's got a cell phone now."

"Is that so?" Nothing really unusual in that. Most people had cell phones. In fact, I couldn't think of anybody besides me and Kelly who didn't have cell phones. Except Eileen.

"Yes," she said. "Sydney gave it to her. He said he wants to be able to get in touch with her."

"Oh." I bit my lip to keep from saying anything. This sounded beyond serious. I couldn't buy her a cell phone. I didn't have one myself. And I couldn't pay the babysitter to come early so I could take her out. Much less get her a car.

Then why the heck was I the one taking care of Kelly's kids now? What kind of emergency could she be having that needed to dump them with me?

The dismal thought that maybe she was just taking advantage of a sucker while she could occurred to me. She knew I had a soft spot for the kids. Maybe she just thought of me as somebody she could dump on when she needed an unpaid babysitter.

Chris reached over and took my hand. "How'd your face get all beat up like that, Jesse?" he asked. "Doesn't it hurt?"

I looked down at him. With his other hand, he was straightening the collar on Brianna's jacket. She was looking up at me with those big, brown, trusting eyes.

Well, if Kelly was playing me for a sucker, she was doing a damn good job. And I wasn't exactly an unwilling victim. I didn't want to see those kids hurt any more than they already were.

"I got in a fight," I said.

"A fight? I thought only kids did that."

"Yeah, well, adults ought to be smart enough not to. I have to remember that," I said.

He nodded solemnly.

"Come on in," I said, starting toward the door. "This is a store, and there's a lot of breakable stuff in here, so you got to be careful."

"A store?" Chris asked. "What do they sell here?"

Hard question to answer, that. I said, "Mostly it's for grown-ups. Tobacco and papers for rolling cigarettes. Funny little statues. Stuff like that."

We went in.

Brianna wrinkled up her nose. "What's that funny smell?" she asked.

"Patchouli," I said. "It's kind of like room perfume or something."

"It's really strong," Chris said.

I had to agree. "Yeah."

"I like it," Brianna said. "Do you think I could get some to wear to school?"

Smothering a grin, I thought her teacher would probably report it to Child Protective Services if she showed up smelling of patchouli. "It's probably too strong for school, honey," I told her. "Some kids might be allergic to it."

"Like it might make them sneeze?"

"Like that. Or even make it hard for them to breathe." Sometimes I felt like I'd choke on the scent.

"Oh." That seemed to satisfy her.

Jumbo George shuffled toward us.

"Chris and Brianna, this is Jumbo George," I said.

He extended a hand the size of a ham toward them. "Pleased to meet you," he said.

The kids were staring in amazement at his incredible bulk. Chris recovered first and took the proffered hand, which completely swallowed his.

"Pleased to meet you, too, sir," he said, nudging Brianna.

She reached out, grasped Jumbo George's pinkie, and shook it.

"You kids hungry? We was gonna have supper. Want some fried chicken?" he asked. "And root beer?"

We gathered around the table in the back room, where he'd opened one of the buckets of chicken. "Get out some of them glasses in the cabinet over the sink, Jesse, would you? Better rinse 'em before we use them."

Chris looked around at the kitchenette and the recliner where George slept, which was piled with a pillow and blankets. "Do you live here?" he asked.

"Yeah. I don't got far to go to get to work."

"You work in the store?" Chris asked.

"Yep."

The boy looked around. "That's really neat. I'd like to work in a store like this when I grow up."

Jumbo George and I exchanged glances.

"And live close to work like this. Then I wouldn't have to be always running late."

"And you wouldn't need a babysitter," Brianna said. "You could just let your kids stay in the back of the store."

Jumbo George laughed. "I wouldn't know about kids. But I got to admit, it's convenient."

The kids each had couple of pieces of chicken and a glass of root beer. It wasn't a particularly nutritious dinner, but it would have to do. Kelly could get them something better when she came and got them.

"How long you kids here for?" Jumbo George asked as he opened the second bucket of chicken, offered them more. They declined, and he grabbed a handful of pieces for himself.

"I dunno," Chris said. "Mom didn't say."

They looked at me. I shrugged. "She didn't say nothing to me about that, either," I said. "Just that it was an emergency, and she needed me to take them for a little while."

Jumbo George raised his eyebrows. "How late do you stay up usually?" he asked the kids.

It was Chris's turn to shrug. "It's not a school night," he said. "So we get to stay up some. Usually, we just watch TV. Unless Jesse's over. Then he reads us stories."

"Well, I don't think I got too many stories to read," Jumbo George said. "There is a little TV, over behind the counter. You can watch that if you want. And if it gets too late, I guess Jesse can take you upstairs to sleep. There's a couple of beds up there."

I turned on the TV, low so it wouldn't bother Jumbo George, and Brianna settled down on the floor to watch it.

Chris peered at the half-done model. 'What's that?"

"It's a castle," George told him. "I'm trying to get it put it together so I can put it in the front window. Jesse's gonna help me. Then I'm gonna decorate it for the seasons. If it gets done in time, maybe I'll put a few Easter bunnies around it. And flowers."

That would look decidedly odd, but I had to admit it would be seasonal.

"Can I try?" Chris asked.

Jumbo George struggled to his feet and lumbered over. "To help put it together?"

The boy nodded. "Yeah."

I almost said, no, that it might break and to leave it alone, but George was quicker than I was.

"Sure," he said. "If you're careful."

Chris picked up an odd-shaped piece and studied the castle. He slipped it onto a slot on the castle wall. It fit perfectly. He picked up another piece and stared at the castle and put it on the front of the keep by the door.

Jumbo George laughed. "Looks to me like the kid's good at this." He turned on an overhead light and settled himself on a stool next to it. "You think if we put Easter bunnies up on the walls, they should have swords?"

"For sure. And wear armor. If you can find any like that."

Scratching his cheek, Jumbo George said, "They sell lots of strange stuff, if you know where to look. I got lots of weird catalogs. I don't get out much, so I buy most of my stock out of them."

I felt a twinge of jealousy—I liked to think it was special when the kids wanted to do things with me. And here was Chris, obviously delighted to be working with Jumbo George. Who'd have thought I was the jealous type? First Sydney, and now Jumbo George.

I squelched that feeling firmly. Very little good would come out of letting the green-eyed monster have his way, and jealousy caused more than its share of problems for anyone who indulged it. Besides, kids always needed people who thought they were special, and no kid ever had too many people who thought that. What with the divorce and battles over custody and child support and the like, Kelly's kids were more in need of support than most.

After a while, Chris started yawning. When I checked, Brianna was asleep on the floor.

"Maybe you ought to think about getting these kids to bed," Jumbo George said.

I glanced at the clock behind the counter. It was shaped like a skull, with the clock face in one eye. After ten. "Yeah. If she's not back here by now, I got no idea what time Kelly's gonna be back for them."

Brianna hardly stirred when I scooped her up. I went to the narrow door beside the refrigerator that led up the stairs to the small apartment on the second floor.

Chris slid down off his stool and followed me. "We don't have pajamas," he pointed out. "Or toothbrushes."

"Well, for tonight, you can sleep in your clothes. Or just your underwear, if you want. And I guess we'll have to skip tooth brushing tonight."

Chris looked around. "Do you sleep down here?" he asked Jumbo George.

"Right here." Jumbo George indicated the recliner. "I used to go upstairs, but the stairs are too tough on me these days. And I can't lie down flat anyhow. I can't breathe."

The upstairs apartment consisted of a central room at the head of the stairs with a kitchenette along the inside wall. Grimy curtainless windows overlooked the alley that ran behind the stores. It had a sagging couch and a rickety kitchen table with four chairs. A bureau that would never fit in either of the bedrooms stood against one wall. It reminded me of the set on the old TV show my foster parents used to watch. *The Honeymooners.*

Dust lay everywhere. The tiny bathroom opened off one corner. A spider had built an elaborate web in the doorframe. Two bedrooms, each barely big enough to hold a single bed, were on either side of the room.

After the airy and well-furnished carriage house, living here was going to be a real come-down when I moved in. But it was a place to stay. After I scrubbed everything down, it would be a bit more livable.

I shifted Brianna's slender body in my arms.

"Mom takes her to the bathroom to pee before she puts her to bed if she's asleep," Chris told me.

Brianna did wet the bed sometimes, but taking her to pee didn't sound like something I would be comfortable doing.

"How does she do that?" I asked him.

"She just carries her into the bathroom and pulls down her pants. Then she sits her on the toilet and she pees. Mom wipes her bottom and pulls up her pants again."

That definitely didn't sound like something I should be doing.

"If I carry her into the bathroom, do you think you could help her pull down her pants and use the toilet?"

Chris looked doubtful, but he said, "I guess I could try."

It was awkward, especially given the lack of space in the bathroom. I lowered Brianna to the floor and held her upright while Chris struggled with her jeans and underpants. When they were around her ankles, I lifted Brianna up and sat her on the toilet.

Sure enough, we could hear her tinkle into the toilet.

I took her off and stood her up again, supporting her so she didn't fall. "Can you pull up her pants again?" I asked.

"Aren't we gonna wipe her bottom?"

That was out of the question. "No."

When her pants were back in place, I picked Brianna up and laid her down on the bed in one room. Untying her shoes, I slipped them off her feet. Then I covered her well. At least she'd be warm.

"You wanna sleep in the other bedroom, or take the couch?" I asked Chris. "There's enough blankets to keep you warm either place."

"You gonna stay here with us?" he asked.

"Of course."

"Where are you gonna sleep?"

"The other bedroom or the couch, whichever one you don't choose," I said.

He frowned. "If I take the bedroom, you're not gonna sneak out early in the morning without me knowing, are you?"

"Nope. If I go anywhere, I'll wake you up and let you know. But I don't plan to go nowhere."

"Then I'll take the bedroom, if that's okay with you."

"Sure." I went in with him. Quilts and blankets were folded on the end of the bed. I laid a few out on the bed for him and took the others to the couch to use myself. He took off his own shoes and lay down. I tucked the bedding around him and squeezed his shoulder. "Good night, buddy."

"Good night," he said. A tear glistened in the corner of his eye. He wiped it away. "Where do you suppose Mom went?"

I shook my head. "That I don't know. She didn't tell us, did she?"

"I wish I knew when she was coming back," he said, rubbing his eye.

"She didn't tell us that either, did she? But don't you worry. We'll make out fine until she comes back," I said with a lot more confidence than I felt.

"Okay."

What the hell was she up to? I wished I had some confidence that she'd be back soon. Or at all.

CHAPTER 17

Morning sun shone through the dingy windows and right into my eyes. Where was I? I resisted moving until I got my bearings.

The apartment above Jumbo George's head shop, where I would be moving when Amanda and Nicole came back and let Eileen move into the carriage house. That would be any day now.

It was morning. Chris and Brianna were still here with me. Where was Kelly? Had she been out all night?

I struggled up and checked on the kids. I didn't want to go downstairs and leave them alone, especially after I'd promised Chris I would stay here with them.

Standing in the doorway, I gently called Chris's name.

He sat up with a start. "Is Mom here?" he asked.

"Not yet," I said, unwilling to put my own fears into words. Kelly loved her children. She would never willingly abandon them. Had something happened to her?

He struggled out from under the covers. "Where could she be?"

I took a deep breath. "It was probably so late when she got done that she decided not to bother us in the middle of the night and just went home. She'll probably be back this morning."

He didn't look convinced, but he climbed out of bed and felt around with his feet for his shoes.

I went over to Brianna's room and called her name. She also woke up with a start.

Hushing the kids in case Jumbo George was still asleep, I ushered them downstairs. If he was still sleeping, I figured I'd write him a quick thank-you note and start the long hike to Kelly's house. I had a little cash, so we could break up the walk with a breakfast off McDonald's dollar menu.

But when I opened the door at the foot of the stairs, the lights were on. Jumbo George was puttering around in the kitchenette, making a pot of coffee. He turned and looked at us, smiling through his beard at the kids. He did look more fierce than friendly, but the kids didn't seem to notice.

"Don't got too much good for breakfast for kids," he said. "They shouldn't have coffee. But there's one of them bottles of root beer left, and I got a whole assortment of different kinds of trail mix in stock. You guys can go over and see if any of it looks like something you'd like to eat."

Root beer and trail mix. Maybe not quite as bad as nothing but root beer and fried chicken for dinner, but even I knew kids shouldn't be eating like that.

"You hear anything from our mom?" Chris asked, trying to hide the hitch in his voice.

Jumbo George took two coffee mugs from the drainer by the sink. "As a matter of fact, I have," he said.

My breath caught in my throat. Why hadn't he called me to talk to her? Or couldn't she talk?

"What did she say?" Chris asked.

"Well, she came by last night, real late. More like early in the morning. She knocked on the door. It took me a little while to get out of my recliner and over to unlock the door. She was a little pissed."

"Yeah," Chris said. "She don't like it when she has to wait for us, either. Was she okay?"

"Yeah. She looked fine. She wanted me to let her in so she could get you guys. I told her it was a hell of a time to be coming for her kids, that you were all upstairs sound asleep, and she ought not wake you up. She should come back in the morning."

So he'd actually seen her, and she'd seemed all right to him, even if she was a bit annoyed. I started breathing again. "So you didn't let her in?"

"No, I didn't let her in. I told her she should go home and get some sleep herself. She looked tired, like she could do with some rest."

"What time is she coming back?" Chris wanted to know.

"I told her we'd call her when you guys were ready," Jumbo George said. "She put you through enough crap. She could wait til you got up and called."

"Can I call her now?" Chris asked.

"Sure. Let me get you the phone." Jumbo George went behind the counter and pulled out an old black desk phone on a long cord. It had a rotary dial. "And tell her if she's coming anytime soon, to stop and get a few dozen donuts for breakfast. Specially some jelly donuts."

"Okay." Chris picked up the receiver and stared at the dial. He may never have seen a phone with anything but push buttons.

"Like this," I said, putting my finger in one of the holes and spinning the dial around. "You do that for each number. Instead of punching them in on buttons."

For what seemed like a long time, Chris stood there, the phone to his ear, no expression at all on his face. Finally, he smiled. "Mom?"

He listened for a little bit. "Fine. Jesse's fine, too. We slept upstairs in the bedrooms. Jesse slept in the...living room, I guess it is. On the couch."

Again, he listened. "Yes. We miss you, too. Could you stop and get some donuts? Jumbo George—he's the guy who let us stay here—wants some. He says a couple dozen. Some of them should be jelly donuts. When are you gonna get here?"

He nodded and hung up.

"She says she'll put on some clothes and be right over," he said.

I accepted a mug of coffee from Jumbo George and tried to think about anything but the image of Kelly before she put on some clothes. I wasn't particularly successful.

Kelly showed up with two boxes of donuts, a dozen in each one. Obviously she had no concept of what Jumbo George meant by "a couple dozen." Or how much he could eat.

A large bruise extended from her cheekbone down to her jaw. I wanted to ask her about it, but not in front of the kids.

Otherwise, she looked like her old self, dressed in a pair of blue jeans and a warm sweatshirt. Her silky dark hair was pulled back in a ponytail, and her face was scrubbed of any makeup. Her nose wrinkled at the patchouli.

She looked great, and I wanted to gather her into my arms, but I stopped myself.

Along with the donuts, she'd brought a half gallon of milk. She plunked them down on the counter and sat down on a stool, resting her head on her hand.

I sat the kids at the table and let them each choose one donut. I rinsed out a few glasses and gave them each some milk. It wasn't a great breakfast, and on top of the questionable supper the night before, I was beginning to have real concerns about how nutritious their diet was. They were, after all, growing kids. They should be eating a lot of fruits and vegetables, not more refined sugar and flour. I started to say something to Kelly, but one look at the expression on her face was enough to shut me up. And remind me that these weren't *my* kids.

Jumbo George said, "You want a mug of coffee?"

She shot him a dazzling smile. "I'd *love* a mug of coffee."

I fixed her a big one and put it in front of her. She downed half of it in one swallow. I flinched. It was hot. But she didn't seem to notice.

Jumbo George took a whole box of donuts and put it in front of him. He glanced at Kelly. "Sorry about sending you away last night," he said. "But it was just too damn late to get those kids up. And you looked like you could use a good night's sleep before you had to deal with them." He stuffed two donuts in his mouth.

"Prob'ly just as well," Kelly said. "It did give me a chance to go home and get cleaned up. And I figured they were in good hands…"

When the kids were finished eating, I gathered up their glasses and our mugs and washed them all out in the sink.

"Thanks, George," I said, "for letting us stay here."

Kelly had the decency to look up at him. "Yeah. Thanks. It was a lifesaver."

Chris was over by the castle, fitting another piece in place. "Can I come over and work on this some more?" he asked.

"Sure," Jumbo George said between bites of donut. "Come over anytime. I could use the help." His beard was sprinkled with powdered sugar.

"Mom, can I get some of that neat perfume?" Brianna asked. "I wouldn't wear it to school. Jesse says it's too strong."

Kelly looked a bit startled. "Perfume?"

"She means the patchouli," I said.

"The patchouli?" Kelly said. "But that's…" She didn't finish her sentence.

Jumbo George laughed and heaved himself out of his chair. He lumbered to the front of the store, got a stick of incense out of a display, and handed it over to Brianna. "Here. You can have that, if you want."

Brianna took it and looked at it doubtfully.

"Smell it," Jumbo George told her.

She put it up to her nose and inhaled and smiled. "Thank you," she said.

Chris was standing there watching, an uncertain but distressed look on his face. I remembered all the times when I was a kid in a foster home and had to watch while other kids got presents, usually from their own families. Since I didn't have a family, I didn't get anything. It always felt pretty rotten.

It wasn't like Chris didn't have a family, but he was still probably felt left out.

I dredged in my pocket for some change. "Hey, Chris," I said. "You go up and choose yourself one, too, if you want." Looking at Jumbo George, I said, "How much?"

He snorted. "Boy don't want no incense stick, I bet. Do you, kid?"

Chris looked stricken, but he shook his head.

"Here. I bet you'd rather have this." Jumbo George took a keychain with a plastic Mr. Natural figure attached to it and handed it to Chris. "That better?"

"Oh, yes," Chris said, admiring the bald head, yellow robe, and long white beard. "Thank you."

"We'd better get going," Kelly said. "Thank you again, Mr..."

"Just call me Jumbo George," he said. "Everyone else does."

She shepherded the kids out the front door.

I stood there watching.

Kelly turned back and frowned. "Aren't you coming?"

"Okay. If you want me to."

"Of course I want you to," she said.

I grabbed my jacket and said to Jumbo George, "I'll be by later in the week. With some money. We can talk about what arrangements we can make then."

"No hurry," Jumbo George said. He was back at the table, examining the remaining donuts.

The red RAV4 was parked by the curb. Kelly had the keys in her hand and punched the button that unlocked it. It chirped.

"It's a nice car," I said. "You gonna keep it?"

She sighed. "I don't know. I like it and all, but the payments are much too high."

"I would bet they're a pretty penny," I said, closing the back door behind the kids and slipping into the passenger seat. "It's brand new, isn't it?"

"Yeah," she said. "Sydney bought it and said he financed it through the check cashing business. He'll make the payments, and I should make arrangements with him to cover them. But I'm not sure that's such a good idea."

I frowned. "I didn't know check cashing places could make car loans. But I guess they make payday loans, so why not? But I bet that isn't cheaper than going through the car dealer or a bank or something."

"Moneywise, I don't know. And I really can't afford an expensive new car like this. But that's not the kind of payments I mean."

"What..." I started to say, but Kelly shook her head and glanced back at the kids.

A chill ran through me. What had Kelly gotten herself into?

"You want to come over to the house?" she asked.

"I can't, really," I said. "I got to go check on the house I'm supposed to be keeping an eye on. If you could drop me off, I'd appreciate it."

"Where?"

"Pretty much anyplace is fine. I can walk the rest of the way."

"How long does it take you to check on it?" she asked.

"Well, usually I'm staying there and I'd probably notice if anything major happened. So I just go around and do stuff like check the locks, bring in the mail, make sure the basement isn't flooded—regular stuff."

"But if you were just going to check everything out now, how long would that take?"

I shrugged. "Maybe twenty minutes, a half hour."

"Suppose I drop you off, take the kids and go do some grocery shopping, and pick you up again?"

Shifting uncomfortably in the seat, I looked over at her. "You want me to come over and keep an eye on the kids?" I asked. That seemed to be the only thing she wanted me for these days.

She bit her lip. "We really need to talk."

I turned to look straight out the windshield. "I'll stay with the kids if you want me to. You don't have to make no excuses or anything." I knew I was setting myself up for some more heartache here, but I liked spending time with the kids. Was I doing them a lot of harm? Much as I didn't want to do it, I couldn't imagine it would be too long before I'd gather my good sense together and tell Kelly I wasn't coming over any more.

"I really do want to talk to you about a few things," she said.

Best bet probably would have been to keep my mouth shut. That's something I learned in prison, that usually nothing good came from saying too much, and I usually managed to keep my thoughts to myself, regardless of the circumstances. But I let my resentment got the better of me. I said, "I'd think Sydney would be the person you'd want to talk to."

When she didn't answer me, I glanced over at her.

A tear was trickling down her cheek.

What, exactly, was that all about?

"Mandy's house is a few blocks down here," I said when she came to the right intersection. "I'll check everything out. If you really want me to come over to your place, come back and pick me up in about a half hour. Won't bother me much, though, if you change your mind."

It would, but letting her know that wouldn't help the situation.

She dropped me off on the sidewalk in front of Mandy's house. I gathered up the mail and went around the back to pick up the keys from the carriage house.

Thirty-five minutes later, I sat on the front steps, just about deciding Kelly wasn't coming back and that was probably just as well, when the RAV4 pulled up.

I got up and went over to it, opening the passenger door and climbing in.

We went over to Kelly's place. I helped her carry in the groceries.

Usually she kept the house in pretty good shape, but today, clothes were strewn on the living room furniture and mail was stacked on the dining room table. In the kitchen, dishes were piled in the sink.

Putting the grocery bags on the kitchen counter, I looked around. What was I doing here?

"I'm gonna take the kids upstairs and make sure they get baths," she said. "And get some clean clothes on them. Their dad's coming over this afternoon to pick them up. They're still wearing the clothes they slept in."

That was true. I was also wearing the clothes I'd slept in, and I could use a shower. I should have thought about that before I came over here, though. I didn't have anything to change into.

"I'll put the groceries away," I said, "and see if I can't fix something for lunch."

She took the kids upstairs, and I started rinsing the dishes in the sink and putting them in dishwasher. It was pretty full, so I started it. Then I unpacked the grocery bags and looked for something for lunch. They hadn't been eating well the last few meals, and they should have something reasonably good for them.

I boiled a few eggs to make egg salad sandwiches and opened a can of vegetable soup.

By the time they got downstairs, I had the food ready and the table set.

We ate in silence.

Finally, Kelly pushed back her chair and gathered up the dishes. "You kids go watch TV, okay?" she said. "I got to talk to Jesse about something."

Chris looked up at her. "Is it okay if I go upstairs and read instead?" he said.

Kelly frowned. "Read?"

"Yeah. Jesse started reading us some books, and I've been reading some on my own, too."

I smiled at him. "'Atta boy," I said. Maybe I was having some positive influence on them after all.

"Yeah," Kelly said. "I guess you can go upstairs and read, if you want to."

When they were gone, she made two mugs of instant coffee and sat down again, pushing one over toward me. She reached across the table and put her hand on mine. I didn't return her hold, but I didn't pull my hand away, either.

"I guess I owe you an apology, Jesse," she said.

Raising my eyebrows, I said, "You don't owe me nothing."

"I haven't been very nice to you."

That was true, but I said, "No reason you got to be nice to me. Like you say, we're not an item. You can do whatever you want."

She sighed. "I do appreciate what you've been doing for me with the kids. I would have been in a fix if you hadn't taken them last night."

"What I do for the kids, I do for them. And for me. I'm not trying to say you're not part of the equation—you are—but I like them and I don't want to see them hurt no more than they already are." I was going to continue and say it might be best for all of us if she found somebody else to keep an eye on them, since obviously the relationship between her and me was going nowhere fast. The longer I stuck around, the worse it would be for the kids when I left completely. Not to mention how hard it would be on me.

But I looked over at her, and she had covered her face with her free hand. Another tear slid from underneath her fingers. My throat closed up, and I couldn't think of anything to say.

"I've messed up bad," she said, her hand still over her eyes.

"How so?"

"You know how I said I was going to be going to the AA meetings?"

"Yeah."

"Well, I went to the first one. And then Sydney took me to the second one. But we went out to get something to eat afterwards."

I remembered the chili I'd tried to keep warm for her but she didn't want. "Nothing wrong with that," I said. "Long as you didn't go out to a bar or something."

"Not exactly a bar. An Italian restaurant. Sydney said we should have some wine with dinner, that one drink wouldn't hurt."

I shook my head. "That's not what AA says."

"But even AA says not everybody needs to abstain completely all the time."

"True. But they do say that the people who need AA aren't the same ones who can have an occasional drink and not spiral downhill. Those are the people get their drinking under control on their own. They usually don't join AA."

Kelly took her hand off mine and traced a pattern on the table with her finger. "I guess."

"The reason people join AA is because they need the support to quit drinking. Ain't no point in going to the meetings and things if you're gonna tell yourself you can have an occasional drink."

"I didn't go to any more meetings," she said. "Sydney said he could help me cut way back on the booze. He took me out a few times. I did drink more than I should have, but I didn't get sloppy drunk or pass out or anything. He said that was proving that he was helping me be in control, not the alcohol."

"And how," I asked, "did that work for you?"

She sobbed once. "Not well."

We sat in silence for a few minutes.

"I ended up going to the liquor store. That time you saw me, we'd been out for lunch. I had two drinks. He said he had some business he needed to take care of and dropped me off at home. I was going to get some sleep, but instead I went and bought a bottle of Southern Comfort."

No point in telling her again it hadn't been me outside the liquor store. If she hadn't believed me the first time, why would she now? "Then what?" I asked.

She shook her head. "I was totally wasted by the time kids got home from school. I'm lucky I got up in time to make it to work."

We both knew how valuable our jobs were. They were steady, they paid well, they had benefits. And had union protection against capricious firings, or I probably wouldn't still be working there. But Kelly had already used up most of her permitted absences. The union couldn't help her if she just didn't show up for work.

"So now what?" I asked her.

"I got to get myself out from under Sydney's thumb," she said.

"How are you gonna do that?" It seemed to me that, what with the cell phone and the car, she'd gotten herself pretty thoroughly mixed up with him.

"I'm trying to figure that out," she said, sighing.

She hadn't really asked for suggestions, but I said, "First maybe you ought to give him back the car. And the cell phone."

"Eventually. But the first thing I've got to do..." She looked at me and took a deep breath. "Jesse, I was over at his place last night."

No surprise there. "Does he live over that financial services place?"

"Yes. That's where we were. He's got an apartment up there. With this photography studio."

"He's got a photography business there, too?"

"Not really a business. More like a hobby. He says he only takes pictures for his own satisfaction and use."

"Like pornography?" I ventured.

She nodded.

"And he's got pictures of you?"

She nodded again.

"Well." I tried to think. "I guess that's not great, but really, so what?" It wasn't like Kelly was an innocent virgin or something.

"He said he might put them on the Internet."

Once again, not great. A little embarrassing, maybe, especially if the kids' friends got hold of them, but not a tragedy that I could see. "So what?"

"Suppose my ex gets hold of them and takes them into court? He's trying to show I'm an unfit mother."

I refrained from pointing out that she might very well be an unfit mother, but it was the drinking, not any pornographic pictures, that would be the problem. "I wouldn't worry about it too much. Have you asked him if he'll give them to you?"

"Even if he did give me copies, he most likely has them saved on his computer."

"I think you're just gonna have to live with that. When are you gonna see him again?"

"When I left last night, I told him I never wanted to see him again."

"Smart," I said. "But you've still got the car. And the cell phone. You're gonna have to see him again."

Kelly rubbed her eye. "Yeah. But maybe not for a little bit, while I get some of these things settled in my mind."

"That might be a good idea, if he don't mind giving you the time."

"Yeah, except…"

"Except what?"

"Except I left my wallet at his place."

"Your wallet? You have a lot in it?"

"Not too much money. But things like my driver's license and my insurance card and my debit card."

I scratched my chin. "That's not good. How are you going to get it back?"

CHAPTER 18

A little while later, I slogged across town in a beginning drizzle, my head down and my hands stuffed into my pockets.

How dumb could I be? Was it because Kelly had smiled at me and said the kids would be gone by the time I got back, and we could climb into her warm, soft bed? When I'd hesitated, she'd pulled me close and kissed me.

Oldest manipulation techniques in the world. I tried to tell myself I would have agreed to go get it anyhow, but I wasn't entirely sure.

If I was that easily manipulated, I suppose I deserved to be on this fool's mission.

Maybe I ought to be letting Kelly get her own wallet from Sydney's car or wherever she'd left it. I didn't want to think about it possibly being in his bedroom.

How did I know Sydney had it? Or that he'd give it to me? Or even that he'd be at the check cashing shop when I got there?

She couldn't give me a ride because she had to wait for the kids' dad to pick them up for their overnight visit. Besides, she probably didn't want to have that car around where he could demand it back. She'd have to figure out what she was going to do about that sooner or later.

The wind picked up, and I pulled the neck of my jacket a bit tighter. I thought about continuing on to Jumbo George's and talking about when I would move into the apartment. I could work on his castle project for a little bit. But I hadn't cashed my paycheck yet, and I didn't have the rent deposit. I'd hoped I could wait for another week. Jumbo George might understand if I asked him.

I was really just looking for a delaying tactic. If I told myself otherwise, I would be lying to myself.

The building with Sydney's check cashing/quick loan/bail bond business stood squarely in the middle of the desolate otherwise razed block. The shades were drawn behind the heavily barred windows on the main floor, but a dim light showed through them. The upstairs windows, also barred, were dark. That was where he lived. The windows to the garage portion of the building were boarded up.

I went past the garage door. It was closed tight. The separate security grate was down and locked. Security cameras, located high on the corners of the building in solid cages, stared down at me with their unblinking red eyes. Additional cameras flanked the sign over the front door. Despite the dimness of the day, the security lights were dark.

The several stone steps up to the front door could use sweeping. I climbed them and looked for a doorbell of some sort. Kelly had said everyone had to be buzzed in, and that made sense. Sydney had to keep a lot of cash on hand.

To my surprise, a slight gap showed between the door and the frame. I looked closer. It was open a crack. That made me very uneasy. I would never have taken Sydney for a careless man.

I shoved the door open with my shoulder. No sense leaving fingerprints anywhere I didn't have to. The interior smelled of dusty paper and car exhaust.

The front room had a long counter that spanned almost the entire room. A heavy plexiglass partition reached from the ceiling to the counter. It was covered with bars. A panel of clearer glass was in the middle, covered with closer bars with a speaker in the middle. A shallow pass-through set in the counter provided a secure way to exchange checks and money. And anything else Sydney happened to deal in.

No one was manning the window.

Raising my voice, I shouted "Hey! Anybody here?"

I was met with silence.

Even more uneasy, I looked around. There were inside security cameras, too. Maybe I should just leave and come back later. Or tell Kelly no one was there and she'd have to go by later and get her own wallet.

But anyone who looked at the images from the security cameras would see that I had been there. I tried to peer through the clearer section of the partition, but all I could see was the empty counter on the other side and a wall behind it. Walking down the room, I came to where the counter ended. It didn't really end; it turned a corner. A door was set in it. Just like the front door, it was open a bit.

Despite the damp chill, I felt a sweat break out on the back of my neck. "Anybody here?" I called. "You need help or something?"

No answer. Again using my shoulder, I shoved the door open enough to go through.

I was in a long space like a hallway behind the counter. It ran the length of the building. At the far end, a door led to the attached garage. It was wide open. I could see the little red sports car parked haphazardly in it.

Another door in the middle of the hallway led to an office. It was wide open, too. I could see a desk with a telephone and a computer. I stepped quietly down toward it.

The office was empty. A coffee mug lay on its side, the coffee in a puddle on the floor. A jar of instant coffee sat there with its lid off. A sugar bowl stood on the desktop; some of the sugar spilled out next to the bowl. A spoon with a little sugar in it lay next to it.

I looked around. The overhead light was out, but a desk light was turned on and the windows let in some light.

At the rear of the room was a big walk-in vault or safe of some kind, its door hanging open. I stepped around the desk and went up to its heavy door.

A man in a business suit lay on the floor, his head at the back of the vault and his well-shod feet near the door. I didn't see any visible sign of injury. It looked like Sydney, but it was too dark to really see.

I fought down rising bile in my throat. I couldn't just leave him like that. Nudging his leg with my boot, I watched for any signs of movement or breathing.

None.

One hand sprawled out from under him and toward me. The skin on it was a peculiar shade of red. I squatted down and put the back of my hand against it.

Cold.

He had to be dead. Much too late for anyone to help.

My breath was coming in ragged gasps. Here I was in the vault of a check cashing business with a dead man. I glanced up. Several metal drawers were pulled open. A fifty dollar bill lay on the floor.

I backed out. I needed to get out of there. Fast.

But the security cameras. I must have seen eight of them. And there might very well be some I hadn't noticed. Of course the police would pull all the tapes and view them thoroughly. No way could I pretend I hadn't been here.

Maybe he'd just had a heart attack. I tried to gather my thoughts. People had heart attacks every day. If I took off without calling for help, they'd say I'd been here and left him to die. No one would care about the fact that I was pretty sure he was already dead. That wouldn't be a good reason for me to leave.

I backed into the office and turned to the telephone. I picked up the receiver. There was a dial tone. I tried to stab at the nine button. My hand was trembling so much that I had trouble punching it in. Finally, I got it and followed with two ones.

"9-1-1," an infinitely calm female voice said. "What is your emergency?"

"Uh, there's this guy lying here. He's not moving," I said, my voice cracking.

"Where are you?"

"Back in his office."

"Give me the address."

"I dunno the exact address. It's Chillington's Financial Services or something."

"Is the man breathing?"

"I don't think so."

"Did you check?"

"No. But his hand is cold."

"Does he have any visible injuries?"

"I don't see none. Maybe he had a heart attack."

"Can you start CPR?"

"I don't know how to do that."

"I can give you instructions."

"No. Just send an ambulance or something."

"One is on the way."

"Oh."

"Make sure the doors are unlocked. Open them, if you can."

"Yes, ma'am."

"Don't go anywhere. Just wait for the emergency crews to get there."

"Yes, ma'am." There was no point in me going anywhere.

"I'll stay on the line in case you want to talk to me again. You go make sure the ambulance crew can get in there easily."

"Okay." I dropped the receiver on the desk and went out of the office, opening the door as wide as it would go. I opened the door in the front room's partition, and went to the front door. That one tended to want to swing closed, so I found a heavy waste basket and propped it open.

Then I went out the door and sat on the front steps. They were wet, and I felt the moisture spreading through the seat of my jeans. I rubbed my face and just rested my head on my hands.

A siren sounded in the distance, drawing rapidly closer. It was joined by another.

He *could* have had a heart attack or something, I tried to convince myself. Somehow, I doubted it.

This couldn't lead to anything good.

CHAPTER 19

A patrol car screeched to a halt. The car doors slammed. I didn't look up.

"You the fella who called 9-1-1?" the cop asked.

I sighed. "Yeah."

"Something about a man in distress?"

"You could say that."

"Where?"

"In the building. Back in the office."

"You got a key?"

"You can just go in. Ain't none of the doors locked."

"In a check cashing place?"

I could hear the surprise in his voice. I shrugged.

"Jeff," he said to his partner, "why don't you go check out the building? I'll keep an eye on this guy."

"Okay, Stan," Jeff said. He dashed up the steps.

To me, he said, "Stand up. Put your hands on your head. I'm going to search you."

I stood up, turned away from him, and interlaced my fingers on the back of my head.

He put one hand over mine. "You got anything I should know about? Weapons? Drugs? Needles?"

"No, sir."

He ran his other hand over my clothes, underneath my jacket, and between my legs. He pulled the keychain and wallet out of my pocket.

Another car, siren screaming, pulled up next to us, blue and red lights flashing against the side of the building.

"What's your name?" Stan the cop asked me, his hand still firmly over mine.

"Jesse Damon," I said.

"That sounds familiar. Do I know you?"

"I don't think so." Of course, when I'd first been released, my name would have come up at the pre-shift meetings.

"You got outstanding warrants?"

"Not that I know of."

"You on probation or parole?"

"Yes, sir."

"Which?"

"Parole."

"For what? Drugs?"

"No, sir."

"Then what?"

"Murder," I said reluctantly.

His hand tightened over mine. "I'm gonna put you in cuffs. For everybody's safety. You're not under arrest. For now."

Not for *my* safety.

He pulled one hand down behind my back, turned it so the palm was out, and snapped on one of the cuffs. He repeated it with the other hand and grabbed my shoulder to turn me around to face him.

I kept my gaze on the sidewalk. Out of the corner of my eye, I could see more vehicles arriving. Among them were an ambulance and an uncomfortably familiar puke green car. Followed by a black Lincoln.

The ambulance attendants pulled a stretcher out of the back and sprinted up the stairs.

The cop named Jeff stepped out of the front door. "This way," he told them. "But I don't think you need to hurry."

I could have told them that. But of course, no one was asking me.

Carissa traipsed up, her camera already aimed at me and clicking away.

One of the cops stepped between her and me. Stan turned me aside so she couldn't get a good shot. "Who's got a cage car?" he asked. "Let's get this guy in it. Now," he said.

"You can use mine." I couldn't see who said it.

Stan, who still had hold of my arm, started steering me toward one of the patrol cars at the curb.

A hoarse voice I recognized said, "Wait a minute."

My heart sank. Detective Belkins. I glanced up to see if I was right about who it was.

I was right. It was Belkins. I looked beyond him, toward the Lincoln, hoping to see Montgomery. But he was nowhere in sight.

Belkins planted himself in front of me and leaned in close. I could smell the stale cigars and sour whiskey on his breath. He had an unlit cigar clenched in his teeth. He didn't say anything for a few seconds, looking me over. And giving Carissa a chance to get a few more photos.

Finally, he yanked the cigar out of his mouth and said, "What did you do this time, Damon?"

I licked my dry lips. "Nothing, sir."

"Nothing, eh? I come up to a crime scene at a check cashing store, and I hear there's a dead man inside. Somebody who, unless I'm mistaken, has been seeing your girlfriend. You're here. I'm supposed to believe you didn't have anything to do with it?"

Shrugging, I said, "I didn't, sir."

His eyes narrowed. "Then what the hell are you doing here?"

I had no good answer for that, so I didn't say anything.

Belkins shook his head. "Take him in. I'm going to take a look around here, and then I'll be down and I'll want to interview him."

"We haven't arrested him, sir," Stan said.

"Don't matter." Belkins snorted. "He's on parole. We don't have to arrest him before we take him in."

Stan tugged on my arm and pulled me over to the patrol car. He opened the door. "Get in." As I slid into the seat, he held his hand to shield me from hitting my head on the doorframe and reached in and buckled the seatbelt. "I'll make sure your wallet and keychain get into a property envelope," he said.

At the police station, the car pulled up to the huge overhead door with a sign next to it that said, "Load and Unload Prisoners." It was big enough to accommodate the prison bus that arrived once a week to take anyone who'd been sentenced to two years or more and thus would be going to the state corrections system. The door slid open, and the car drove in.

Stan helped me out of the car and escorted me through a door, where he turned me over to another officer. "Belkins says he'll be right down to talk to him."

The new cop rolled his eyes, but he said, "Okay." He took my arm.

I looked back at Stan, who was walking away. "Thanks," I said.

He stopped short. "Thanks? For what?"

"You know. For not giving me a hard time. For being professional."

Shaking his head, he said, "Just doing my job. You didn't give me a hard time; I don't give you one."

"Well, it don't always work like that. So thanks."

I ended up in a dingy interview room yet another time, minus my jacket, belt, boots, and hair tie. Two battered wooden chairs sat on either side of an equally battered wooden table. I didn't care to speculate on how they'd gotten that battered. I shifted uncomfortably in the hard chair. At least they'd switched the cuffs to the front and attached them to a waist chain. When my nose itched, I could even scratch it if I bent my head down enough. I've never figured out why the only time my nose ever itched was when my hands were cuffed.

Belkins said he'd be right down to the police station, but there was no telling how long that might be. Especially since his little sweetheart was apparently covering the situation for the *Rothsburg Register*. Belkins was certain to pose for a couple of photos at the scene.

Maybe Montgomery would show up, too. I could only hope. Belkins wasn't especially fussy about how he got his evidence. I was too experienced to blurt out incriminating statements, but whatever I did say would be twisted against me. I was well aware that Belkins wasn't above using physical force and intimidation to try to get information that he wanted.

In theory, I could ask for a lawyer before I answered any questions. In practice, since I was on parole and had signed away most of my rights, it wouldn't do any good. If I refused to answer his questions, Belkins would report that I'd been uncooperative, and Mr. Ramirez, my parole officer, would want to know why. And he'd think about violating my parole.

It might not matter at all, I thought glumly. Even without knowing for sure how Sydney had died, Belkins was looking at me as an obvious suspect. Unless the coroner ruled that he died of natural causes, I was in for a rough time. And even then, I could see Belkins trying to make the case that I'd intimidated or frightened him into a heart attack.

If I picked up another homicide conviction, I'd likely be looking at a life sentence. Combined with the twenty some years backup time I had on the last conviction, I'd never see the outside of a prison again in this lifetime, even if I got life with the possibility of parole.

The door opened behind me. I didn't turn around to look. Someone flicked on the bright light overhead. The odor of an unlit cigar and clothes in need of laundering reached my nose and announced Belkin's approach.

He walked around to the other side of the table and stood there, glaring at me. I kept my gaze on the stains on the tabletop.

"So," he said, chomping on the cigar.

I didn't respond.

"What have you got to say for yourself?" he asked.

He didn't really expect me to answer a non-question like that, did he?

Getting up, he came around to my side of the table and clenched his fists. Without visibly moving, I tried to brace myself for a blow to the head.

Instead, Belkins put his fist under my unshaven chin and lifted my unresisting head. He bent down so his face was inches from mine. I continued to look impassively toward the tabletop, although he was standing so close that it was no longer within my view.

With his other hand, he snatched the cigar out of his mouth. "Look at me," he commanded.

I could feel his spittle on my face and smell the sour scent of stale whiskey on his breath. Concerned that he might react badly if I didn't follow his commands, I raised my eyes and focused on a spot on his blotchy red forehead beneath his greasy black hair.

"You think you're so smart, don't you?" he sneered. "Well, this time we got you good to rights. You're going back to prison. For a long time."

Still no direct questions that I had to answer, so I just sat there, trying to breathe through my mouth so I didn't have to smell his funky breath.

He shifted his hand so he could grasp my chin between his thumb and forefinger. He squeezed and shook my head roughly. Then his hand moved down on my throat and his grip got tighter.

I tried not to react, but I gagged.

The door opened again. This time, I glanced toward it and saw Montgomery, impeccably attired in a striped charcoal gray three piece suit, lighter gray shirt, and dark red tie.

He eyed us.

Belkins's hand dropped away from my throat like it had been burned.

"Get anywhere?" Montgomery asked smoothly.

"Nah." Belkins coughed. "I was just getting started."

Montgomery turned to me. "You want a cup of coffee, Jesse?"

I would have loved a cup of coffee. But I knew better than to start the sequence of events that was designed to make me feel grateful and indebted to him.

"No, sir," I managed to say. "Thank you."

Belkins snorted. "Think being polite is gonna help you, do you? You're wrong."

Montgomery and I both ignored him.

Perching on the edge of the tabled, Montgomery folded his manicured hands on one knee. The green gem in his ring winked in the light.

"You want to tell us what you were doing at Chillington's Financial Services?" he asked.

Too direct a question to ignore. I sighed. "I went over to try to get Kelly's wallet back. She'd left it over there."

Montgomery's eyebrows arched on his smooth dark forehead. "Your girlfriend Kelly?"

"Yeah. Only she's not really my girlfriend."

Belkins snorted. "She come to her senses, or you two just fighting again?"

I didn't dignify that with a response.

"So you knew she was seeing him?" Montgomery continued.

"Yeah."

"How did you feel about that?"

I shrugged. "Not real happy. But she can see whoever she wants."

"But you weren't happy about it."

"No. Of course not."

"Were you unhappy enough to do something about it?"

"No. What could I do?"

"You tell me."

I shrugged again. "Not a whole hell of a lot."

"Maybe you went to talk to him? Tell him to stay away from her?"

"No."

"Maybe you just went to talk, but he wouldn't agree not to see her. Maybe he even laughed at you. Told you what he'd done with her. Anybody'd get mad at that. Is that what happened?"

"No."

Montgomery stood up and walked behind me. "Your girlfriend's seeing this other guy. He's got some coin. Drives a sports car. You don't even have a driver's license. You thought maybe you'd have some money from that reward for the cat collar, but it's never shown up. So you go over to his place. And things get a little out of hand."

"I told you. Kelly left her wallet over there. She asked me to go get it for her." Even as I said it, I realized how lame that sounded.

"And why," Montgomery asked, "couldn't she go over and get her own wallet if she'd left it there?"

I sighed. "Her ex is coming over to pick up the kids. Overnight visit. She had to be home when he got there."

"Overnight visit, huh? No kids? Was she planning on making a big weekend of it with Sydney?"

"I don't think so. She asked me to come back to her place."

"Yeah, right. With her wallet that you were supposed to get from Sydney."

"She told me she didn't really want to see him again. At least not right now. And she had to get the kids ready to go to their dad's. Give 'em baths and stuff like that." I didn't add that they'd slept in their clothes. At Jumbo George's. In my care.

Montgomery walked around, back into my field of vision. "I thought I had a pretty good handle on you, Jesse. I even went to bat for you when the prosecutor was thinking about bringing charges against you for the ATM break-in. The video was pretty good, but the guy in it did have a dark hoodie pulled over his head most of the time. You had an alibi for the time it said, and the security company said that was accurate. So I convinced them it must be somebody else."

"Of course it was him," Belkins said. "I don't know how he managed it, but he got away from work for long enough to do it. And he figured he could dodge the blame for it. He was almost right, that time. Probably had that girlfriend of his to pick him up and run him over to the ATM."

"The girlfriend works the same shift he does," Montgomery pointed out. "They're the only forklift drivers. I don't think both of them could be gone with no one noticing."

"Well, maybe she lent him her car. And covered for him."

They were trying to get me to respond, to defend Kelly. Or say anything. I would never leave Kelly hung out to dry, if things got serious. But I didn't see that this was anything but speculation, so I kept quiet. I knew they'd twist anything I said so I sounded guilty anyhow.

"I suppose that's a better possibility," Montgomery said. "But it's been a few months since he was released, and up til now, he seems to have been pretty much following the requirements of his parole. Why would he do something like that now?"

Belkins snorted. "We can be pretty sure he's been up to stuff before this. We just haven't been able to catch him at it. And now—he thought he was gonna get that reward. Carissa told me the insurance company is still investigating. But I bet he thought he was gonna get it right away, so he went and spent money he didn't have. And then had to get money quick somewhere."

I let my chin fall down on my chest and closed my eyes. Mistake.

Belkins grabbed me by the shirt with both hands. "You listen to us. But this time, we don't need you to say nothing. We got you on tape going into that check cashing office. You can't deny you were there."

"I didn't deny that I was there," I said. "I was the one who called 9-1-1. And I stuck around. Wouldn't be no point in leaving. The surveillance tape was recording the whole time."

"Damn straight," Belkins said. "Both times."

Both times? Was he referring to the ATM tape?

"And the first time," he said, his face so close to mine that I could see the enlarged pores on his pasty white skin. "The first time you were wearing that same dark hoodie you did when you broke into the ATM. You thought that, because you got away with it one time, you'd get away with it another time?"

This didn't make sense to me, but I knew better than to ask any questions. They would either enlighten me or they wouldn't, but it would have nothing to do with anything I said.

"Do you have a hoodie?" Montgomery asked.

Belkins took one hand off my shirt and moved back a bit.

"Yeah," I said. "But it's not real dark, more of a light gray."

"Why did you go back the second time?" Montgomery asked. "If you were going to call 9-1-1, why didn't you do it the first time you were in there?"

"I was only in there once."

"Was it—" Montgomery leaned closer "—that he wasn't dead yet the first time?"

"There was no first and second time. Only the once." What were they getting at?

"How much do you remember about the body?" he asked. "When you went back to check on him? Were you pretty sure he'd be dead by then?"

"I didn't know he was gonna be dead when I got there."

"He drink any coffee while you were there?"

I shook my head. "He was dead. He couldn't drink anything."

"The first time."

"There was no first time. Just the once."

"He usually drink a lot of coffee?"

"I dunno. I mean, he was in AA. Those guys tend to drink a lot of coffee. Switch from booze to caffeine. So maybe he did."

"He take sugar in his coffee?"

"That I don't know."

"So you just went over there to pick up something your lady left there. A wallet, you said?"

"Yeah." Saying it again didn't make it sound any more believable.

"Didn't it strike you as odd, a check cashing place like that, lots of money around, not locked up tight?"

"Sure did. I wondered should I go in, but it seemed like something must be wrong."

"So you jimmied the lock and went in?"

By my own testimony, they had me on the entering half of a breaking and entering charge, and now they were trying to get me to admit to the breaking part. "Doors weren't locked. They weren't even closed tight."

"And then what?"

"I called out to see if anybody was around."

Montgomery looked at me intently. "Did anybody answer?"

"No."

"So what did you do?"

"I looked around."

"See what you could find to steal?"

"No. See if I could find anybody."

"And did you?"

"All I found was the dead guy."

"This guy Sydney?"

"I thought it might be him, but I couldn't be sure."

"And you were sure he was dead?"

I shrugged. "I was pretty sure he was when I saw him. I mean, he was cold."

"So you touched the body."

"Yeah. If he had of been warm, he might of been still alive, and I would have told the dispatcher he needed to send an ambulance."

"Notice anything unusual about him?"

"Sydney?"

Belkins rolled his eyes in exasperation. "Yes, Sydney."

"Well, he was dead. That was unusual."

In spite of the situation, Montgomery smiled. "Anything about his complexion?"

"He's a white guy. That what you mean?"

He smiled again, stroking his dark cheek with his equally dark hand. "Light skinned white, or darker?"

I thought back. "Kind of reddish, I think."

With the hand still on my shirt, Belkins pulled me closer to his face. "Reddish is right. You know what makes somebody reddish like that?"

"No."

"Cyanide poisoning, that's what. And who do we know who's had access to cyanide lately?"

I didn't answer that one.

"Potassium cyanide crystals look just like sugar, don't they, Jesse?" Montgomery asked, his voice soft and menacing.

Of course they did. "I guess," I said.

"And don't you think they're going to be testing that spilled sugar on his desk? Right next to the overturned coffee mug?"

"Yeah. I expect they would."

"And don't you think there's gonna be an autopsy?"

I shifted in the chair. "I'd think so."

"For sure there will be," Montgomery said. "And can you give us any clue as to what they'll find?"

"I dunno."

Belkins reached over and gave my shirt a shake. "I got a pretty good idea."

They both stood there, looming over me. I tried to keep all expression off my face.

"What I don't understand," Montgomery said, "is why you went back there. I thought you were pretty smart. You had to know it wouldn't take us long to piece all this together. Why didn't you just take off?"

"Because," Belkins said, "he's been getting away with so much, he figures we're really stupid."

Montgomery sighed. "Obviously, Jesse, you're not going to be cut loose on this one. Let's get you booked. Murder, to start with. First degree. Breaking and entering. We'll see what else the state's attorney's office wants."

"Is there some way I can make a phone call?" I asked. Kelly was the only one I could think of to call. I could let her know I wouldn't be bringing her wallet over and ask her to maybe check on Mandy's house and leave a note there saying where I was. Mandy and Nicole would be disappointed in me. But right now, that was the least of my worries.

Montgomery checked his watch. "I'm sure you'll get a phone call," he said. "But not right now. Shift change—they've got to do roll call and head count and all that good stuff."

Belkins dropped my shirt and went to the door. He stepped out and called down the hallway.

A uniformed correctional officer stepped in. Belkins and Montgomery left.

"Stand up," he said.

Reluctantly, I got to my feet. He took me by the arm and hustled me through the hallway, paused briefly at a grill for control to open it, and down a metal staircase. I felt every tread of the steps through my socks.

We stopped at the doorway to central booking, but the room was filled with milling police officers and a bunch of sullen tattooed young men who sported shaven heads and camouflage vests. Their hands were secured behind their backs with bright yellow plastic flexible cuffs.

Most of the officers didn't wear regular uniforms, but had on dark T-shirts that said, "Police" in florescent letters. It was apparent that they had on bulky body armor underneath.

The disposable flex cuffs instead of metal handcuffs argued for a planned raid, as did the presence of so many cops in the dark T-shirts. The emaciated look of some of the prisoners argued for a meth lab.

The clerk at the counter was shuffling through a pile of paperwork. The CO caught her eye. She looked at me, frowned, and shook her head.

He tugged on my arm. "Come on. We can take care of this later."

We stopped at a holding cage just outside booking.

It'd be a while before anyone was ready to process me.

Unlocking my handcuffs, the officer removed them and the waist chain. Lifting his radio, he said, "Holding one."

The door slid open.

"In you go," he said. "Now be nice to the other guys."

Two surly black teenagers sprawled on the bench near the door. They didn't look up.

On the bench across the cage, a man lay, taking up the entire space. His face turned to the wall.

I stepped inside. The door clanged shut behind me.

The guy lying on the bench rolled over, sat up, and looked at me. He staggered to his feet, took a few steps toward me, and said, "Jesse?"

I froze.

I felt like I was looking at a distorted image of myself in a funhouse mirror. He was thinner than me, his curly brown hair cut short, and his face was lined and weathered. But he definitely looked one whole hell of a lot like me.

CHAPTER 20

My eyes had to be playing tricks on me. I shook my head.

"Ah, come on, Jess," the guy said, sweeping the fringe of hair on his forehead to one side. "You haven't forgotten your big brother, have you?"

I stood stupidly, unable to believe what my eyes were telling me. His ragged blue jeans and sweatshirt hung on his spare frame. His hands were almost completely engulfed by the sleeves of his stained gray sweatshirt, and he'd made holes in the cuffs for his thumbs. On his feet were a pair of work boots that looked suspiciously like state issue, the kind the prison systems provide for released inmates who don't have any clothes of their own. Since they weren't steel-toed, like mine, he'd been permitted to keep them. The laces had been removed, though, undoubtedly confiscated along with his belt. If he'd had one.

He needed a shave even worse than I did.

"Will?" I choked out. "Denny?" Those were my two older brothers.

He laughed. "Denny. You got to remember me."

I sure did. Last I saw Denny, I was sixteen, standing lookout on a derelict, dark street in Baltimore while he and Will went into a drug house to make a buy. Or so I thought. We'd agreed that, if anybody got caught holding, I'd take the blame. Both of them already had extensive drug records and were looking at three-time loser charges. I was a juvenile. The most I'd pick up was probably six months in juvie hall. Or even rehab. I'd take that, even though I didn't do drugs myself.

As I stood there shivering, wearing a dark hoodie identical to the ones he and Will wore, they had dashed past me, shoving a few plastic bags into my hands, and warned me not to follow them.

Our dad was recently out of prison. He'd reclaimed me from the foster care system. Not because he wanted me, or even because he cared about me, but because of the food stamps, Social Security payments, and Section Eight housing vouchers that came along with me.

That was the beginning of the end of my plans to go to college. I was pulled out of the Colemans' supportive foster home in a decent school district and plunged into an inner city, where the high school had a sixty percent dropout rate and the guidance counselors laughed if a student mentioned college.

Dad picked up his old heroin habit again almost as soon as he hit the street. Will, my oldest brother, said we had to keep him supplied or he'd go out looking himself and do something that would get him locked up again right away.

At first, Dad getting locked up again didn't seem like such a terrible idea to me, since it would mean I'd be returned to foster care. I knew I'd probably end up in a group foster home instead of being returned to the Colemans', in whose foster home I'd been thriving. Not ideal, but living with my father and brothers was a nightmare.

But in only a few weeks of hanging around with my brothers, I found myself in trouble with the juvenile justice system.

I wasn't actually in the apartment when the dealer got shot. But other people were. One of them was an undercover cop.

My brothers managed to get out of the apartment and shove the bags into my hands, but didn't tell me what happened. Just left me holding the bag. Literally.

Since I didn't know about the shooting, I didn't deny it when the undercover cop identified me as being one of the people in the apartment. By the time I figured everything out, I was looking at adult murder charges. Nobody wanted to listen to me, including my public defender, who just tried to get the best deal possible for me. So I was convicted and sentenced as an adult. Forty years was a long time, but it beat life, and it definitely beat the death penalty.

Over the years in prison, I'd learned a lot about myself and how to control my feelings, both in formal anger management groups and by observing other inmates. In the beginning, I gave into blind fury a few times, but that led to nothing good. Usually a quick trip to a segregation cell, where I could cool down at my leisure. I'd have thirty days to do it. With not much but my permitted three library books, paperbacks only, per week to occupy me. That's where I began to really appreciate libraries.

But I felt unreasoning rage building in me as I looked at Denny's lopsided grin. He was missing a few of his front teeth.

I closed my eyes, trying to relax my tight muscles and take deep breaths.

"Ah, come on, bro," Denny said. "It's been a long time."

"Twenty years," I said through clenched teeth.

"Guess so. I been doing nickels and dimes, in and out of jail. Never had a chance to look you up."

"I shouldn't have been too hard to find," I said. "Just had to contact Department of Corrections and find out which prison I was in. Nowadays, they even got an inmate locator on the Internet."

He raised his eyebrows. "I don't know nothing about how to use the damn Internet. But you was locked up the whole twenty years?"

"The whole twenty years. I picked up forty, so I got another twenty backup time. I'm on parole now."

"Wow. And here I figured you was kicking around and I just never came across you. Who knew?"

I knew. "Who do you think took the rap for killing that drug dealer?"

"But you was a juvenile. And you wasn't even in the apartment when he got shot."

"I know that. And you know that. But the cops didn't get a good look at the shooter. They thought it was me."

"Really? But you was a juvenile."

"A juvenile charged as an adult with murder."

"We figured you'd get stuck in a kiddy jail, maybe a camp, and released when you turned eighteen. Didn't you tell them you never even went inside?"

"I tried. But a fat lot of good it did. I was involved in a felony that resulted in a death. Technically, I'm guilty of murder. And I was definitely convicted of it."

Denny scratched his head. "I never knew that. Me and Will, we took off for Florida. Figured we'd stay there till the heat died down. Will got locked up down there, and I came back after a year or so. Never did find out what happened to the old man. I figured you'd gotten hooked up with him again and you'd gone somewhere. Or that he got locked up again."

"The old man was a druggie. He never should have gotten custody of a kid, even a sixteen-year-old one. They should have left me in foster care. I have no idea what happened to him."

Denny sighed. "Prob'ly dead. Or in prison somewhere."

The mindless fury inside me was subsiding. I unclenched my fists, took another deep breath, and went over to sit on the bench.

Denny came over and sat next to me. As he moved closer, a sour odor reached my nose. He was badly in need of a shower. I needed one, too, but he smelled like he hadn't washed himself or his clothes in a few weeks. And may well have puked on himself at some point. As well as peed his pants.

That wouldn't be a problem for long, for either one of us. We'd get a shower and a delousing as part of the intake process. Whether we wanted it or not. Then they'd issue us underwear, orange jumpsuits, and flip flops.

"I was in the bus station in Hagerstown," he said. "Just got released, and they dropped me off. I picked up a copy of a newspaper somebody left on a seat, and there, right on the front page, was your picture. It looked like a mug shot, so I figured you'd been picked up for something, but when I read the article, it said you'd gotten a big reward of some kind. And that you was working steady."

"Yeah. I seen that article, too."

Denny ignored what I said. "Well, I figured, ol' Jess has got hisself established. And I haven't seen my ol' bro in a coon's age. Why don't I just head up that way and look him up? He'll be happy to see family."

"You was wrong about that."

"About you being happy to see family?"

"About most of it. I do have a steady job. Or I did—I'll prob'ly lose it now. But I never did get the reward. And established?" I tried to laugh, but it came out as more of a snort. "I been struggling since I hit the street."

"It don't look that bad to me. I been trying to check things out, before I came up and said anything to you."

"What do you mean?"

"I finally figured out where you worked, so I hung around watching for you. How was I supposed to know you worked the overnight shift?"

"It's a good job. And midnight to eight pays ten percent shift differential."

"Yeah. Well, I did see you eventually. But you're a hard man to pin down. I tried to follow you a couple of times, but you never seemed to go straight home, and I never did find out where you stayed at most of the time. I found out you had appointments at the parole office, so I figured you hadn't been exactly walking the straight and narrow, but I didn't know you been locked up for the last twenty years."

"Well, I was."

"Damn. And all because of that little incident with me and Will. Who knew?"

I sure did.

"At first, I thought maybe you stayed with that broad, the hefty one with the long dark hair. I followed her a few times."

My face flushed. "You followed Kelly?"

"I did." He nudged my side with his elbow and winked. "She's stacked, ain't she? Not like one of them skinny chicks—she's built! A real armful."

Not trusting myself to respond calmly to him, I moved a few inches away on the bench. I sat on my hands to keep them from flying up and punching him in the nose. All that would get me was locked in a segregation cell. And much as my insides were boiling with conflicting feelings, I realized this might be my only chance to hear what Denny had to say.

"So I followed her a few times. But she never did go to where you're staying at. And she was seeing somebody else, too—did you know that?"

I licked my dry lips. "Yeah."

He grinned. "I always figured that wasn't a bad bet. If a woman's only seeing you, she's gonna expect a lot. But she's got somebody else, he's got to come up with something for her, too. If you're just the side dish, you get the benefits without the demands. And it gives you the green light to have your own little bit on the side. Less intense all around that way."

That didn't sound like any type of relations I'd be interested in. Cocking my head so I could see his face sideways, I asked, "You got a woman?"

"Me?" He laughed. "Hell, no. I ain't been on the street that long. And it's tough out here. I'm having enough trouble finding something to eat and a place to stay."

"So where have you been staying?"

He shook his head. "Mostly at the Rescue Mission. But you got to be sober or they won't take you in. Then I sleep under one of them railroad bridges. But that's cold. I was hoping to find where you stayed and see if I could move in, for a little while. But I never been able to do that."

Thank goodness he'd never managed to follow me to Mandy's place. I said, "I used to have an apartment. It wasn't much, but it was a place to stay. It got flooded out, and I don't think the landlord's gonna fix it. Haven't had a whole lot of luck finding a place I can afford." I wasn't about to mention Mandy and the carriage house. With her nice house full of valuable antiques and easily salable knickknacks, that would be an invitation for disaster. Better Denny shouldn't know about it.

Or even Jumbo George's place. He didn't need the kind of grief that would come from somebody like Denny hanging around. I said, "Just staying a night here and night there. Or, actually, day here and a day there, since I work most nights."

He nodded knowingly. "I been trying to get a handle on things. This is a rough town to make it in. And that damn flood only made things worse. Can't even find a long-term bunk in the homeless shelter. It's full."

The bars of the holding cage formed a striped shadow pattern on the floor. I stared down at it. "Don't think finding a place to sleep is gonna be a problem for a little while. For either one of us."

He chortled. "Yeah. For now, at least, I got me three hots and a cot. Don't know how much they're gonna be able to pin on me, but they're gonna try. And I sure ain't gonna make bail."

I started to say, "One of the things they might pin on you wouldn't be breaking into ATMs, by any chance, would it?" but decided not to.

"Just been trying to get by," Denny continued. "Got a little cash, but not a whole lot. I was gonna see if you wouldn't stake me out of that reward money."

"But I told you, I never got none of that," I said.

"So you say. We can talk about that when we get all this sorted out."

"I got a feeling that ain't gonna happen anytime soon. What did they pick you up on?"

Denny sighed. "They got me breaking into an ATM."

"Oh?" That answered one of my unasked questions.

"Yeah. Pretty stupid of me. I should have waited till it was dark. Somebody must of seen me and called it in. And of course the alarm went off. A whole slew of cop cars showed up before I could get around the corner."

"Was that the first time you'd tried something like that?"

He shook his head. "Nope. First time worked like a charm. That was nighttime. Early morning, really. I was long gone by the time anybody showed up. I heard the sirens, but I hustled away as fast I could without being spotted and worked on getting as far away as I could. I got a couple hundred bucks."

"That should have kept you for a while," I said.

"Well, yeah. But it's not my town. At least not yet. I didn't know where to get good weed cheap. So I ended up paying top dollar."

"Just weed?" I asked.

"A little meth, too, but I didn't really know where to get that, either, at least at first. So I was going through that little stash pretty fast. Then, last night, I was too wasted to go to the Rescue Mission. I fell asleep under the railroad tracks, and some bum rolled me. I needed to get a little coin fast."

"Is that why you hit the ATM?"

"Well, yeah. But it wasn't the first thing I tried. I figured I'd see how tight it was at the check cashing place where that guy your lady's been seeing stays at. Gotta be a lot of cash money in a place like that. If I could figure out a way to get any of it."

"True, that." And security should be really tight. But it wasn't—and I didn't want to say much that might stop him from telling me what happened.

"I thought I'd really lucked out. The guy was just pulling into that garage that's attached to the building when I got there. The door was coming down, but I slipped in under it."

"It was daytime. Didn't he see you?"

Denny shrugged. "He might of seen something. He did turn around and look. But I ducked down next to one of them big green recycling containers in the corner, and he didn't see me."

"Did you get anything there?"

"Not really. For a while, I thought it was gonna work out good. I picked up a tire iron from the garage and followed him. He went into his office and made himself a cup of coffee. There's a big vault in the back of the office. I figured it had to have a lot of money in it."

I remembered the office. And the vault. "Was the vault open?"

"No. But I don't think it was locked good, neither. He sat down at the desk and drank his coffee. I just about decided I was gonna go in and tell him he'd best come up with some money if he knew what was good for him when he got up. He went to the vault and pulled the door open. His back was to me, so I hit him with the tire iron. But not real hard. He never seen me."

"What do you mean, not real hard?"

"Enough so he fell down and was knocked out. He's gonna have a big bump on his head and a headache when he wakes up, but prob'ly not even a good concussion. Weren't even no blood I could see."

I kept my hands clenched on the edge of the bench. "Then what?" I asked.

"I figured I'd hit pay dirt. I stepped over him and went into the vault. But you know what? There wasn't a whole lot in there. Mostly papers. And some kind of video cassettes or something. And a stack of CDs. But only a few fifties in cash."

"So you didn't get much?"

"Well, there was these locked drawers in the back of the vault. I figured that's where the money was, so I broke into them. The tire iron wasn't great for that—crowbar would have been better—but I got the tops of them smashed in, then I could pry them open. I did get about two hundred dollars or so, but you know what?"

"No. What?"

"They was mostly signed checks and blank money orders. I took a handful of the money orders, but I'm not even sure what I could use them for."

"They didn't take them when they busted you?"

"Nah. I stashed them behind a loose concrete block under the railroad bridge. Figured later maybe I could find somebody to take them off my hands for a few bucks."

Sydney—if it had really been Sydney—wasn't just knocked out when I'd gotten there. He was dead and cold. "You sure he was still breathing when you left?" I asked.

"Yep. I mean, his chest was moving, so he must have been breathing. I had to step over him again to leave, and he kind of moaned."

"So how'd you leave?"

"I was gonna take that fancy little car." He grinned. "I know I couldn't keep it too long—once he'd reported it stolen, it'd be easy to spot. But it'd be fun to drive it for a little while. Maybe dump it in the river or something when I was done with it. The keys was on the desk. So I took them and went out to the garage and started it up."

The car had still been in the garage. I wondered how to ask him about that. But I didn't have to. He told me himself.

"Then I couldn't figure out how to open the garage door. There was some kind of remote control thingie in the glove compartment, but I couldn't make it work. I heard a siren and got a little spooked, so I just left it and went through the building and out the front. I had to bust the lock on the front door to get out."

"Did you lock the doors behind yourself?"

"Nope. I did try to close the front door, but with the busted lock, it didn't close tight. I didn't want it to be super obvious it was open, but I didn't want to spend too much time trying to make it look locked."

"How about the siren?"

Denny shrugged. "False alarm. It turned out to be an amb'lance. I seen it down on the next street. But by that time, I figured I'd better not go back."

I thought for a few minutes. "Did you leave the car running?"

"You know, I'm not sure if I did or not. I'd started it when I got in to look for the door opener, but I couldn't make the door open. So it must have been running when I got out to try to make the damn opener work, but it wouldn't. I don't know that I went back and turned off the car."

An odor of car exhaust was one of the things I'd noticed when I was in the building.

"Is that when you hit the ATM?" I asked.

"Yeah. I still had the tire iron, but it didn't work near so well as a crowbar would've. That makes two times I should have had a crowbar. But you got to make do with what you can find."

A cart pushed by a CO rolled up to the door of the holding cage. It held a stack of covered food trays. A cafeteria smell of gravy and boiled vegetables wafted off it. "You guys want to be fed?" he asked.

Denny sprang up. "Yeah!" he said eagerly.

The two teenagers wrinkled their noses. "What ya got?" one asked.

The CO lifted the lid of one tray. "Looks like meatloaf and mashed potatoes and corn," he said. "And juice and coffee."

"Nah," the teen said, turning his back.

Denny sniffed. "Can I have his if he don't want it?" he asked.

The CO shrugged. "Don't make me no never mind. But he got to come over and get it and give it to you. I can't give you two."

"Hey, dude, can you do that for me?" Denny asked.

The teenager looked surprised. "I guess," he said, scrambling to his feet.

"You want mine, too?" the other one asked.

"Oh, wow, I'd be much obliged," Denny said, wiping his mouth with the back of his hand, which was still covered with the sweatshirt sleeve.

The second teen stretched and looked bored. "Hey, knock yourself out, dude."

They both went to the door to get their meals.

I followed to get mine.

The CO passed each tray through a slot in the door, one at a time. Denny took his and put it on the bench. Then each of the teens took theirs, handed them to Denny, and went back to their sullen conversation in the corner.

I took my tray and carried it over to the bench. Denny was already shoveling the food into his mouth with his hands. "Haven't eaten since yesterday," he said with his mouth full. "Or maybe it was the day before."

For a jailhouse meal, it wasn't bad, and I knew enough to eat whatever I could when I had a chance. But I was nowhere near as ravenous as Denny seemed to be.

He drained his coffee. "You guys don't even want your coffee?" he asked, looking at the other paper cups with hungry eyes.

"No, man," one of them said. "We're gonna be out of here in time to get a steak dinner tonight." His buddy laughed.

Denny upended first one and then the other cup.

I finished my meal except for my coffee, which I put on the bench. I piled the trays, the plastic spoons, and the empty cups in a neat stack and put it on the floor next to the door.

The teens watched me. "Hey, dude. Why you doing the cleanup for the man?"

I shrugged. "If I got to be in here, I'm gonna make it as livable as I can. You live in a cage for long enough, you at least want it to be clean and neat."

"You do much time?" the kid asked, eyeing Denny, who was anything but clean and neat.

"Twenty years," I said.

He raised his eyebrows. "Wow. That's a good bit."

I nodded and picked up my cup of coffee. It was strong and bitter, but I drank it slowly, savoring its warmth.

"That was good," Denny said, wiping his mouth again with the sleeve-covered back of his hand. He belched.

CHAPTER 21

How much should I tell him about Sydney? Should I let on that I knew he was dead? Denny had been really unwise, telling me all he had. And it put me in an awkward position. What would I do if I had to make a choice between turning state's witness against Denny and going back to prison myself?

I could only hope it wouldn't come to that.

"What do you think's gonna happen to you now?" I asked Denny.

He grinned. "Back to prison, I imagine. They got enough for some pretty good charges. Ought to pick up a long enough bit to be sent back to the state system. Don't want to do no real time in a county lockup. That's no life."

I could agree with that. "What if they pin the whole thing at the check cashing place on you? That was violent—it'd carry a heavier bit."

He nodded. "Yeah. Then for sure I'd end up back in the state. No place I ain't been before."

Frowning, I said, "You don't mind going back to prison?"

"Well, when you put it like that..." He scratched the side of his scrawny neck. "I guess no, I really don't mind. I'm getting too old for this. It's tough enough to make it when you're a kid with a future. I ain't got no future. Locked up, I'll get fed, I'll have a place to stay that's at least dry, even if it ain't real warm. I won't freeze. When I get sick, they'll find me a doctor."

I guess, to a certain extent, I could understand. But I would do almost anything to avoid being locked up again. What kind of a life had Denny been living that he saw prison as a possible alternative?

"S'pose the guy at the check cashing place is hurt real bad? Or worse?"

"Worse? You mean, like dead?"

"Yeah."

"Shouldn't be. I mean, he was fine when I left."

"Fine?"

"Well, not fine, exactly. But not dead. And I didn't hit him hard enough to really do that much harm, I don't think. But if he died, well,

I guess I'm looking at a murder charge." His grin widened. "Like you been doing time for."

A CO came up and opened the door. "You. Damon. Come on."

We both looked at her. "Which one?"

"Damon." She looked at the paper in her hand. "Dennis Damon. Which one of you is that?"

Denny stood up and stretched. "That'd be me, I guess."

She peered at us. "What, are you guys brothers or something?"

Denny nodded.

"Both Damon?" The CO shook her head. "We're gonna have to real careful about that one."

Denny turned around and let her put cuffs on him. Her nose wrinkled as she got close enough to catch a whiff of him.

"Hey, Jess," Denny called.

I looked up from my seat on the bench. "Yeah?"

"Look me up if you can, huh?"

I almost said, "Why the hell would I do that?" but there was no point making him feel worse. "Okay," I said. That didn't mean I had to do it. "But chances are pretty good I'll be locked up, too. I got that twenty years backup time, and if I pick up a new conviction..." I let that thought hang in the air.

He ignored what I said. "And when you get back out on the street, send me a couple bucks of that reward money. You know, the money you didn't get. Okay? You know how much difference having a little coin in your commissary account can mean when you're locked up."

I did know, although nobody ever sent me anything. I'd earned every cent that ever showed up in my commissary account. "I really didn't get no reward money," I said. "But if I can, I'll send you something. Won't be a whole lot—I don't never got that much myself."

A little while later, a uniformed sheriff's deputy came and got the two teenagers. He didn't put them in handcuffs.

"About time," one of them said, smirking.

I didn't move from where I was sitting on the bench, but I watched out of the corner of my eye as they were led, not toward the booking room, but through the sally port that led out. I hoped they were right and on their way to that steak dinner.

Then someone came for me. Handcuffs, of course. And straight to booking.

Standing in front of the height lines painted on the wall, holding a placard with my new commitment number, while they got the mug shot, I wondered if Carissa had gotten wind of this yet.

"Push your hair back off your face. I need to get a better picture." They had taken extra care about the paperwork and now were being very fussy with the pictures. Everybody, inmates and staff alike, knew the stories about mix-ups with inmates who were similar in appearance to one another. Add to that the similarity of names, and the fact the Denny and I would have commitment numbers very close to each other, and the possibilities for error multiplied. Nobody wanted to be the one who made the error that released the wrong inmate.

Usually they attached the ID bracelet loosely, so it could be slipped off for showers and things. The clerk pulled mine fairly tight and secured it. It would be tough to get off. "Don't lose that," she said. "There's a twenty dollar charge for a replacement."

Denny was already through the medical department before I got in. "Put all your clothes in that bin," the nurse said. "I'm sending them to the laundry man before they go to the property room. Don't want them all packed up and festering."

I didn't think they were that bad—Denny's had been, and mine weren't exactly clean, but they were wearable. All I could do was follow instructions, though. I hoped they got them in the right property bags. Although if things went really badly, I wouldn't have to worry about having my own clothes for a while. Maybe ever.

After the shower, delousing, physical exam, and body cavity search, I was given jail issue underwear, an orange jumpsuit that was a bit too big, and flip flops that were also too big. Better too big than too small, though. I was handed a stack of folded bedding and a hygiene kit. Then I was escorted toward the housing units.

I was hoping I'd end up in the general population, but of course that didn't happen. My violent conviction, coupled with the murder charge I was looking at now, were enough to put me at a higher security level. My assignment was a cell in a closed unit, where I'd be locked in about twenty-three hours a day. Twenty-three long, dull hours.

The CO assigned to the desk checked my ID against the paperwork on his clipboard and radioed in to have the cell door opened.

It was a four-man cell, but I was the only one in it right now. That wasn't likely to last. I unrolled my mattress on the bottom bunk on the darker side of the cell. The lights in the central area would be dimmed at night, but the security lights would be on twenty-four-seven, and I wanted to be where they didn't shine right in my eyes.

Well, at least I wasn't housed with some of those meth addicts they'd busted. As time went on, those guys would become increasingly agitated and some of them would take it out on their cell mates. The worst ones might be moved to detox or medical cells, but there were only so many of them available.

The CO was sitting at his desk, his eyes on what looked like a computer screen. But it could have been a monitor to the security system. He didn't appear to be paying much attention, but I knew not much would get by him.

A couple of inmate kitchen workers came by, supervised by a bored CO. They passed a covered food tray through the port in the door. I lifted the lid. Some kind of stew. I looked quizzically at the workers, who were sorting out trays for the other cells.

"Venison," one said.

"Yeah. Prob'ly road kill," said the other. "A few too many carrots in it, if you ask me. But it ain't bad."

He was right. It wasn't bad. I ate it, mopped up the gravy with the slice of plain white bread, and drained the cup of coffee. There was also a square something that was probably supposed to be cake. It was a little crusty around the edges, but it was sweet. I ate that, too, and put the tray on the floor next to the cell door.

My mind reeled. I had the answers to a few of the puzzles that had been nagging at me, but what was I going to do with them? Snitch out my own brother? I kicked off the flip flops, lay down on the thin mattress, pulled the rough blanket over me, and fell asleep.

* * * *

"You Jesse Damon?"

I struggled to wake up enough to make sense of the question. I rolled over and sat up. "Yeah."

A CO was standing outside the cell. "Lemme see your ID."

I stood up and passed my hand through the bars. "I can't get it off," I said. "It's too tight."

He grabbed my wrist and twisted it up so he could read it.

"Okay," he said. "Somebody wants to see you."

"Who?"

Shrugging, he said, "I dunno. And why would I tell you if I did?"

He mumbled something into the radio as I scrambled under the bunk for the flip flops. The cell door slid open, and he stepped back, giving me a lot of room to step out. Another few words murmured into his radio, and the grill between the housing unit and the hallway slid open.

I glanced back. The officer at the desk didn't look like he'd moved.

One of the too-big flip flops slipped off my foot.

"Come on," the CO escorting me growled. His keys jangled and boot heels rang on the highly-polished hard floor.

My feet made no noise, and I struggled to keep from slipping or losing the flip flops.

We stopped at a door. I was beginning to know my way around this place. It was an interview room. The door opened, and I stepped inside.

Montgomery was sitting on the edge of the table, swinging his long leg lazily. His normally unreadable face looked grim.

"Sit down, Damon," he said, indicating the chair next to where he was perched.

I sat.

"There's a couple of things you haven't been exactly straight with me about," he said.

That was true, but I wasn't sure which ones he was thinking about, so I didn't say anything.

"You've been living in that carriage house all this time, haven't you? The one where you got in trouble with that woman. Am I right?"

"It was more like her husband I got in trouble with," I said. "At least as far as I know," I added as an afterthought. Maybe there were charges pending there I wasn't aware of yet.

He returned to his main point. "But you were living there. And you told me you were spending a night here and a night there. You want to explain that?"

I sighed. "It wasn't like it was a permanent place to stay or nothing. I think Eileen's gonna move in there, if she hasn't already. And I'll have to get my stuff out and find someplace else."

Glancing up at his frown, I said, "Unless, of course, I get locked up for a while."

He nodded. "I'd say that's true. But you stayed at the carriage house for maybe, what, a month?"

"More like three weeks."

"But why did I have to find that out for myself? And not even from your parole officer?"

Why, indeed? I hadn't told some people because I didn't want to make Mandy's beautiful house and valuable possessions a target of any of my low-life acquaintances if they realized the house was empty for a while. But Montgomery and my parole officer hardly fit into that category.

"That was the nicest place I've ever stayed at," I said. "And I knew it wouldn't be for long. I couldn't let myself think of it like I was *living* there. 'Cause it's gonna be downhill from there." As I said it, I realized that was the truth.

Silence stretched between us. Montgomery's voice was a little softer when he said, "So you couldn't bring yourself to say you were living there?"

I rubbed my cheek nervously against my shoulder. "Something like that."

"And," he said, shifting position, "what have you got to tell me about one Dennis Damon?"

"My brother?" I said stupidly.

"Yes. Your brother. Were you ever planning to mention that he was in town?"

"I didn't know anything about him. I didn't know he was in town. I didn't even know that he was still alive."

He raised his eyebrows. "Don't you think you would have heard something if he'd died?"

"Not necessarily. Why would I? I haven't seen or heard from him in over twenty years. Not till I got thrown in that holding cell with him." I looked at my hand and took a deep breath. "You're prob'ly not gonna believe that."

"That is hard to believe," Montgomery agreed. "Especially since he seems to have been hanging around your girlfriend and the guy she was two-timing you with."

"Nobody calls it two-timing anymore," I said, trying to get a few seconds to think. "And you can't say it's cheating when we didn't have no exclusive agreement. You already asked me about that, last time you were interrogating me."

"Interrogating?" Montgomery said, mock hurt in his voice. "I don't interrogate you. Interviewing is more like it."

I glanced up at his face. "Yeah. Right."

"And as I recall," he continued, "you admitted that you weren't pleased with the situation. And that you didn't like this Sydney Jameson person."

"True, that. But that don't mean that I was gonna *kill* him."

Montgomery leaned back and changed the subject. "Are you sure he's dead?"

I looked up quickly. "I guess not. If that wasn't Sydney in the office, maybe Sydney isn't dead. But the guy in the office, he looked a lot like Sydney. And I'm pretty sure *he* was dead."

"And the guy in the office, do you know how he died?"

"Not really."

"Can you make a guess?"

What did I have to lose at this point? I shrugged. "I bet they think it was potassium cyanide poisoning."

"Oh? And why would anyone think that?"

"The guy had a reddish color. There was spilled sugar all over, and potassium cyanide looks like sugar crystals. And we just had that spill at work."

"Did you have access to the spilled potassium cyanide?"

He knew I had. I said, "Yeah. So did a bunch of other people."

"There weren't that many. How many of them had a beef against Sydney Jameson?"

No good response came to mind, so I just kept quiet.

Montgomery stood up and started pacing behind me. "And do *you* think the person, whether he was Sydney Jameson or not, died of potassium cyanide poisoning?"

"Not really."

"What do you think it was?"

"I don't know for sure. But maybe carbon monoxide."

"And what would make you think it was carbon monoxide?"

"Well, when I first went in, it kind of smelled like car exhaust. That makes you look reddish, too. The door from the garage was open. And I think the car was left running."

He stopped pacing. "The car wasn't running when the emergency responders got there."

"No. It wasn't running when I got there, either. I think it ran out of gas."

"You went into the garage and looked at the car's ignition? Is that why you think it was left running?"

Now I was in dangerous territory. Not for me—I was pretty well screwed no matter what—but I didn't want to say anything about Denny being there. I didn't know how clear the security tape would be. Could they tell us apart?

I just shook my head and didn't say anything.

He resumed pacing. "Where are the blank money orders?"

"Huh?"

"You know, the money orders that were taken out of the vault."

Again, I shook my head and didn't say anything.

"Even if somebody manages to put amounts in on them that looks authentic—and that wouldn't be easy, although it could be done—they have to be activated by the cashier. They're useless. All anybody would get out of trying to cash one would be a whole bunch of trouble."

That made sense. I nodded.

"So wherever they are, they're worthless. Except maybe as a ticket to jail."

Denny had said he'd stuffed them behind a loose block or something under a railroad bridge. It wasn't like he'd hidden a gun or drugs where kids could find it. If somebody found these and was dumb enough to try to cash them, that was on them.

He stopped behind me. "Have you got anything to say about the ATM break-ins?"

"Wasn't me."

"You've said that. Anything else you want to tell me?"

"Not that I can think of." I didn't know if Denny's account was accurate or not, but according to him, they'd caught him practically red-handed on the second one. Couldn't they figure out he was responsible for the first one, too? What did they expect me to say?

"What, you can't tell me what you know? You got some kind of sense of loyalty or something, just because he's your brother?"

I shrugged.

"How loyal has he been to you all those years you spent in prison? Did he ever once visit? Or send a money order? Or even a Christmas card?"

There wasn't much I could say about that, so I just sat there.

"You know, they keep records of visits. And your commissary account. It's not hard for me to check up on those things."

"So go for it," I said. If that was true, he would have found out I'd never had a visit. Or any money in my account that wasn't my dollar a day pay from the prison laundry. But so what?

"You realize you and your brother look a whole lot alike?"

"Yeah." That had been a crucial factor in my murder conviction. It was maybe not quite as true now—I thought Denny looked a whole hell of a lot older than I did, but I could have been wrong—there was still a strong resemblance.

"And on those security videos, it's really hard to tell the difference."

I'd suspected as much.

"Only real difference I can see is the hair," Montgomery said.

He circled back around to where I could see him. I glanced up at him.

"You usually have your hair pulled back in a ponytail. If you don't have a hair tie, like now, your hair's sprung all out around your head. Denny's is just as bushy, but it's cut a lot shorter. And he's got bangs, so it falls into his face."

Where was this going?

"When I realized that," Montgomery went on, "I went back and reviewed the videos. I could tell the difference."

I took a deep breath.

"So now I know who was where when."

"And?" I asked.

"You're right, it wasn't you on the ATMs."

"Told you."

"I have to admit, I was kind of surprised when I thought maybe it was you. I mean, you've been working hard to make it. You had to know you couldn't get away with something like that. So you'd have your parole violated and be back in prison so fast, it would make your head spin."

"Yeah. I kept looking over my shoulder. I thought I was gonna be picked up on for a violation hearing any minute."

Montgomery laughed. "You almost were. A couple of times."

"So you intervened?" I asked.

"You might say that. I don't make these decisions, but I do have a certain amount of influence when I'm investigating a case."

"Why did you do that?"

He leaned against the table. "I thought I had you pegged. If you were going to violate your parole, you wouldn't be found around here easily. You'd just take off."

I had to admit that thought had occurred to me. If I knew I was going to be locked up again, I'd want to take the chance to see as much of the country as I could before they caught up with me. Which, I had no doubt, would happen sooner or later.

"So," he said, "I don't see much point in keeping you locked up. Just costs the taxpayers money, and it wouldn't prevent any crimes."

"You seem awfully concerned with the taxpayers these days," I said, not expecting an answer.

But he gave me one. "I have my reasons."

Emboldened, I looked up at him. "Where's Belkins? I'd of thought he'd want to be in on this interrogation."

Montgomery raised his eyebrows. "'Interrogation?'"

I grinned. "That's right. 'Interview.'"

"It's Saturday night. Now that he has a girlfriend, he has plans for Saturday night. Unless it's super important, I'm not going to bother him."

"Anyone ever figure out how Sydney died?" I asked.

"Are you sure it was Sydney?"

"Well, not one hundred percent, but pretty sure."

"And are you sure he was dead?"

"That, I'm sure of. Unless they got some way to bring somebody back, he was cold and dead."

Montgomery stroked his chin and looked at me, thinking. "Nothing official yet. But every indication is carbon monoxide."

"Not potassium cyanide?"

"Doesn't look like it."

I relaxed a bit and sat back in the chair. "So what happens next?"

"We continue the investigation. Try to determine what happened."

"I figured that. I mean, what happens next to me?"

"You were going to be held for a hearing tomorrow, or Monday at the latest. But since there's a death involved, the state's attorney's come in to work on it, even though it's a weekend. Looks to me like they don't think they have a case against you."

"At all?"

"Not unless there's something I don't know. You know anything I don't?"

"No, sir."

"Then they'll probably cut you loose. I can't say the same for your brother, though."

Not much I could do about that. Montgomery was being surprisingly forthcoming with information. "How come you're telling me all this?" I asked.

He smiled. "I was hoping to get you to roll over on Denny. But that's not going to happen, is it?"

I shook my head. "No."

"I didn't think so. And I don't think we'll need it anyhow."

"He gonna cop a plea?" I asked.

"What do you think?"

"I think, yeah. He's not been doing so well, out on the street. He's pretty much been thoroughly institutionalized."

"You could have helped him out some."

"If I'd of known he was around, I might have considered that, although I for sure wouldn't have let him stay with me. Which is what I think he wanted."

Montgomery stood up and glanced at his watch. "I'm late. I've got a date with my wife. I'm not in charge of it, but I think they're going to get an order to release you. Try to keep out of trouble, okay?"

"I'll do that," I said.

He went to the door and called for a CO. Then he turned back toward me. "Just so you know, Jesse. I'm going to be resigning."

"Resigning? As in, you're not gonna be a cop no more?"

"That's right."

"I thought you were bucking for a promotion. I thought that was why you were such a stickler for getting good evidence that wouldn't be overturned in court."

"I was."

"Then how come you're resigning?"

"I've decided I can have a bigger impact by running for office."

I frowned. "You mean, like a politician?"

He laughed. ""Don't make a face like that. Yes, a politician. I'm going to be running for mayor. Can I count on your vote?"

"Well, you could. Only I'm a convicted felon. I don't got a vote."

"You do once you're off parole."

"Yeah? That'll be another twenty years."

"Maybe by then I'll be running for something bigger."

"You mean, like, Congress?"

He smiled. "Something like that."

"Well, okay. Of course I'll vote for you. If I can."

"Oh, by the way. I told your girlfriend you'd probably be getting out sometime tonight. She said she might try to pick you up."

CHAPTER 22

Of course, it took a while to come up with my clothes, which had never made it down to the property room. The shift had changed, so nobody knew anything about where they'd gotten to. Finally, someone thought to ask the inmate who had been on laundry duty before the evening feed up, and he told them to look in one of the dryers.

At least they were clean, if a bit wrinkled. I changed into them, glad to hand over the orange jumpsuit and the flip flops.

I shoved my hair back out of my face and waited at the sally port. I let my hair grow primarily because haircuts are expensive and it didn't make any difference at work, as long as I kept it tied back. Who'd have thought that the uncut hair would have saved my bacon?

When I got into the public entryway of the jail, no one was sitting on the hard benches, waiting for anybody. Definitely not Kelly. Oh, well, what did I expect? It was too late for the kids to be up, even if she'd really told Montgomery that she might pick me up.

I debated between the carriage house and Jumbo George's. The carriage house was a lot closer. Mandy and Nicole were due back soon. If they'd driven straight through, they'd be back by now and might very well have let Eileen move in. Maybe I should just walk by and see if there were any lights or anything on in the house or the carriage house. I could spend the night and get my stuff out in the morning.

If that didn't seem like a good idea, I could head straight for Jumbo George's. That was a lot of walking. But I'd spent most of the day in a cell, without being at all sure I wasn't going to be locked up indefinitely, and the free night air, even though it was cold, smelled good to me. I hated to get Jumbo George up, though. He had a tough time bedding down in his recliner every night, and getting up wasn't any easier.

When I got halfway down the stairs, I turned to look at the jail and the police station behind me. I shivered and stuck my hands into my jacket pockets. I'm not a praying man, but I said a quick one for Denny. I didn't think he'd be getting out anytime soon.

As I stepped down onto the sidewalk, someone called, "Jesse!"

I froze, taking my hands out of the pockets so no one could think I was going for a weapon. It was a female voice. At least it didn't sound like Carissa. Thank goodness.

"Jesse! Over here!" Cautiously, I turned to look. It was Kelly, climbing out of the RAV4. She gestured to me to come over. I hesitated at first, but I went over.

"When Montgomery told me you were going to be released 'right away,'" she said, "I figured it might be a couple of hours. I know how these places work. So I told the kids to bring some blankets and pillows. They're dead asleep in the back seat."

Sure enough, I could see them bundled up, Chris's arm protectively around Brianna. Their eyes were closed, and I could hear their regular breathing.

"I thought they were supposed to spend the weekend with their father."

"He never showed up to pick them up," Kelly said. "Get in. We're going home."

That solved the problem of where I was going to go right away. I hoped it would also solve the problem of where I was going to spend the night.

When we pulled up to Kelly's house, for once, Chris was as dead asleep in the car as Brianna was. I gathered him in my arms and turned him so his head was on my shoulder.

Kelly dashed on ahead, opened the front door, and turned on the porch light.

I carried him upstairs and laid him in his bed, removing his shoes but not bothering with his clothes. Tucking him under the covers, I smoothed his hair and slipped his teddy bear in next to him. "Good night, Tiger," I whispered.

I heard Kelly struggling up the stairs, Brianna cradled in her arms. I considered taking her, but when Kelly turned into the bathroom, I figured I'd best leave that to Kelly. I went downstairs to switch off the light and make sure the front door was closed and locked.

"What do you want to do now?" Kelly asked, hugging herself and shivering. Her makeup was smeared, and she looked cold in that flimsy blouse.

"Truth be told, I'd like to take a shower," I said. "Wash off that jailhouse stink."

She nodded. "You do that. I could make us some coffee. And something to eat, if you're hungry."

"I'm not hungry," I said. "One thing they do is feed you, even if it's not gourmet."

"Okay."

She didn't offer to join me in the shower, but I was telling the truth about that jailhouse stink. I think it's got something to do with the disinfectant and stale air and the polyester jumpsuits.

I went back upstairs and stripped. I didn't have another set of clothes, but these had just been laundered.

It wasn't a long shower, but the warm soapy water and the privacy made it a luxurious experience. I dried off with a fluffy towel and pulled on my clothes again.

Carrying my boots in my hand, I went down to the kitchen.

Kelly had brushed her hair back into its usual ponytail and scrubbed off the makeup. She was wearing a bulky warm sweater that emphasized her ample bosom.

"Shall we go sit in the living room?" she asked, pushing a full coffee mug toward me.

"Why don't we stay here until we finish the coffee?" I said. If we went and sat on the sofa, Kelly would slide over against me, and I knew the temptation to cuddle and smooch would be overwhelming, at least for me. We had a couple of things we needed to talk out.

"What's gonna happen to your brother?" She picked up her mug and took a sip.

I shrugged. "Cop a plea, I imagine. Maybe settle for involuntary manslaughter. After all, he didn't mean for Sydney to die. They may fold all the other charges in. Might get away with ten years or so."

"Really? Just ten years?"

"Yeah." I shook my head. "But he'll prob'ly do every minute of it. Ten years is enough for you to think things through and maybe decide you're gonna change your life. More than enough."

"You think he wants to make some changes?"

I shrugged. "Who knows? Right now, I think he's just happy not to have to think about where his next meal is coming from or where he's gonna sleep. He may be sorry later, but it'll be a bit late to worry about it."

"He gonna survive?" she asked.

"Oh, yeah. He's spent most of his adult life locked up, one place or another. It's living on the streets he don't know how to handle. Hard to just get by. People don't want to hire you. Or rent you a room. And heaven knows you haven't got enough money to make it without a couple of breaks. So next thing you know, you're doing something that's gonna get you locked up again."

"Maybe." Kelly warmed her hands on the coffee mug. "But killing Sydney—that's kind of extreme, don't you think?"

"True, that. But he didn't mean to actually kill him. If the car hadn't been left running, Sydney wouldn't have died."

Kelly's eyes hardened. "He deserved to die."

I looked at her. "Maybe. I don't pass judgment on whether anybody else should live or die. I got enough trouble with just me. But I don't think Denny's all bent out of shape over it. Maybe he's a bit concerned to be looking at murder charges, but he don't care that Sydney's dead."

"You mean, just kind of closes his mind to his role in it?"

"Yeah. And to the possible consequences. It just seems that things happen, not like he's done anything."

Kelly nodded. "Almost like my dad. He can never handle it when he's out on the street. All he wants to do is party. So he ends up doing something stupid that gets him locked up again."

"Yeah. And your dad even has some support. He can come stay with you."

She snorted. "Gonna be a cold day in hell before I let him try that again."

I grinned. Kelly's dad's bike club had more or less taken over her house. "I can see why not."

Gathering up the now-empty coffee mugs, I carried them over to the sink To give Kelly a few minutes to think.

She barely moved.

I rinsed out the mugs and put them in the dishwasher. It was almost full, so I started it.

Finally, she looked up. "I really made a mess of things this time."

Although I didn't disagree with the general statement, I wasn't sure what she meant. "How so?" I asked.

"You were right. I should have stuck to going to the AA meetings."

I winced. "You really didn't?"

She shook her head. "I did, at first. That's where I met Sydney. And I went to a few with him. Or one. But after that..." Her voice trailed off.

"What did you do instead?"

"We went to his place. You know, over the check cashing office. He said he'd been sober for a long time, and he knew all about AA. He said it's true some people can't ever drink again, but that's not true of everybody. He said he thought I could have an occasional drink and not have it bother me." She wiped a tear away from her eye.

"So did it?"

"Did it what?"

"Bother you?"

"Yeah. I'd think I was just gonna have one drink, and the next thing you know, I'd be on the third or fourth. Then Sydney could talk me into almost anything."

I didn't want her to tell me that they'd had sex. Of course they had.

"Then we'd have sex," she said.

My chest tightened.

"Then he'd bring me home." She looked at me expectantly.

My mouth was dry. I licked my lips. "Yeah," was all I could say.

"First he bought me a cell phone. He said he wanted to be able to get in touch with me whenever he wanted."

That made a certain amount of sense.

"Then he got me some nice stuff. Clothes. Perfume. Makeup. I never been able to spend much on stuff like that, and I always thought I didn't much care. But it was nice."

I nodded. I could never afford to buy her much stuff like that.

"Then the clutch finally went completely on the station wagon. I *needed* that car."

"True, that." What with the kids and where she lived, she did need a car.

"So he bought the RAV4 and handed me the keys. A real new car. I never had a new car before."

I'd never had a car at all, but it didn't seem to be the time to point that out.

"I told him I couldn't afford to make payments on an expensive new car. He said maybe we could work something out."

"Like what?"

She shivered. "I feel so dirty. He wanted to make videos."

"Porno?"

"Not really, I don't think. At first he said it was just for him, and he set up a camera. Then this one time, he had somebody else there, he said so he could get better videos. I wasn't thrilled, but it didn't seem so bad. But then the other guy—Demitri is his name—wanted to have sex with me, too. And Sydney told him he could. Nobody asked me."

"And you didn't protest?" I asked.

"I was pretty out of it," she said. "I had a headache, and Sydney gave me some kind of pill he said would take care of it."

"Did it?"

"You mean, as in, did it take care of the headache? Yeah, I guess. I didn't have a headache any more. Or, if I did, I didn't notice it. I felt a little woozy."

I could just imagine what he had given her. "And did you have anything to drink?"

She looked away. "Just two drinks. Then he gave me the pill."

I deliberately changed the way I worded it to put more of the responsibility on Kelly, where at least some of it belonged. "And after you took the pill?"

She didn't seem to notice. "One more. Or maybe it was two."

"Or more?"

She shrugged.

"Was that last night?"

"No, the time before. But Demitri was there last night, too."

"And what happened?"

"Not much. Sydney was mad at me. And the other guy told him to let it go, they could deal with it later."

"Why was he so mad at you?"

Kelly hung her head. "He'd told me to bring the kids. That he wanted to take pictures of them, too. He said not pornographic, but…"

I took a deep breath. Thank goodness she'd found me. "Is that the 'emergency' you were talking about, so you needed someplace for the kids to go last night?"

She nodded.

"That's why you left them with me?"

"Yeah. I didn't want to take them anywhere near Sydney's place."

"So why the hell did *you* go?"

A tear rolled down her cheek. "By that time, I was into it too far. I *owed* Sydney. I didn't know how to get myself out of it. But I sure as hell wasn't going get the kids mixed up in it."

"You owed him? You mean, like the car and the cell phone and things?"

"Yeah. I figured I was just gonna go this one last time, do whatever he wanted me to, tell him he could have the damn car and the phone back and I'd pay him whatever he said I owed him." She wiped her eye with the back of her hand.

"How were you gonna do that?"

"I dunno. But I'd find a way. Sell the house, I guess. But I was in it way too deep. I had to get myself out." She was crying, and started to hiccup.

I got up and got her a glass of water.

She took a drink. "Like I said, the other guy was there, too. Sydney was mad that I didn't bring the kids. But Demitri, he said I was too upset to get good pictures anyhow, just let me go home."

"And Sydney did what he said?"

"Yeah. Sydney grabbed me and wanted me to have sex with him. With them. But then Demitri said they weren't ever gonna force me to do anything I didn't want to do. He said they should just let me go home and we could all discuss it later when everybody had a chance to think it over."

"So that's why you didn't want to go over there this morning?"

She nodded. The tears were coming freely now.

"So how'd you lose the wallet?" I asked.

"I guess when Sydney tried to grab me. It was in my purse. When he reached for me, I stuck the purse between us, right into his hand. He snatched it and threw it aside. Prob'ly the wallet fell out then."

"Did you get the purse back?"

"Yeah. Demitri picked it up and gave it to me. But I didn't look inside till I got home."

"So that's why you wanted *me* to go over and get the wallet?"

"Yeah. I was still trying to figure out what to do."

"Don't you think it would have been a good idea to tell me what I might be getting into?"

She sniffed and reached for a paper towel to wipe her nose. "You're right, Jesse. I should have. I wasn't thinking straight at all. It didn't really occur to me that you might have any problems there."

In the end, it hadn't really made a difference. I'd had problems, for sure. But not the ones I would have expected if she'd told me all that.

"How about some more coffee?" she said.

Sighing, I got two more mugs out of the cabinet, filled them with water, and stuck them in the microwave. I stayed over there, across the kitchen from the table. It would give both of us a few minutes to think. When the water was hot, I put a spoonful of coffee crystals in each mug, stirred, and carried them over to the table.

I sat down at the table and took a sip of my coffee. It was too hot to take a big gulp.

"You want a slug of Southern Comfort in that coffee?" she asked. Her tears had stopped.

"No." I looked at her. "You know it would violate my parole. And you shouldn't have any alcohol in the house at all. Too easy to add just a little bit to your coffee, and then the next thing you know, you're drinking it straight from the bottle. Didn't you learn anything from AA?"

She sat up. "I didn't go to AA but a few times, remember? After that, I was out with Sydney."

"Yeah. And he said you could drink in moderation, right?"

"Well, a lot of people can."

"I know. And those people don't need AA to stop drinking. But so far, it doesn't look to me like you're one of those people."

"Are you saying you think I should start going to the meetings again?"

"Yep. And this time, look for a sponsor who doesn't think you can take an occasional drink. Or offer to buy alcohol for you. Preferably a female sponsor."

She shifted in her chair. "Why don't we go sit in the living room?" she said. "It's more comfortable there."

I was still concerned that she was going to try to get me to forget we still had things to discuss, but to tell the truth, I was not in any mood to give into her charms. "Okay." I took a gulp of my coffee. It was still too hot. I put the mug down on the table and stood up.

Kelly stood up, too, and drained her mug. I marveled that she didn't burn her mouth. She took me by the hand and led me to the couch. Sure enough, she cuddled in close to me. I put my arm around her shoulder, but that was as far as I was willing to go.

She snuggled in closer, taking my hand and squeezing it. I squeezed back. She leaned her head on my shoulder and nibbled at my neck. I didn't respond to that.

"What's the matter?" she whispered. "Don't you like it when I kiss you?"

"Of course I like it," I said. "But I think we've got a few more important things to talk about first."

Dropping my hand, she pulled away and sat up. "Like what?"

"Like whether we're acting like responsible adults."

She burst into tears. "You think I'm a slut because of the stuff with Sydney and Demitri. And you don't want to have anything to do with me."

I did think that her behavior with Sydney and Demitri was kind of slutty, but that didn't mean I didn't want to have anything to do with her. Lord knows, we all do things we're not proud of. I took her hand back in mine and said, "That's not true. Of course I'd much rather you hadn't slept with them. But that's over and done with and can't be changed. I am, though, concerned about the drinking. That can lead to some pretty bad decisions." I didn't add, "And it certainly has here," even though I thought it.

"Don't you think that's my business?" she said, sniffing.

"Yes."

"Then maybe you should butt out."

I dropped her hand. "Maybe I should. If that's what you want. It's only my business if you make it my business."

Angrily, she swatted at her eyes with her other hand. "Don't you love me?"

We'd never bandied around the "love" word before. "Maybe," I said. "I don't know. I care a whole lot about you. More than I've ever cared about anybody before. But I'm not sure I know what love is."

"What do you mean?" she asked.

"I do know I can't stand by and be an enabler."

"Enabler? What's that supposed to mean?"

"That means that just because I really care for you, I'm not going to let you manipulate me."

"You *don't* care about me."

"If I didn't care about you, I wouldn't worry about it. I'd just have sex with you, like Sydney and that other guy did. But if we're seeing each other, I want it to mean more than that."

"You're not mad at me?" she said.

"No. I'm not mad at you. You have to decide what you want. If it's the alcohol, okay. Well, not okay, but it's your decision and your life. If you keep on drinking, I'm not gonna be a part of your life."

"And if I stop drinking?"

"If you stop drinking and start going to AA again, I'll be as supportive as I know how. But I still won't be an enabler."

She leaned her head back on my shoulder. "I don't know if I can get a handle on this."

"You can if you want to. Just not by yourself. Remember the 'higher power?' You got to find your higher power."

"It might take a while."

"It probably will."

"Will you wait?"

"I'll wait."

We sat in silence for a few minutes.

"I got a lot of other problems, too," she said.

"I know you do. You can handle them."

"I can start going to AA meetings again."

"That's a good first step."

"You keep an eye on the kids for me while I go?"

"You know I will. But you got to figure out how to get there. What's with the car? Can you get your old one back and get it fixed up?"

She sighed. "That's a story. We used my old one as a trade-in on the RAV4."

"That's too bad."

"Well, it wasn't worth putting a new transmission in. So it's no real loss."

"So what're you gonna do for a car?"

She shrugged, "I haven't figured that one out. I'm gonna drive the RAV4 for a few days, at least. While I think it through."

"And the phone?"

"I already dropped that off at the store we got it from and explained. They weren't happy—said there was a year-long contract, with a termination fee, but I pointed out that the contract was with a dead man, not me."

I sat back. Kelly rested her head on my shoulder.

"Well," she said. "If I'm gonna start going to a couple of meetings a week, you're gonna be over here a lot with the kids."

"Yeah."

"And with Mandy back, you don't have to stay over there and keep an eye on her place."

"I don't know if Mandy's back yet."

"She is."

I looked at Kelly. "How do you know?"

"After I heard you got arrested, I drove by her house."

"How'd you know I got arrested?"

"You don't think they didn't haul me in and talk to me for a few hours? After all, I was right in the middle of everything. When I asked if I could talk to you, they said to check with the jail about visiting hours. So I figured you'd been locked up."

That made sense. "So you went over to Mandy's?"

"Yeah. I told her what happened and that you might not be around for a while."

"What'd she say?"

"Just that she knew that might happen. She said she'd hang onto your stuff for you. And that woman, Eileen, was going to stay in the carriage house."

"I figured as much."

"So…" Kelly snuggled up against me again.

"So…what?"

"So, why don't you just move in here?"

My stomach lurched. I hadn't seen that coming.

Wasn't it what I'd been wishing for ever since I'd spent the first night in Kelly's bed? That she'd commit to a serious relationship and ask me to move in? The kids would love it.

Why didn't it feel right? And it didn't.

"Kelly," I said. "I'd like nothing more. But I don't think we're ready."

Pulling away, she said, "What?"

"Look at it. You've just been pretty thoroughly traumatized. And you haven't even started your AA meetings again." And since I didn't see it would do any good, I didn't add, "And not a half hour ago, you wanted to put booze in your coffee."

She turned her head away. "And you haven't got issues?"

"Of course I have issues. I just got out of jail. For now, it looks like I'm not gonna get charged. But Mr. Ramirez might still violate my parole. Nothing's settled. So *I'm* not ready, either. This is too important a move to make until we're sure it's the right thing to do."

She looked at me with clouded eyes. "I'm sure."

"You can't be sure right now. How can you even be thinking straight? I know I'm not."

She stood up. "So where are you going to live?"

"Jumbo George's. The place where I stayed with the kids."

"You don't *want* to live with me?"

"I'd love to. But even more, I want it to work when we make the decision. I can't see that it would work now."

Turning her back on me, she said, "Are you going over to Jumbo George's now?"

"If you want me to," I said.

"I want you to stay."

"For overnight? But not move in?"

She looked around the room. "I guess."

I stood up and gathered her into my arms. "I'd like that very much." I kissed her.

"But first," she said, pulling away, "let's go get that bottle of Southern Comfort and pour it down the drain."

ABOUT THE AUTHOR

KM Rockwood draws on a varied background for stories, among them working as a laborer in a steel fabrication plant, operating glass melters and related equipment in a fiberglass manufacturing facility, and supervising an inmate work crew in a medium security state prison. These jobs, as well as work as a special education teacher in an alternative high school and a GED teacher in county detention facilities, provide most of the background for novels and short stories.

www.kmrockwood.com

www.ingramcontent.com/pod-product-compliance
Lightning Source LLC
Chambersburg PA
CBHW031425250626
47155CB00004B/1623